P9-EGK-116 -- 2021

Praise for Sonya Lalli

"Sonya Lalli's charming novel explores how our relationships define us. Through honesty, humor, and vulnerability, Serena Singh reminds us that new, fulfilling connections are possible at any age. This equal parts relatable and entertaining story is a delight from start to finish!"

—Saumya Dave, author of *Well-Behaved Indian Women*

"Heartfelt and forthright, Lalli's culturally rich work of women's fiction is exceptional." —*Booklist* (starred)

"From yoga studios to finding oneself in trips abroad to online dating, Lalli gives readers a wonderful novel about love and belonging and meaning of happiness and home."

—Soniah Kamal, award-winning author of *Unmarriageable: Pride and Prejudice in Pakistan*

"Anu's struggle to find herself is wrought with obstacles, and sometimes frustrating, but the resolution of her story is both satisfying and realistic. A moving look at one woman's journey between her family and her desire for independence."

—*Kirkus Reviews*

"Sonya Lalli offers up a tale of familial pressures, cultural traditions, and self-discovery that is equal turns heartbreaking and hilarious. . . . Lalli tears down stereotypes with humor and warmth." —*Entertainment Weekly*

OCT - - 2021

"An engaging love story that delivers on the promise of true love forever. . . . *The Matchmaker's List* comes through in spades (and hearts)."

—NPR

"Lalli's sharp-eyed tale of cross-cultural dating, family heartbreak, the strictures of culture, and the exuberance of love is both universal and timeless."

—*Publishers Weekly* (starred review)

A Holly Jolly Diwali

SONYA LALLI

BERKLEY · NEW YORK

BERKLEY
An imprint of Penguin Random House LLC
penguinrandomhouse.com

Copyright © 2021 by Sonya Lalli
"Readers Guide" copyright © 2021 by Sonya Lalli
Penguin Random House supports copyright. Copyright fuels creativity,
encourages diverse voices, promotes free speech, and creates a vibrant culture.
Thank you for buying an authorized edition of this book and for complying
with copyright laws by not reproducing, scanning, or distributing any part of
it in any form without permission. You are supporting writers and allowing
Penguin Random House to continue to publish books for every reader.

BERKLEY and the BERKLEY & B colophon are registered trademarks of
Penguin Random House LLC.

Library of Congress Cataloging-in-Publication Data
Names: Lalli, Sonya, author.
Title: A holly jolly Diwali / Sonya Lalli.
Description: First Edition. | New York: Berkley, 2021.
Identifiers: LCCN 2021022207 (print) | LCCN 2021022208 (ebook) |
ISBN 9780593100950 (trade paperback) | ISBN 9780593100967 (ebook)
Subjects: GSAFD: Love stories
Classification: LCC PR6112.A483 H65 2021 (print) |
LCC PR6112.A483 (ebook) | DDC 823/.92—dc23
LC record available at https://lccn.loc.gov/2021022207
LC ebook record available at https://lccn.loc.gov/2021022208

First Edition: October 2021

Printed in the United States of America

1st Printing

Title page art: Lanterns © Marish / Shutterstock
Book design by Elke Sigal

This is a work of fiction. Names, characters, places, and incidents
either are the product of the author's imagination or are used fictitiously,
and any resemblance to actual persons, living or dead, business
establishments, events, or locales is entirely coincidental.

R0460696946

For Simon

CHAPTER 1

*W*e need to talk."

I paused the television just as Matthew McConaughey pressed his palm against Jennifer Lopez's flawless cheek. Mom and Dad stood at the bottom of the stairs dressed up for the party I'd already thought they'd left for. Their faces were stone, and when Dad put his arm protectively around Mom's shoulder, my stomach bottomed out as I imagined the reasons for said "talk."

1. They were getting a divorce.

I sank farther into the couch, mentally shaking my head. This was unlikely. Most Indian couples their age, however miserable and fluent in English, refused to learn the d-word. Besides, my parents' marriage seemed to be a happy one. Trust me. My bedroom was just down the hall from theirs, and sometimes I could hear how *happy* they still made each other. Ugh.

2.   One of them was sick.

My hands trembled just thinking about this scenario, but then I remembered they'd both had physicals the month before, and their doctors had said everything was just fine. I should know. I drove them both to and from their appointments so they didn't have to pay for parking.

3.   Jasmine.

Yes. *Jasmine.* My whole body relaxed when I realized the most likely scenario was that my older sister was up to something again. On the verge of a scandal. Had broken up with her deadweight boyfriend du jour. (Oh god. Let it be that!) Or maybe she was just being a run-of-the-mill *pain* yet again, and my parents wanted to vent about it before they ran off to whatever function was on that evening.

"Yes?" I asked, satisfied I was ready to hear the answer.

Silently, they trundled toward me, but instead of taking one of the many seats in our living room, they chose to stand directly in front of the TV.

"What is up?" Dad asked cheerfully. "Busy?"

"Very." I laughed. "What is *up* with you?"

He glanced at my mom, who was clearly about to do the

heavy lifting. I blinked at her, and although I was curious what it was Jasmine had done to upset them again, I was ready to get back to *The Wedding Planner*.

"We are worried about you, Niki."

I scrunched up my face. Hold on a second. They were worried about *me*?

"You are?"

A knowing glance passed between them.

"Care to elaborate?" I asked.

"Niki, it's Saturday night," Mom said. There was a tinge of annoyance in her voice, like when I didn't rinse my plate before putting it in the dishwasher. "Why are you home?"

"What is *that* supposed to mean?" I scoffed, oblivious to the point she was trying to make. "Mom, I—"

"Enough is enough." She held up her hand like a conductor, waving me off. "Niki, you are very . . . very . . ."

"Successful?" I volunteered. "Obedient? *Lovely*—"

"Single," she interrupted.

Wow. Mom burn.

Yes, I was single and had been for a while, but I didn't know how the "very" played into that.

I tucked my legs under me. "What's your point?"

"You know," Dad continued, "there are apps for dating. Have you heard?"

"No," I deadpanned. "What's a dating app?"

"*Well*," Dad started, but then Mom cut him off.

"She knows very well what a dating app is. Niki, are you on the Tinder? The Bumble? The Hinger?"

I smiled, even though I was irritated. Clearly, they'd done their research before the big talk.

"I am not," I said flatly. "TBH, I don't like the idea of meeting people online."

"TBH?" Mom echoed.

"To be honest," I explained.

"*Ah*, so you would prefer to meet people in person?" Dad gestured at Matthew McConaughey. "I see you are meeting so many good candidates."

Mom grinned, and even I had to laugh at that one.

Dad burn. Very nice.

"Niki, we are not upset with you—" Mom started pacing, she always enjoyed theatrics. "We are *so* proud. But we have been thinking you should be . . . putting yourself out there. You understand?"

"Like, I need to start dating."

"*Hah.*"

"Maybe I'm already dating. How do you know I don't have a secret boyfriend?" I crossed my arms. "Or girlfriend, for that matter? Maybe I have several. *Maybe* I'm a total player."

Mom narrowed her gaze at me. "And when do you see all these boyfriends and girlfriends? On the bus home from work? Do you sneak them into your *parents'* house after you come straight home every day?"

I groaned, burrowing my face into the pillow. Another mom burn. But this one stung.

You see, they weren't totally wrong. My friends *constantly* told me that I would never meet anybody if all I did was work, (occasionally) go to the gym, and socialize with the same group of people—which these days was usually in someone's living room rather than out at bars. Diya, who was one of my best friends from college and lived on the other side of the world in Mumbai, was particularly hard on me during our weekly video chats. Her glamorous Indian wedding was just a few weeks away, and before I'd declined the invite because I couldn't get the time off work, she'd even threatened to fix me up with one of her cousins or friends.

But what happened to the good old-fashioned meet-cute? Maybe in the produce section of my local grocery store, or if I were to drop a pile of papers in front of the office hottie, regardless of the fact that my office was, uh, paperless.

Now I was twenty-nine years old and getting zinged by my parents, the same parents who used to stomp their feet whenever Jasmine flitted in and out with a new guy. The same mom and dad who, up until today, seemed *thrilled* that I still lived at home, that I wasn't in a relationship they needed to worry about.

I sighed, glancing up at them. I was annoyed but not surprised, as far too many of my South Asian friends were starting to sink in an all-too-similar boat. One day we're practically barricaded inside with our textbooks, "boys" not only not a subject worth discussing but, more often than not, entirely off limits.

And then?

And then, as if overnight, we're of marriageable age. Suddenly, we're not girls in need of protection but women, and being *very single* was our very own fault.

"I'll make more of an effort," I said finally, because I did want to get married one day, and there was no point in fighting the inevitable. "But I don't like the apps."

"Fair." Dad nodded. "Thank you."

I grabbed the remote, ready for the conversation to be over, but they didn't budge. Oh great. The talk wasn't yet over.

"Yes?"

I was looking at Mom because she was the one who clearly had more to say. Her mouth was weirdly tense, and she was playing with the buttons on her cardigan as if they were puzzle pieces.

"*Beti,*" she said affectionately, which was strange, because her love language was sass. "Do you . . ."

"Mom, please. Just out with it, OK?"

She nodded primly. "OK? OK. I am *outing* with it. I am . . ."

"*Mom!*"

"Do you want us to set you up?"

My jaw dropped. Like, to the *floor.* I could practically hear it land on the hardwood, my jaw shattering every which way.

"But . . ." I sputtered. "*You* didn't even have an arranged marriage!"

Mom and Dad snuck a look at each other, sly and knowing and with so much intimacy they really shouldn't have expressed in front of their own child. They were both in their early twenties when they moved to the US, and their (very) old-fashioned meet-cute took place at the local *gurdwara.* They weren't introduced by family or friends, so it was technically a love marriage, but from the stories I heard, they matched so well they might as well have been arranged. They were both raised in the Sikh faith. Tick. They both valued their Punjabi heritage and family values. Tick tick. So within five months of first laying eyes on each other over plates of *aloo paratha* in the *langar* hall below the prayer room, they were married.

Triple tick.

"We didn't have an arranged marriage, no," Dad said, looking back at me. "And we are not suggesting this for you."

"Exactly." Mom cleared her throat. "We are just saying *if* you were to be interested in meeting someone, outside of the apps, then maybe we know somebody." She paused, searching my face. "Maybe you could go for coffee, and if you like each other, you can—"

"Bang?"

Dad blushed, while Mom pretended not to hear me.

"Niki, you can date *normally*. We will not interfere. We don't even know the boy." Mom sighed. "He is nephew of our friends. Apparently, very sweet. *Modern*. A doctor—"

"Wow, a doctor? Sign me up!"

"We do not approach you with this lightly," Mom continued, ignoring me. Her voice was suddenly small and weak, and it made me feel terrible. Like a terrible daughter who, despite every effort to the contrary, had somehow still managed to disappoint them.

"You know"—she turned to Dad and placed her hand tenderly on his beard—"we were Niki's age when we were married."

Their body language mirrored the romantic cheek hold going on in the background between Matthew and Jennifer, and for the first time in a long time, I *felt* very single.

Were my parents trying to make me feel worse than I already did?

No. They weren't cruel. They were a little cheeky, intrusive, and condescending at times, but they were good parents. The best, actually.

And I, being the good daughter that I was, told them to give their friend's nephew my phone number.

CHAPTER 2

J glanced at the clock in the top-right-hand corner of my monitor. I still had twenty-two minutes to go, and so I decided to go through my Asana task board.

- Assign engineer to ETL script for bimonthly reporting data
- Oversee networking and SSH keygen for the Hadoop hardware
- Chase DBAs to set up SQL credentials for new co-op
- Check in with Oliver about CRM reporting design for marketing team

I was the data analytics manager at a start-up that sold e-products I didn't fully understand, and while the work was challenging enough, it didn't exactly stimulate me anymore. I'd been hired straight out of college as an analyst, and last year, when my former boss was poached by Microsoft, I was promoted to manage the entire team. Now I reported directly to Oliver Chu, the VP of R&D, or Research and Development.

For anyone not in my field, R&D was the only acronym worth explaining. My team used so many in our day-to-day work that we'd gotten into the annoying habit of abbreviating whatever words or phrases we could. There were the millennial staples like LOL, TBT, and ICYMI. The ones we'd invented ourselves, such as WNMC? (Who needs more coffee?) or WWSJD? (What would Steve Jobs do?)

And *then* there was the acronym I'd been using a lot these days.

FML.

I'd double-checked that I'd completed everything I needed to do that morning, and I still had twenty minutes to spare. I glanced out the window, praying for a distraction, and just my luck, Romeo was back. He was wearing his predictable uniform of jeans, a ball cap, and a bright orange safety vest, and I leaned closer to the window and rested my forehead against the cold glass as I watched him saunter up to Juliet's coffee cart.

I didn't know their real names, but here were the reasons I knew their love story, which played out at the coffee cart outside my office window, was as worthy as—although hopefully less tragic than—their namesakes'.

1. It always took Juliet less than a minute to serve most customers, but she dallied when whipping up

Romeo's order. Last Friday, it took her *five* whole minutes to make what looked like a straight-up Americano.

2. Without fail, for the past six months, Romeo had been coming by Juliet's cart every single day. And it cost a pretty penny for one of her hipster coffees.
3. Their chemistry was palpable, even from my stalking viewpoint one floor up. The lingering. The smiling. I could practically *smell* the pheromones.

Why didn't they just *go* for it?

I frequently found myself watching Romeo and Juliet chat each other up whenever I needed a mental break. Or, like today, when I had time to kill before my first date with the eligible doctor my parents wanted me to marry.

Three days after *the big talk* with Mom and Dad, I'd gotten a friendly, if overly eager, text from one Dr. Rajandeep Singh Sahota. He'd recently moved to Seattle for his residency in internal medicine, and after a weeklong text conversation that straddled the line between dull and mildly amusing, he'd asked me out on a low-pressure lunch date, even offering to come meet me in the lobby of my building on his day off work.

While I wasn't necessarily looking forward to the date, from his social media I'd gleaned that he was rather handsome, so I wasn't *not* looking forward to it, either. It was a humdrum, rainy day in late October, and I'd dressed up accordingly. Black boots and tights. A dark corduroy skirt, mock-neck blouse, and my favorite raincoat from Zara. Even though I hadn't been on a date in over a year, or in a real relationship since my early twenties, I'd slept soundly the night before. Whether Rajandeep Singh Sahota turned out to be my future husband or a hilarious anecdote I told my friends, I was under no pretense that I was about to get swept off my feet. That I'd get bested by true love and romance.

Because it was starting to dawn on me that those romantic fantasies weren't real. They were something we made up in our heads.

I swiveled in my ergonomic chair, still staring out the window. Romeo and Juliet were flirting *hard*, and I wondered why neither of them had ever made a move. Did one or both of them have a partner? That was the most realistic explanation, but in my head, they were my Barbies, and I got creative, sometimes going so far as whipping up a narrative that involved war, evil twins, even amnesia.

Juliet laughed at something Romeo said, and I let myself get carried away, down to their conversation. (I frequently daydreamed conversations as I people-watched. Sometimes I even made up silly little songs to go along with them.)

"I thought you might turn up today." Juliet tossed back her hair, laughing gregariously.

"Would I ever let you down, sweetheart?"

"Sweetheart!" Juliet held their eye contact. *"What else do you call me?"*

"What else do you want me to call you?"

"Oh, Romeo . . ."

"Hey, Niki."

Huh? How did they know my name?

"Niki?"

I snapped upright, out of my daydream that had been about to verge on NSFW (Not Safe for Work!). It wasn't Romeo and Juliet calling out for me to be their throuple but my *boss*.

I whipped my head around, and came to face-to-face with Oliver's crotch. *Oh god.* As quickly as I could, I flicked my eyes upward.

"Hey, Oliver." My face was still uncomfortably close to his groin region, and he took a giant step backward just as I stood up from my chair. "What's up?"

"Do you have a minute?"

I glanced at my watch. It was now 12:19 p.m., and I was supposed to meet Rajandeep in the office lobby on the half hour.

"I have eleven," I said to Oliver. "Is that enough?"

Oliver grunted a nonresponse. He looked like he was in a mood, a real pivot from the jolly dad vibe he usually sent out. "Just follow me."

"So, how was your daughter's soccer game last night?" I asked him once we were seated in his office.

"They lost. Ten to four. But who's counting, right?"

I laughed. "*You're* counting."

"I know I'm not supposed to be, but this whole 'no one wins' and 'it's all about participation' ethos really bugs the hell out of me." He shook his head. "But what do I know? I'm kind of an old fart."

"You said it, not me."

Oliver grinned, and momentarily, his body relaxed. But then he seemed to remember he was supposed to be in a grumpy mood, and the smile dropped from his face.

"Anyway." Oliver cleared his throat. He took the chair directly beside me. "I called you in here because, well, I have some news."

"Good news?"

He shook his head. "Bad news. The board didn't approve our budget."

My eyebrows furrowed. I'd heard rumblings that the company board meeting a few weeks earlier hadn't gone "well," but no one with a cup was willing to spill the tea.

"I guess we'll have to cut costs. Are we switching to single-ply toilet paper?" I joked.

Oliver's mouth twitched. Usually, he was all about the jokes—especially childish ones—but nothing.

I gulped. "Are there going to be layoffs?"

I said it out loud because I wanted him to jump in and say, "Of course not." But he didn't. He sighed, leaned forward on his desk. And I knew what was coming before he said it out loud.

"I am so, so sorry, Niki. If I could keep you, I would."

If I could keep you.

"We have a mandate to cut ten percent of the staff."

I choked, and I could feel my whole body start to shake.

"I feel terrible, Niki. You have to know, I really didn't want this—"

"Who else is being cut from analytics?" I whispered, somehow finding my voice.

"It's just you."

My stomach somersaulted, and it took everything to hold

myself together. *Just me?* As in the five analysts who reported to me weren't being let go, but *I* was?

"This doesn't make any sense," I stammered, refusing to cry. "You promoted me *last* year, Oliver. Because I was the best. So why *me?*"

Oliver hesitated. "We're required to let go of everyone in middle management. You know. The more expensive roles."

I pressed my hands into my face, and I could feel the floor spinning out from under me as I tried to remain calm.

This couldn't be happening to me. Because I had done everything . . . *right.*

I'd majored in computer science because it was a booming field. I'd taken a job as an analyst at a thriving yet soulless start-up because there was room to grow. And I'd spent years working my *ass* off to get that promotion so I could save responsibly for my future, so I could move out of my parents' house unburdened by student debt.

And for what? So I could be let go from a job I'd earned that was now suddenly too expensive? So I could do every little thing right only to be royally fucked over?

"You're upset," Oliver said after he gave me a minute to compose myself.

"No shit." I was on the verge of tears, and I bit down on my lip hard. "Sorry. I know it's not your fault."

"I hope you know," Oliver said, clearing his throat. He sounded emotional, too. "That I'll write you the best goddamn reference letter you'll ever read."

"Thanks," I said flatly.

"I'm serious, Niki. Shakespeare will roll in his grave. You better believe it."

I smiled despite myself as I thought of my Romeo and Juliet at the coffee cart. Would they ever get together? Probably not. But now, I'd never know for sure.

I had sat at the same desk for more than seven years, and all my personal items fit into two canvas tote bags.

Wasn't *that* depressing.

I could almost hear the montage of sad-ass music as I left the office for the very last time. Radiohead. The Cranberries. Iron & Wine. Rationally, I knew I'd been let go, that I'd just said goodbye to *my* team for the very last time, but it still didn't feel real. I walked to the bank of elevators on my floor, pushed the button I'd touched thousands of times before.

Was this it? I didn't want to believe it. I still couldn't.

My phone buzzed in my back pocket as I stepped into the elevator. I quickly scrolled past several notifications to the most recent alert. Jasmine had just posted on Instagram. I swiped through, and when the app opened, a burst of color filled the screen.

Jasmine worked in animation at a trendy mixed-media company, and she frequently posted graphics from her portfolio. I liked the post, and after commenting with several fire emojis, I found myself wondering what she was doing this very minute. She'd be working away in her gorgeous open concept office in

Pioneer Square, sipping on an oat milk latte. She'd be having a meet and greet with a cool client while wearing her new blue-light glasses and an impossibly cool yet professional BoHo outfit, because being comfortable in her skin came so freaking naturally to her—

"In or out?"

I looked up, my hands trembling. The elevator had stopped at the ground floor, and there were several women waiting to get in. I smiled in apology, slipped my phone back into my pocket, and then brushed past them.

After thinking about Jasmine, the reality of my situation was starting to feel very, very *real*. The company to which I'd devoted most of my twenties had pushed me out the door, and I had to leave. But where would I go? Tomorrow morning, when my internal clock woke me up at six thirty, what the hell was I supposed to do?

I trudged through the lobby, the heavy totes banging against my hips. I was never coming back. I would never eavesdrop on strangers' conversations as they raced past me to a meeting or conference call. I would never again shoot the shit with the friendly building staff. Tim the security guard or Jeb at reception or Tess, who sold magazines, coffee, and cigarettes at the kiosk.

Or . . . Dr. Rajandeep Singh Sahota?

I stopped dead in my tracks as the fog cleared and I watched him walk briskly toward me.

I'd totally forgotten. I had a *date*.

"Niki, hi!"

Stunned, I stood there like an idiot as he closed the gap between us and wrapped me in a hug.

"How are you? I was worried I got the time wrong."

"Hi . . ." I glanced at the giant clock by the elevator bank. It was now 12:45 p.m., and I was a full fifteen minutes late. "I'm so sorry—"

"Don't be. When duty calls, it yells. So tell me. What do you feel like eating? Sushi? Burritos?" He gave me a quizzical look. "*Sushi* burritos?"

"I . . ." I trailed off, trying to decide whether to bail or push through. "Rajandeep—"

"Call me Raj."

"Raj," I repeated, and for the first time I took a good look at him. There was no doubt about it. He was handsome all right. Tall. With a thick beard and glasses that made him look like a sexy English teacher.

"Is everything all right?" he asked me.

I bit my lip, stalling. Raj looked genuinely concerned, and his feelings were valid. I was entirely frazzled, and while I couldn't see what expression my facial muscles were up to, I suspected I looked like I was wearing the mask from *Scream*.

Data analytics was high pressure and demanding, and while the stress of my old job didn't get to me, the stress of suddenly not having one was coming at me like a hurricane. I shifted my weight between my heels, utterly torn. I was clearly not in the proper headspace for a first date, but what difference would it make if I went home and crawled into bed with a box of Oreos?

I still wouldn't have a job. And I would still be, in Mom's words, very single.

"Sushi," I said finally, because *fuck it*, right? "Let's go for sushi."

*L*uckily, Raj was a chatty guy and took the lead in the conversation as we walked to my favorite sushi bar two blocks over. We talked vaguely about the weather, the latest Seahawks game, and then how he was enjoying Seattle so far. I didn't volunteer much, and by the time our bento boxes arrived, the conversation had come to a lull. The food here was excellent, but even though I hadn't eaten since seven in the morning, I wasn't hungry. I could barely stomach a single bite.

"You're nervous," Raj said, watching me pick at my seaweed salad. "Have you ever done this before?"

"Eaten out with a man? Never."

He chuckled softly.

"No," I said a beat later. "My family hasn't set me up before. You?"

"Not until recently. I'm the oldest child, and they're desperate for me to get married." He sighed, setting down his chopsticks. "And it's not that I don't want to get married; I just wish they didn't care so much."

"Bingo," I said flatly.

"You must have it a bit better than your older sister, right— what's her name again?"

"Jasmine," I said, each syllable rolling slowly off my tongue. Over text, Raj and I had gone over the basics of each other's lives and family, but I was impressed he remembered I'd told him I had a sister.

"Are your parents setting her up, too?"

"God no. She would never agree to that." I shrugged. "But it doesn't matter because she has a boyfriend." I raised my left eyebrow at him. "And they live together."

He clutched his palm to his lip. "No. A *live-in* boyfriend?"

"I know, right? She's ruined the family name."

He smiled, creases forming in his beard. It was oddly pleasant to look at.

"Anyway, she'll probably never marry him just to spite my parents. She's always been more of a rebel." I scoffed. "Her boyfriend is actually kind of a dick. I think she started dating him in the first place to piss them off."

Raj nodded. "There's one in every family—"

"For example," I said, leaning in. "Jasmine majored in art—which almost *killed* my parents. But it worked out for her. She has this amazing job and can afford to live downtown."

"That's—"

"*And* she travels. Like, everywhere. She's been to every continent except Antarctica. Can you believe it? With a freaking art degree? And . . ." I swallowed hard. A wave of emotion came over me so suddenly and with such force I dared not speak. I swallowed hard, but I could feel myself shaking, everything threatening to spill out.

"And . . ."

And it simply wasn't fair. I did everything right, and she did everything *wrong*.

Jasmine spent all her money to live *that city* life and travel the world over, while I dutifully stayed home to save money for the future, to be there for our parents.

Jasmine was gainfully employed by way of an art degree, while I had set music aside for a practical career path that had only left me *unemployed*.

Jasmine was shacked up with a guy named Brian, who she claimed to be the man of her dreams—a man nobody in our family actually liked very much—while I would inevitably marry whomever my parents wanted for me. A sensible, marriage material man like Dr. Rajandeep Singh Sahota.

I looked up at my date, whose gaze had shifted to the wall beside him. My face heated.

Jasmine was off living her best life, and I was here, acting like a total bitch. I wouldn't want to look at me right now, either.

"I'm sorry," I said, my face collapsing into my hands. "Fuck."

"It's OK." I felt Raj's hand on my shoulder. "Sibling relationships are complicated."

"Yeah." I'd started crying, full-on guttural sobs that had no business on a first date. (Or tenth, for that matter.) I grabbed a wad of paper napkins and blew my nose, feeling terrible.

"Our issue isn't actually that complicated," I said finally.

"You're jealous," Raj said plainly, and I welled up again, hearing someone else say it out loud.

"Niki, it's natural. And inevitable." Raj skewered a maki roll, popping it into his mouth. "Everyone feels it. Hell, I feel it right now."

"Toward?"

Raj gestured to the table next to us, where a server was setting down a giant boat of every sort of sushi roll imaginable.

"Order envy," he said. "That shit is real."

I smiled despite myself. The tears stopped again, and I set the napkins down.

"I love Jasmine. A lot. And we're close, honestly. But after today . . ." I trailed off, words escaping me.

Raj chewed thoughtfully on his food, urging me on with his eyes.

"I got let go," I said finally. "From my job."

He swallowed, his eyes bulging. "When?"

"Today." I glanced at my watch. "About twenty minutes before our date was supposed to start."

Raj extended his hand, and I took it. "I'm so sorry."

"It's OK—"

"It's not OK," he said. "We could have postponed . . ."

Raj's voice was steady, calming, and so I told him about what happened at work. Like word vomit, I told him about how I'd worked so hard to get promoted only to be in an even less secure position as a middle manager. How I'd based every decision in my life on what was most practical, on how my parents would have wanted both their daughters to behave.

Only to end up let go.

"I'm sure you've made the right decisions, Niki," Raj said afterward. "Even if it doesn't feel like it right now. I'm sure you'll find another job soon."

"Thanks," I said, feeling bad for complaining so much. However much time I put into my career, training to be a doctor would have been a million times harder. In his first year of residency, Raj still had years of long hours in front of him to become a full-fledged specialist in internal medicine.

"Do you . . ." I didn't know where I was going with this, and suddenly remembered that I was on a first date and not in a therapy session with a close friend.

"Do I . . ." Raj prompted, and so I decided to just roll with it.

"Do you ever feel like you missed out?"

"No," he answered plainly.

"*Really*." I crossed my arms in front of me. "You don't have FOMO after spending your twenties in classrooms or a hospital. And you don't feel like you missed out on anything."

"Not at all." Raj swallowed the edamame he'd been chewing. "I may work hard, but I have a lot of fun, too, Niki. When I have a week off, I travel. When I have the day off . . ." Raj smiled at me. "I go on a hot date."

I pointed to my disastrous self. "Me? So hot."

"I think so."

My face burned. Thank god I had dark skin and my cheeks never colored.

"Nothing wrong with having a solid life plan," he said. "It's good, in fact. But you can take a break sometimes, Niki. For, you know, some *fun*."

I stared down at my food. These words were sounding all too

familiar, and I wasn't sure I wanted to hear them again, and from a total stranger.

"Sake?"

I looked up. The waiter had appeared, and when Raj ordered a whole bottle, my heart thumped in my chest.

"What are you doing?"

Raj's eyes sparkled. "We're taking a break."

CHAPTER 3

*A*fter the second bottle of sake, we were both certifiably drunk and ready to go to a bar. There was only one problem. It was 4 p.m. on a Wednesday.

"Should we go back to my place?" Raj asked, as we were both furiously scrolling through our phone for options.

"Sure," I retorted. "Do you have a condom?"

Raj didn't respond, and I fleetingly worried he wouldn't find my joke funny. Or worse. Think I was serious. But when I looked up, he was smiling over at me fondly. I couldn't tell if we were digging each other or if the alcohol just made it seem that way.

"We could just stay here," I said. The waiter looked over at us. We were smack in between the lunch and dinner rush, and the only customers still here. "Beer?" I mouthed at him.

The waiter laughed and then gave me the thumbs-up.

"We're sorted," I said, looking back to Raj. "The bar will come to *us*."

"If we tip generously, do you think they'll turn down the lights and turn up the music?" Raj grimaced. "Well, not *this* music."

I scrunched up my nose. Taylor Swift wasn't everyone's cup of tea, and decidedly mainstream, but I respected her talent and actually really loved this song.

"We can have a dance party," I said finally. My words came out heavy and slow. "We can get *wild*."

"Do you consider a dance party wild?" Raj asked me. Beneath the table, I felt his foot against my calf.

"Depends on who I'm dancing with."

"I went to a full moon party in Thailand. That was pretty wild." Raj smiled to himself, at whatever memory had just popped into his mind. "What's the craziest thing you've ever done?"

I shrugged, trying and failing to think of a single story. Like many college kids, I'd been to my fair share of parties. I danced and sometimes I even drank a little too much, and on the very rare occasion, I even smoked a joint.

But to be honest, that was about it. I'd had fun, but it was wholesome fun, and in every single situation, I always had a safe ride home back to my parents' house. I said no when a flirty guy wanted to hook up or asked me out on a date, because if I couldn't see him instantly as a potential long-term partner, then what was the point?

I said no when friends rented a house together over in Wallingford and offered me a room, or invited me along on a trip, so I could finish paying off my loans and start saving for a down payment. I even said no when Diya, one of my favorite people in the entire world, told me she was getting married.

Our beer had arrived, and I took a long swig.

"One of my best friends is getting married soon," I said. My head had started spinning. "Her name is Diya. We were inseparable in college."

Raj spread his arm along the back of the booth. He looked a little drunk himself. "Oh yeah?"

"She's amazing. I miss her *so* much." I ran my fingers through my hair. "She grew up in Mumbai, and moved back there after graduation. She's having this big fat Indian wedding soon, and I'm not going to be there."

"Why not?"

"Because I said *no*," I said, my head bobbing around in a haze. "But I should have said yes, Raj. I should have done something *wild* and said yes."

"Yeah, but *why*—"

"Because . . ."

Because my company was notoriously stingy with vacation days in the months leading up to Christmas. Because after a twelve-year relationship, Diya and Mihir had a very short engagement and gave us less than six months' notice. Because flights to India were expensive. Because . . . a lot of reasons that didn't seem so rational or compelling anymore.

"You could still go to that wedding, Niki." Everything was so fuzzy it was as if he were speaking to me through a glass divider. "It's never too late. Call your friend. Ask her if you can still come."

The beer was causing a new, second wave of inebriation, one that I could feel cascading through my limbs and into the very tips of my fingers.

"Take a *break*, Niki," Raj said. I felt his hand squeezing mine on the table. "Go have some fun. Your life will still be waiting for you when you get back."

I looked down at our hands, intertwined on the table. Even though my nervous system was registering the touch, the temperature of his skin, I could barely feel him.

Jasmine said yes to everything, and I *always* said no. Maybe that was the problem. Maybe Raj was right, and sometimes I needed to take a break.

Sometimes I needed to say *yes*.

On an impulse, I grabbed my phone and called Diya. I had no idea what time it was in Mumbai and doubted she would pick up, but right there and then, I decided that if she answered and said it was not too late for me to RSVP, then I'd go. I had the time. And because of the severance pay that Oliver said would be landing in my bank account later today, I had the money, too.

"Hello?"

She answered on the fifth ring and sounded as groggy as I was feeling.

"Sorry," I said. "What time is it there?"

"Niki?" Diya paused. "Nearly five in the morning."

I shook my head. "Sorry—"

"What is it?" She interrupted. "Are you OK, girl?"

"Yeah. I'm fine. Well, actually, I'm *drunk*. I just got laid off. Which means I can—"

"Come to the wedding?" Diya squealed. "Don't toy with me, yeah? Are you *really* considering attending? I am *so* sorry you were fired. But I am not that sorry if it means you will be coming."

I laughed. "Well, do you even have room to squeeze me in?"

Diya laughed. "Niki, there will be fifteen *hundred* people at my wedding. Of *course* I can squeeze you in! Have you booked a flight?"

"I'll book a ticket as soon as I get home," I said, smiling from ear to ear. "Promise."

"Where are you?"

I looked up. Raj was reclining lazily into the booth. He looked about as drunk as I felt.

"I'm on a date," I whispered loudly.

"A *date*?" Diya's voice was so loud I nearly dropped the phone. *"Drunk?"*

"Shhh. Yes. It's a first date. He said I needed to get drunk and take a break from being a cal-cu-la-tor." I paused, my eyes locked with Raj's. "It's going well. Right?"

Raj winked at me, and then tried to give me a thumbs-up, but his arm was shaking, and it looked more like a hang-low surfer sign.

"When you sober up," Diya laughed, "call me. I want *all* the details. Actually, no. Put your date on the phone. I want to thank him for talking some sense into you."

I was too out of it to disagree, and so I tossed Raj my phone.

As Diya chatted away, I smiled lazily at him, at the thought of seeing her again so soon.

"Yes, well, I think so, too," Raj said when he finally managed to get a word in. "Yes," he repeated a minute later. "Yes. OK. I'll tell her." He laughed again. "OK, nice to meet you, too. You're welcome. Bye, Diya."

Raj hung up the call and then handed me back my phone.

"What was that all about?" I asked.

"Diya told me to tell you that . . ." He paused. "She likes me for you."

I smiled, crossing my arms. Diya was one of those effervescent, delightful people who somehow had the confidence to say anything to anyone.

"Anything else?"

"Yeah," he answered, as I felt his leg rub against mine beneath the table. "That you should come home with me right now."

I rolled my eyes. "Ha, ha."

The waiter returned, offering us another round of beer, but I knew my limit, and I'd had enough. Raj also declined and then asked for the check, waving me off when I offered to pay for my half.

"You can treat next time," he said, reaching for his wallet. "When you're back from India."

I smiled, our eyes locking across the table. There were no butterflies, but that's because I wasn't nervous.

I'd go to India. I'd have a bit of fun. And afterward, my practical, good-Indian-girl life would be right here waiting for me.

CHAPTER 4

*M*om?"

She didn't answer, and I fell back into the soft material of a Kashmiri scarf I definitely wouldn't need in hot and humid Mumbai. Mom had offered to help me pack, although rather unhelpfully, she'd brought the entire contents of our storage closet up to my bedroom so we could decide, outfit by outfit, what clothes I should take for Diya's wedding events. I glanced at my alarm clock, sighing. We'd been going at this for three hours, and only half the suitcase was packed.

"Mom," I called again, louder this time. "Mom, it's getting late—"

"*Aacha*. I'm here. I've found it." She came into view, her gold-toned evening bag tucked beneath her armpit. But that wasn't all she had with her: stacked precariously in her arms was a pile of small, paisley-printed boxes.

I sprung from the floor, lunging for the boxes just as the top few were about to topple over. We managed to get them on the bed without any falling to the ground.

"Here," Mom said, handing me the purse. "Don't lose. It's my favorite."

"Thanks," I mumbled, gently setting it in the suitcase. "What's in the boxes?"

"*Pinni.*"

"For?"

"What do you mean *for*?" Mom bent down to the floor and started riffling through a heap of saris. "They are *for* taking with you. No daughter of mine will turn up to a host family empty handed."

I groaned. *Pinni* was a common sweet in Punjab, and my mom made giant batches for every holiday, birthday, or gathering of more than ten people.

"My suitcase isn't that big," I said, careful not to whine. I hated when Mom assumed I'd forget something so obvious. I may not be Indian per se, but I still knew that hospitality was a pillar of our culture. "And besides. I already bought Diya's family a present."

I held up a box of a scent diffuser I'd picked up that morning while running errands at the mall. I'd managed to get a last-minute flight deal for a ticket to Mumbai, but it had only left me with two days to pack and break three pieces of news of various proportions to my family.

1.   The layoff.

They were enraged on my behalf, but very supportive.

2. I was going to India.

They were *surprised* to say the least, but again, very supportive.

3. I'd gone on my first date with Rajandeep. I meant, *Raj*.

I'd shared this piece of news with them at breakfast that morning using a total of seventeen words, when they both had their mouths full of *dalia*. Although I yet again anticipated a favorable response, I'd left the kitchen before they could interfere, which Mom had promised they wouldn't.

"What is *that*?" Mom asked, eyeing the gift.

"It's a diffuser." I clicked my tongue as she stared at me blankly. "Mom, we *have* one."

"Give them both gifts. You are arriving just before Diwali, Niki." She turned back to the saris. "You must bring sweets. It is holiday tradition. And Punjabi sweets won't be so common in Mumbai. I know they'll enjoy."

"Do I need to bring them *eight* boxes, though?"

"You don't know who else you'll be meeting. Where else you'll be staying after the wedding. And you must take some to your *buaji* and cousins . . ."

I grimaced. Mom and Dad had convinced me to visit Punjab after the wedding to visit our extended family, but I'd never met any of them in person before and felt strangely resistant to the idea.

"I was thinking of sending a full dozen, but I ran out of brown sugar." She tossed me a canary yellow sari. "Hold that up against your face, *hah*? Let me see what it looks like on you."

I sucked in air between my teeth and dug deep for patience. There was no point in arguing with Mom, so obligingly, I held up the sari. Mom's face instantly lit up.

"Gorgeous. Absolutely perfect. You must wear on Diwali."

I turned to face the mirror. It was true. The contrast of the yellow and my dark skin looked great—all bright colors were my color—but I'd already packed away my standard *little black dress* for the occasion.

"Just take it and decide what to wear later," Mom said, as if she could read my mind. "You don't even need to wear the matching blouse. All the girls these days just wear bralettes underneath, or those"—she gestured ambiguously to her chest—"those tops. What do you call them? Tunnel tops?"

"Tube tops?"

"*Hah*."

I tossed the sari into the suitcase, smiling. "I haven't owned a tube top in about fifteen years. And when I did, you never let me wear it because it was too revealing."

"Well, you're old enough now. I'm not so worried about you getting pregnant."

I laughed. "Were you really that worried?"

"About you? *No*. Your sister on the other hand . . ." Mom threw me a side-eye, and we both broke out into a fit of giggles. And as I watched her lovingly sort through outfits, it occurred to me that I wasn't just going to India but that I was going alone.

My parents couldn't afford to bring Jasmine and me with them when we were younger. They didn't go very often, either, perpetually putting their savings toward their house, children, and building a life in America rather than costly international flights. By the time they could afford the long-promised family trip to Punjab, Jasmine and I didn't want to go. We were in high school or college by that point, but now I couldn't remember what was so important that we missed visiting where Mom and Dad came from. And these days, I felt embarrassed about the fact that I was Indian but had never been to the country my family was from. (I also barely understood Punjabi, nor did I speak Hindi or any of the hundreds of languages spoken across the subcontinent.) It was a land of unknowns, a place that in my mind existed in the past, a history book of where our family came from. The thought of facing the place for the first time without my parents was suddenly making my heart race.

"You should come with me," I said to Mom, squatting down beside her. "I know Diya would love to have you, too."

"I wish I could, *beti*." She brushed my cheek. "Celebrating Diwali in India will be a *wonderful* experience."

I smiled, thinking about the way our family celebrated Diwali. Every year, we got together with dozens of other families in the community and set off sparklers and firecrackers, ate, drank, and sometimes even danced until the wee hours of the morning. It was the Festival of Lights—that I knew—but I suddenly realized I didn't have a clue what the holiday was really about.

"Mom?" I sat down next to her on the floor, cross-legged. "Embarrassing question . . ."

"Do you want to have the sex talk?"

"Mom!" I sputtered.

"Because we don't do that in our culture. You know that." She playfully covered her ears. "So just go about your business in private and don't be an idiot."

I groaned, covering her mouth with my hands until she laughed. I wondered if joking around like this was her way of trying to get me to talk about Raj, but I decided to brush past the comment.

"Actually," I said, "I was curious about Diwali. Why do we celebrate it?"

Mom gave me a look, and I could tell immediately she didn't really know, either. Our family was Sikh and went to the *gurdwara* a few times a year, but my parents had always taken a laissez-faire approach to religion and spirituality. To them, it seemed to be an all-you-can-eat buffet, and they encouraged Jasmine and me to pick and choose whatever we felt was right for us.

"Do you know why Sikhs celebrate Diwali?" I asked again.

"Yes," she said, lines appearing on her forehead. "Of course!"

"Really?"

She pursed her lips. "Really . . ."

We ended up googling it, and apparently, people of the Sikh faith traditionally celebrated Diwali alongside many Hindus, Jains, and Buddhists, but for different reasons.

Sikhs had originally decorated the Golden Temple in Amritsar with lights to commemorate the release of one of our gurus from prison in the 1600s. Now the holiday had merged into a Christmas-like festivity that transcended religions, cultures, and borders, and was generally a time to get together with family and friends, exchange gifts and sweets. To have an excuse to be together and have a party.

There was a lot of background information online about how the holiday originated and was celebrated by Hindus, which was a much more ancient religion, but Mom closed the browser before I had a chance to read it closely.

"Diya's family is Hindu, *hah*? Just ask them when you get there," she said, putting the phone away. "Or you could ask your new friend. He might know."

I chuckled softly as I realized, yet again, Mom was trying to change the subject to Raj.

Mom hummed, avoiding eye contact. "Rajandeep seems like a worldly person . . ."

"Does he?" I said flatly.

"Have you . . ." She trailed off, and I bit my lip to keep from smiling. Mom attempting not to interfere with my life was rather entertaining to watch.

"Have I what?"

"Niki, you know what I'm asking—"

"*Mom*, leave her alone, would you?"

I smiled at the sound of Jasmine's voice just outside the room and looked over just in time to see her throw herself through the doorway. It had been a few weeks since we'd seen each other, and I was hoping she'd come say goodbye before I left for Mumbai.

"It looks like a tornado passed through here," she said, looking around my room. Indeed, there were clothes, jewelry, and odds and ends everywhere, only a fraction of which had actually ended up in the suitcase. "Ooh, what's that?" She reached for the canary yellow sari, and then held it against herself in the mirror.

"Damn, this is my color." She turned to Mom. "Can I have it?"

"No." I laughed. "It's mine."

"Actually, it's *mine*. Niki is borrowing it and then giving it straight back." Mom grabbed the sari from Jasmine and tucked it back in the bag. "Have you eaten?"

"Sort of," she answered. "I had a bag of chips in the car—"

"That's not dinner," Mom said flatly.

"It has the same amount of calories, though."

Mom turned to me, her eyebrows raised, but all I could do was shrug. When I was feeling lazy and my parents weren't home, I'd also been known to eat an entire bag of chips instead of dinner.

Mom went downstairs mumbling about nutrition and promises to return with leftover *subji*, and I watched Jasmine rummage through my things. She stopped beneath the window at my full-sized electronic keyboard. It was dusty AF, and I winced as she plopped down on the stool and started banging away on the keys.

"Can you not?"

"Well, *you're* not playing."

As Jasmine played "Chopsticks," I crawled up from the floor to the bed and curled myself into a sideways fetal position. A minute later, she stopped playing and flopped down next to me.

"So, what's new?"

"You know what's new."

"Yeah," she giggled. "You're going to India. And you're dating an *Indian* doctor all of a sudden. Way to show me up."

"It's not exactly hard." I nestled into her, her chest rising and falling as she laughed. "And we've only been on one date, remember?"

"Want to talk about it?" she asked, and I shook my head.

"Not much to say. I'll see him when I'm back." I paused. I could hear Mom and Dad banging around in the kitchen downstairs warming up Jasmine's dinner, and I knew we had only another minute together, just the two of us. "Any advice for traveling?"

"I brought you my plane pack," she answered. "It's downstairs. Don't lose it."

I laughed, remembering the dorky purple fanny pack she took on all of her travels abroad, full of everything from pressure socks to ginger chews, which helped with upset stomachs and nausea, to a deck of Uno cards.

"Thanks." I breathed in and got a whiff of the weird organic shampoo she used.

Jasmine went quiet, and when I looked up at her, she was studying me like a chemistry textbook—a high school subject both of us nearly failed. Her jaw was tense.

"What?"

"I'm worried about you."

I guffawed. Mom and Dad had said the exact same thing.

"Is everything OK?" She paused. "Planning an overseas trip on two days' notice is very unlike you—"

"Yeah," I said. "Well, being *me* hasn't exactly worked out, has it?"

She reached her hand out and started petting my hair like I was a cat. It was kind of weird, but she did it all the time, and I'd actually grown to find it comforting.

"I'm really sorry you got laid off," she said. Her voice was small, but I knew she felt terrible. That was the thing with Jasmine. She was wildly unpredictable, but she was incredibly genuine, so when she said something you knew she meant it.

I wrapped my arms around her, cuddling up the way we used to when we were kids. "I'm sorry, too."

"Why?"

I shrugged. I still felt horrible for bad-mouthing her to Raj during our date.

"You said your boss is a nice guy, right?" Jasmine smiled. "He'll write you a good ref—"

"Let's not talk about me," I interrupted, forcing out a smile. "How are you? What are you working on these days? I really liked that video you posted this morning."

"You mean the talking fish with the beanie?"

I nodded, even though I'd been thinking about something else. "What was that about?"

"Oh!" Jasmine beamed. "Well, the city is launching an environmental justice campaign in public schools this spring. And they hired *us* to animate a video for it!"

I swallowed hard. "Really?"

"Yeah! It's so cool. Right now, we're still in the planning stages. We're working with a bunch of producers and scriptwriters, and we'll have to make sure it's super shareable and social media friendly, you know? Like, it would be so great if we could get it trending as some sort of TikTok challenge . . ."

I listened to her talk about the video until my parents came up with dinner, and Mom and I resumed packing while Jasmine ate noisily on my bed.

Jasmine had a job she was passionate about. A boyfriend she loved, even though the rest of us didn't. She was happy and *free* and comfortable in her own skin and—

I stopped myself before that very unflattering train of thought could run away again.

I loved Jasmine more than anything, honestly. I didn't actually begrudge her happiness. I just wished that I had managed to find some happiness, too.

CHAPTER 5

$\mathcal{E}$ven though I'd made the plans, secured a visa, packed, and said all my goodbyes, it didn't really hit me that I was going to India until twelve hours later, when I found myself at the very back of the biggest jumbo jet I'd ever been on.

I'd never traveled alone before, let alone gone on an international flight that took me to the other side of the Pacific Ocean, but I was prepared. I had Jasmine's fully stocked plane pack and snacks galore, and had downloaded the entire discography of Lady Gaga, Kendrick Lamar, and Metric to keep me occupied if I found myself awake and bored on the fourteen-hour flight to New Delhi.

I glanced around at the nearby passengers. Everyone seemed to be playing with the screen on the headrest in front of them. Curious, I spent the rest of the boarding period scrolling through the in-flight entertainment options, quietly fist-pumping when I discovered it had the first few seasons of *Sex and the City*.

Plugging in my earphones, I picked one of my favorite episodes and happily sank into my seat. I was very aware the show hadn't aged well, and Mr. Big was a *big* dick that Carrie shouldn't have pined over, but I still loved it. Years ago, when Mom and Dad were asleep, Jasmine and I would sneak down to the living room and binge episodes until we got caught.

I settled in, barely even registering when the plane took off as I watched Carrie sneak away from her friends to go over to Big's apartment and then throw her arms around him in a passionate embrace.

My eyelids felt heavy as my daydreams merged with the show. Kissing her deeply, he steered her toward the bedroom. I squirmed in my seat, imagining someone's arms around me like that. Peeling off my dress—couture, of course—twisting my ponytail into a knot as he pulled me closer to him.

For a moment I thought that, maybe, it could be Raj. I blinked, but his face disappeared; it wasn't him.

No. It was someone else, a man I'd never met but who conveniently had the looks and general *sex god* aura of Chris Hemsworth and Riz Ahmed combined. My breathing turned shallow as I imagined us together, rolling around, our limbs intertwined, his mouth wet against my neck . . .

Niki, I love you, baby.

Oh, Chris/Riz, I want you—

I felt something shift next to me. I blinked, trying to ignore the passenger next to me and stay focused on the moment. But they moved again, and hesitantly, I glanced their way only to discover my immediate neighbor was about eight years old.

And he was watching Carrie and Mr. Big *seriously* get it on.

I panicked, pressing my hand against the screen. Still, between my fingers, I could see their limbs moving. Damp, bare skin. I tugged out my earphones and fumbled with the control buttons, sighing in relief when I finally managed to get the show turned off.

"You shouldn't be watching that," I stammered. My face was hot, and I was too embarrassed to look at the kid. "Where are your parents?"

"Up there. We couldn't get any seats together." He gestured vaguely toward the front of the plane. "Where's your husband?"

"I don't have a husband."

"Do you have a boyfriend?"

He blinked at me, his eyelashes annoyingly longer than my own.

"You shouldn't ask people that," I replied, eyeing him. "But no. I don't have a boyfriend."

"Is that why you're watching porn?"

My mouth dropped.

Damn it. Maybe the kid was onto something.

*T*he kid, Vivek, wasn't so bad in the end (especially when he was asleep). But for the few hours we were both awake, he let me watch a new Disney movie on his iPad with him, and I shared some of my snacks. We high-fived when we parted ways. He also asked me on a date when we both got back to Seattle. (With the heaviest of hearts, I had to tell him no. I also texted Dad to make sure he knew I was still capable of meeting people in real life, even if they weren't Matthew McConaughey or of legal age . . .)

As I went through customs and navigated the massive airport, my head felt foggy. I was both overheated and chilled to the bone, and wandered aimlessly through the terminal while I waited out my layover. My parents had warned me not to drink the water in India, as my stomach wasn't used to it, and so I cautiously brushed my teeth and washed my face in the restroom with bottled water I bought from a vending machine.

I slept like a rock on the two-hour flight to Mumbai and woke up feeling slightly refreshed. I picked up my suitcase from baggage claim and, with a spring in my step, made my way outside the terminal.

I didn't know what to expect, but what I found outside wasn't it. The bright sun and humidity. The smog. The sheer noise and volume of people standing outside in the collection area was overwhelming. I felt dread and excitement in equal measure hanging thick in the air like a noxious cloud of emotion. I waited outside, my skin damp beneath my sweatshirt. Should arriving in India have felt like I was coming home?

Because it didn't. I'd never even been here.

*D*iya eventually found me at the airport, and we caught up on the drive back to her apartment. Even from the car, I could tell there was a pulse to Mumbai, quick and unpredictable. Until you are stuck in an Indian traffic jam of speeding cars, rick-shaws, scooters, and occasional livestock, you can never really know what it's like.

The city, or at least the parts I was seeing speeding by in Diya's red Hyundai, was hard to describe and impossible to compare to anything I had ever seen before. It was a hodgepodge of apartment buildings and shop fronts, markets and thoroughfares, a devastating collision of both unimaginable wealth and poverty.

"You get used to it," Diya said at one point, catching me staring at a makeshift shelter by the side of the road. Beneath it were several families, including small children playing in the ditch.

I didn't respond, unsure about what to say.

"Inequality is everywhere, Niki," Diya continued. "Even in Seattle. Some countries are simply better at hiding it."

I smiled weakly. She was right. But it didn't make it any less difficult to see up close.

Diya's family lived in a three-bedroom apartment on the twentieth floor of a high-rise apartment building. She'd moved back in with them after college abroad, and it was wonderful to see her parents after so long. They'd visited Diya at least once a year in Seattle and always took us out to dinner and insisted I call them by their nicknames—Auntie Jo and Uncle Jo. (Their last name was Joshi.) They took me on a tour of the place as lunch was being prepared, and when Uncle Jo caught me admiring the view during the tour, he tracked down a map to orient me.

They lived in a western suburb called Bandra, neighboring both the ocean and glamorous South Bombay. With a pen, Auntie Jo drew an X through all the places she recommended I visit during my time with them, everything from their favorite Marathi restaurants to Chowpatty Beach to Colaba at the southernmost tip of the peninsula, which still had strong elements of Bombay's history as a Portuguese colony. I was surprised to see them call their home Bombay instead of Mumbai, even though the name had switched back from the British's botched pronunciation decades ago. I suppose that's what they were used to calling it.

"How was the drive from the airport, Niki?" Uncle Jo asked me after we ate. I was *stuffed*. Their cook was a lovely woman named Pinky, and she'd prepared a delicious fish curry dish, which we ate with rice. For dessert, Auntie Jo laid out the box of chocolates I'd brought and Mom's *pinni*, which I'd given them immediately on arrival and seemed to be a big hit.

"We could have sent our driver," Auntie Jo added. "However, my bullheaded daughter *insisted* on picking you up herself."

I knocked shoulders with Diya, silently thanking her for the hours she'd spent in the car to come get me.

"The drive was . . ." I hesitated, trying to come up with the right word. "Exciting."

"So diplomatic!" Uncle Jo exclaimed. "There is a saying here in India. While driving, all you need is good brakes, a good horn, and good *luck*!"

I laughed. Auntie Jo and Diya looked like they'd heard the joke before.

After lunch, Diya insisted I try to nap, as we'd be out late that night celebrating Diwali. I slept deeply until midafternoon, waking up to Diya and her parents exclaiming loudly in the kitchen over wedding plans, which was only a week away.

I felt guilty arriving as a houseguest at such an inconvenient time, but when I mentioned this to Diya, she rolled her eyes and told me to "chill," and that they were excited to have me around to keep the family sane during what promised to be a hectic time. Still, I'd booked myself a room at a hotel for once the wedding festivities commenced, one where a lot of their out-of-town guests were staying.

I felt like a new woman after showering, and Diya and I got ready together in her room like we did back in college for a night out, sharing makeup, hair products, and Diya's curling iron while sipping on cold beer as we chatted our faces off. We covered the topics all old friends talk about when they haven't seen each other in a while. Family and friendship. Love and careers. For about ten minutes, when both of us were feeling particularly existential, we even brushed up on the meaning of life. (And didn't come to any profound or even sensible conclusions.)

Even though it stung, it felt good to talk about the layoff and my nervousness about finding a new job, and Diya cathartically vented about how challenging it had been the past six months balancing familial expectations for her traditional Hindu wedding and working seventy hours a week.

"It's like my managing partner is waiting for me to screw up or miss a day of work." Diya stopped abruptly, riffled through her closet until she found the pair of heels she was searching for. "I could not miss even one beat, Niki. Do you know what he said to me when I announced the engagement?"

I shook my head, watching her.

"He did not even congratulate me. He said, 'When can I expect your notice now that you are taken *care* of?'"

My jaw dropped. "He said *what*?"

"I will show him," Diya muttered, as she pulled out a pair of nude heels. "Pretty soon, I will be taking *his* job."

I stood up and gave Diya a high five and told her I was proud of her. Even though Diya was privileged, she was still a woman, and sexism cut through everything—class or caste or socioeconomic status—no matter the industry. No matter the country. Back home, tech was notoriously male, and although strides were being taken to make the industry more equitable, there was still a way to go. At my old company, the board of executives that had mandated that ten percent of the company be laid off was made up of one hundred percent men.

"*Bus*. I have a few weeks off now," Diya added. "And I am *allowed* to be excited for my own damn wedding. *Finally*."

I winked at her. *Finally* was right. She and Mihir had been together since high school, and long distance at least half of that time. *Finally* they'd be "allowed" to share a bed or go on vacation together without lying to their parents about how many hotel rooms they were getting.

"What about you," Diya said, switching gears. "Do you have further updates on Raj? Have you texted him to say you arrived safely?"

I shook my head, applying Diya's cream eye shadow to my lids. I'd checked in with my family, but that was it.

"Niki," she warned, causing me to look over. Diya was standing in front of the mirror, adjusting the rose gold *dupatta* that matched her *lengha*. "You don't want this to fizzle out, do you?"

I hesitated, about to say one thing but then opted on another. "I guess I don't."

"Then text him." She smiled. "Let him know you are thinking about him."

"Now?"

"Now."

I obediently texted Raj and then tossed my phone on the bed. I'd done my hair and makeup and even had jewelry on, but I was still wearing Diya's bathrobe over my undies. I still hadn't decided whether or not to wear Mom's canary yellow sari or my standard black cocktail dress that I'd worn at least fifteen times.

"Question," I said, thinking about what would best fit the occasion. "I know Diwali is 'the Festival of Lights' and all, but what exactly are we *celebrating*?"

"Me, of course." Diya pouted her lips at the mirror. "You know that essentially *diya* means 'light' in English?"

I nodded. My vocabulary was poor, but that word I knew.

"So there you go. It is the Festival of Diya." She winked at herself in the mirror. "It is the festival of *me*!"

CHAPTER 6

$\mathcal{I}$n the end, I went with the sari after watching Diya gush at the detailed gold-and-saffron-colored embroidery. After everyone was ready, we gathered in the *mandir* just off the main room, and Auntie Jo invited me to join in on Lakshmi Pooja. She explained it was a Hindu ritual performed on Diwali that invited the goddess into their homes to bless their family with prosperity, peace, and happiness. I happily agreed and enjoyed witnessing the custom. After, I asked her about the origin of Diwali, and as we rushed out the door, she quickly told me the festival also celebrated the return of Lord Rama from exile after fourteen years. I was curious to hear more, but as we were already late for the party, I made a note to follow up later.

Auntie and Uncle Jo didn't plan on staying at the Diwali party very long, so Diya and I took our own car. We left just after dusk, and by then, the city was lighting up with firecrackers and sparklers, lanterns, string lights, and floral garlands hanging from doorways, windows, and shop fronts.

I was in awe. I loved Diwali, but I'd never seen it like this. It was in the air we were breathing, permeating everyone it touched with music and laughter and something I even found vaguely spiritual. People were spilling out onto the streets, dressed in vibrant colors, and there were markets everywhere, hawker stands and bazaars selling everything from clothing to *paan* to sweet *burfi* of every kind and color imaginable.

The India I'd arrived at this morning had me feeling queasy, uncertain about the world and my place in it, but the last remnants of my unhappy mood cleared as Diya and I blared India's Top 40 music and cruised down Marine Drive toward the party.

It was already in full swing when we arrived at a hotel in South Mumbai. There were *diya* everywhere, covering every free surface with flickers of warm light, and fairy lights stretched across the ceiling every which way. There was a stage with live music and, behind that, a double doorway leading to a gorgeous terrace. I snuck a peek outside. Artists had decorated vast swaths of the ground with *rangoli*, powders of every color sprinkled into vibrant murals of peacocks and mandala, lotus flowers and *diya*. Knowing she would appreciate the craft, I surreptitiously took a few photos and texted them to Jasmine, who responded thirty seconds later with ten starstruck emojis.

Diya and I tracked down her parents by the bar, and they introduced us to the hosts, their close friends. I thanked them for letting me tag along and gave them a box of Mom's *pinni* before

Diya dragged me away to grab glasses of prosecco and do the "rounds."

Over the next hour, Diya introduced me to a barrage of aunties and uncles in her Mumbai community. When Diya's fiancé, Mihir, arrived, who I hadn't seen since our college graduation, we went outside to the terrace to hang out with their friends.

In very quick succession, I met the bridesmaids, six girls who grew up with Diya here in Mumbai and most of whom still lived in the city. (Diya introduced me to them as the honorary bridesmaid, as she sweetly said I would have been included if she'd known I was able to come.) Then there were the groomsmen, Mihir's friends, and after that came *the spouses*. The husbands, wives, partners, boyfriends, and girlfriends of the aforementioned.

I helped myself to my second glass of prosecco even though we hadn't eaten yet, because it was a bit overwhelming meeting such a big group. I couldn't keep track of anyone's name except Masooma, who was the most welcoming of the bunch and lessened the blow of being the outcast with such a tight-knit group of people. I didn't begrudge any of them—I'm sure Diya would feel equally left out if, one day, she was required to hang out solely with my group of school friends—but still, it made me realize that I wouldn't really know anyone at the wedding except the two people who'd be busy getting married. None of our mutual college friends from Seattle were able to come.

Masooma pulled up a chair next to me during dinner. She told me that she and her husband, Tahir, were Muslim, but they enjoyed celebrating Diwali in the same secular way many of us who weren't Christian enjoyed Christmas. Quickly, I discovered Masooma and I had a lot in common. She worked in business development for a tech company here in India, and I had a great time talking to her about the industry, Mumbai, and our love for our zany, spectacular mutual friend Diya.

I was reluctant to leave the conversation, but my bladder was about to burst, so I excused myself shortly after we'd finished eating. I practically ran to the restroom, but luckily, there was only one auntie in there and nobody ahead of me in line.

After, while drying my hands, I smiled at the auntie, who was still there fixing her lipstick in front of the mirror. She was small and round, and kept looking over at me with a sour expression on her face.

"Hello." I made eye contact with her and smiled brightly. "Are you having a nice evening?"

She smacked her lips together, turning to me. "You are Diya's American friend?"

"That's me. I'm Niki." I smiled again. "It's nice to meet you, Auntie."

"Your parents are from India or Pakistan?"

I hesitated. Technically, they were from both. "I'm Punjabi. My dad grew up near Amritsar, and my mom—"

"What is your surname?"

"Randhawa."

"Ah." She paused. "Your family is . . . *Jat*."

My jaw stiffened. She didn't say it like a question but a statement. A proclamation of what my family name said about our caste.

"You are staying on how many weeks?" she asked.

"Three," I said stiffly.

"Have nice time." She clutched my wrist, brushing past me, but not before she inspected me from top to toe. "Be advised. You must cover yourself properly in this country. The sun is very bright, *nah*?"

"I . . ." I stammered, staring after her as she walked away from me. I was enraged. Humiliated. And I stepped forward, ready to tell this sour-faced auntie how backward she was for making a dig at my dark complexion, for asking about my family's lineage, for feeding into a colorist, casteist, staggeringly broken system.

But when I opened my mouth to say something, I couldn't get a word out. Not even a grunt. This woman was a friend of Diya's parents. She was an auntie.

And even though I'd never felt that Indian, I was Indian enough to know that I had to respect her.

CHAPTER 7

Fifteen years ago

Jasmine . . ." Dad turned around from the passenger seat. "No drinking tonight. *Aacha*?"

Jasmine scoffed. "Obviously."

Mom eyed her in the rearview mirror. "We. Are. *Serious*."

Usually, I was able to duck out of the room whenever tensions ran high, but unless I wanted to throw myself out of a moving vehicle, I was stuck here.

The silence was deafening, and I shifted uncomfortably in the backseat. Mom had forced me to wear an embroidered *lengha*, and although it was pretty enough and didn't look secondhand, the fabric made my skin itch. I unbuttoned my coat, scratching at my sides where the loose threads prickled me the most. It felt like spiders were having a party in there.

"Niki," Mom snapped. "Stop scratching yourself. Are you a girl or an ape?"

I tried not to roll my eyes as I withdrew my hand. "Technically, I think I'm both?"

"Have you heard us, Jasmine?" Dad warned, ignoring me and my joke. "Have you understood? You must be on your *best* behavior."

Jasmine rolled her head away from me until her forehead was flush against the window. A beat later, she replied, "Understood."

Jasmine had missed her curfew the weekend before and spent the next morning barfing into the toilet, so needless to say, Mom and Dad were furious with her. All week, Jasmine hadn't been allowed to hang out with her friends and was ordered to come straight home after school, which meant I had to come straight home from school, too. She wasn't allowed to use the phone or computer and had been tasked with doing the dinner dishes and the whole family's laundry. I was excited to have my chore duties reduced until Jasmine threw all my clothes into the dryer and shrank my favorite pair of pajama pants.

Oh, and I forgot to mention the *lectures*. Every night before bed, Mom and Dad had sat *both* of us down on the couch and gone off about the ways of the world, spending hours bemoaning and monologuing and pleading about things that could really be boiled down into three simple points.

1. Jasmine and I were too American.
2. Jasmine and I had it too easy.
3. Jasmine and I needed to be good Indian *daughters*.

Why *I* had to sit through these sessions was beyond me. Yes, like Jasmine, I'd never been to India, and in Dad's words "had never learned how hard life could be working on the family farm," but I *was* a good Indian daughter. I'd never disobeyed them. I'd never *not* done exactly as they said. Yet here I was, lumped in with my rebellious, selfish older sister.

We arrived at the banquet hall, late as usual, and were immediately ushered to our tables. I had expected to be split up from Mom and Dad, who were led to a table with other couples their age, but I was disappointed to not even be sitting with Jasmine, who blatantly swung by the open bar on the way to her seat at the "older kids" table. I wondered if Mom and Dad saw her. In that moment, I wondered if I hated Jasmine or was in awe of her.

The speeches started, and the evening droned on, and on, and on. Until the dancing started, wedding receptions were always a snooze fest, and I passed the hours whispering with the other girls at my table. Well, I more so listened to the other girls. They were talking about Bollywood movies, and I had nothing to contribute.

"Niki?" someone said after a while. I sat up straight, having zoned out on the conversation.

"Sorry . . ." I stammered. It was Radhi speaking. She was also thirteen years old but went to a different school, so I only ever saw her at Indian functions. "What did you say?"

"Have you seen *Deewane Huye Paagal*?"

"Not yet." I cleared my throat; I'd never even heard of it. "But I've been meaning to. Who's in it again?"

"Shahid Kapoor. Oh my god—he is so good looking." Radhi paused. "Do you like him? Who's *your* favorite actor?"

I glanced around the table. All the girls were waiting for my answer, trying to include me in a conversation I had no interest being in. I knew most of them, sort of, but I didn't exactly fit in with this crowd. They all lived within a stone's throw from the *gurdwara*, went to Punjabi school twice a week, and hung out together afterward at one another's houses—watching Bollywood movies or Punjabi dramas, or practicing *bhangra* dances they made up and performed at folk festivals and celebrations.

I knew this because they used to invite me along, and I'd joined them a few times, but the *gurdwara* was thirty minutes away by car and seventy-five minutes by bus, and Mom and Dad didn't have time to drive me there, let alone pray themselves. Mom's employer paid double wages on Sunday, and so she always volunteered for those shifts, and Dad had never really been a religious man. As a family, we attended *gurdwara* only for the most auspicious occasions. Weddings and funerals. Or when Dadima, Dad's mother, who visited once a year from Punjab, was in town and forced us to go.

"My favorite actor is . . ." I trailed off, as Orlando Bloom came to mind. I'd seen *The Lord of the Rings* four times since it came out.

"Shah Rukh Khan," I said finally.

"Shah Rukh?" Radhi narrowed her eyes. "Really?"

I kicked myself. I should have known better. Picking Shah Rukh as my favorite actor would be like if I picked Brad Pitt with my white friends at school. Shah Rukh was too obvious a choice because he was everybody's favorite.

He was pretty much the most famous man in India.

Our table was one of the last to be called to the buffet. I was starving and piled my plate high with *aloo mataar*, *raita*, *saag paneer*, *daal*, chicken curry, and *naan*, the gold standard of wedding dinners in our community. I returned to my seat, and for the first time all evening, I felt like I was on the same page as the Punjabi girls. Even though our lives were totally different, and I didn't have anything in common with them, every night we all ate the same things for dinner.

"What do they put in Indian food?" Radhi exclaimed suddenly. "It's *so* yummy. Is it crack?"

"It's the *ajwain*," I blurted proudly, before anyone else could come up with the answer. "And *dhaniya* and *jeera* of course."

Two of the girls across the table giggled. My shoulders slumped.

"What?" I asked, suddenly doubting my answer. It was those three ingredients—carom seeds, ground coriander, and cumin—that made the cuisine so distinctive, right? Wasn't that what Mom put in basically every dish?

"Uh," one girl answered. "That's not how you say *jeera*."

I squirmed. "*Jee-rdaa*?"

The girl shook her head, pressing a hand over her grin.

"*Jee-rdhaa*," I said again, harder on the second syllable, but it just made the girls laugh even more.

"You sound like you're speaking Spanish or something," another one said. "That's *not* Punjabi."

My cheeks heated up as I glanced over at Radhi for backup, but she, too, was in stitches. She and all the other Punjabi girls, the more *Indian* girls, were laughing at me.

My chest tightened, and I felt the tears forming at the corners of my eyes. I blinked, swallowing hard, and refused to cry. To embarrass myself any further.

Luckily, Radhi changed the subject, and the conversation carried on, but inside I was fuming.

If Mom and Dad didn't want their daughters to be so freaking "American," then why hadn't they taught us to speak Punjabi properly? Why hadn't they rented a house closer to the *gurdwara* so they could *physically* be part of their diaspora community? Why did they never play the music or movies that showed us where we came from?

If Mom and Dad wanted us to be good Indian daughters, then hell, why had they even left India?

CHAPTER 8

$\mathcal{T}$he tears started to fall as soon as the auntie left the restroom. Thank god no one else was nearby. Thank god Diya's eye shadow was waterproof.

I flopped down on a velvety fainting couch near the sinks, patting my eyes delicately with tissue so my makeup wouldn't run.

Why was I so upset? Why did I give a flying fuck what that auntie thought of me? Although I'd had insecurities when I was a teenager and used to hide from the sun, I'd since learned to love the deep tone of my skin. And I was *proud* of my family history, my agrarian roots. The caste system was illegal and *backward*; who even cared anymore if *Jat* was the label attached to my family?

I sank deeper into the couch, my head falling into my hands. It felt heavy, like a bag of wet sand. Was the jet lag making it worse?

"Beti," someone said suddenly. "What is the matter?"

The voice was soothing and filled with so much concern that when I opened my eyes, I thought I'd see Mom. But of course it wasn't her. It was another woman, the silhouette of an angel backlit in the doorway, and I tried to get a better look at her as she rushed to my side. Her hair was cropped short at her chin in a salt-and-pepper bob, and she had an elegant maroon sari draped around her voluptuous figure. She was anywhere from forty to sixty, and one of the most beautiful women I'd ever seen in my entire life.

"Here," she said, taking the tissues from me. "I will help."

We sat together in silence as she gently patted my face. After, she stuffed the tissues in her blouse and cupped my face in her hands.

"Now you are *perfect*," she said, beaming.

"Thanks . . ." I snorted, withdrawing from her grasp.

"You don't have to tell me what's wrong. But I am sitting here a moment longer regardless."

She turned away from me and started rummaging through her purse. Her gold-toned bag was very similar to the one Mom had lent me, which I'd left in the glovebox of Diya's car.

"Thank you," I repeated, remembering myself. "I'm sorry about that."

"Why are you sorry?" she said, her eyes still down. She opened a small tube of lotion and squirted some on her palms. "Would you like some? I am Aasha, by the way."

"Niki," I replied. "It's nice to meet you, Auntie. And sure. Thank you, I'd love some."

"Ah. You are Diya's friend." She squeezed some of the hand cream onto my palm. "I thought it might be you. Would you like me to fetch her?"

"No," I said, a little too loudly. It was the Festival of Diya, and I didn't want to ruin her night. "I mean. No. But thanks. I'm OK."

Aasha Auntie looked at me skeptically, the same way Mom would if I told her something wasn't wrong when it clearly was. I sighed and reluctantly told her about the incident.

"Which lady was this?" she asked, her voice wavering. I could tell the story genuinely troubled her, and so I described the sour-faced woman. Aasha Auntie nodded in recognition.

"Ignore her. She is a very ignorant person." Auntie tutted. "No wonder her children secretly go to therapy."

"I can usually ignore people like that," I said tentatively. "I guess I just wasn't expecting to hear it."

Or what I was expecting coming to India in the first place.

"It is women like that who give the aunties a bad name," she said after a moment. "We are not all *so* bad."

"I know," I laughed, suddenly feeling shy. "I feel better just talking to you."

Aasha Auntie narrowed her eyes, and I caught her giving me the familiar up and down.

"You know," Aasha Auntie purred, "I have a son."

I cleared my throat. Uh-huh. Of course she had a son. Even the nice aunties had a *son.*

Suddenly, she started. "Now *I* am sorry, *beti.* I am being silly only." She ran her fingers through her hair. "Ignore me. You are much too sensible for my son."

I smiled awkwardly.

"I just miss my boy. I wish he would find a nice girl and move *home*." Aasha Auntie stood up from the couch, a wistful look on her face. "Anyway. *Aaja*," she beckoned. "Let me introduce you to my friends. I will steer clear of any aunties who have sticks up their bottoms."

I laughed. "I don't know . . ."

"Please? Let me show you off." She ran her fingertips over the embroidery details of my outfit. "You look beautiful, *beti*. And what a lovely sari."

I smiled bashfully. "It's my mom's."

"I think I would like your mother. She has *impeccable* taste."

*A*asha Auntie was a blast. She drank. She smoked. She talked my ear off about everything from the state of Indian politics to her failing herb garden to the latest gossip from their social circle. After introducing me to one person or another, she immediately told me everything she knew about them. The fact that sour-faced auntie disapproved of therapy sessions was only the tip of the iceberg. She knew about all sorts of taboos and skeletons in her community's closet—affairs, divorces, broken-off engagements, bad investments, drug abuse. I jokingly said to Aasha Auntie that she should star in her own reality TV show, and she told me that she'd been invited—but turned the offer down!

When I had a moment, I also asked Auntie about Diwali. She was Hindu, like Diya's family, but originally from West Bengal. She told me that in her community back in Kolkata, their *pooja* on Diwali worshiped the goddess Kali.

The evening wore on and the party got louder. There were fireworks going off outside in all directions, and so the band turned up the speakers inside the ballroom, and at some point, Aasha Auntie and I ended up close to the stage. It was impossible to have a conversation without screaming at each other, and so we stopped gabbing about the Patel-Mehta Feud of 2012 and started enjoying the music.

The band was incredible. All night, I'd been vaguely aware they'd been covering popular Indian and Western songs, but up close, many of them sounded better than the originals. The arrangements they picked were unusual, funky, totally out of left field, but they somehow seemed to work. Who knew the song "All of Me" sounded better as indie rock with a quick tempo than the original John Legend power ballad?

Aasha Auntie and I watched the band from down below, and a few minutes turned into a few more, and the longer we watched them, the more my eyes kept flicking toward the back of the stage. Toward the guy behind the bass guitar.

God, he was hot.

Not exactly the Chris Hemsworth slash Riz Ahmed dreamboat I'd been caught fantasizing about on the plane, but pretty damn close. Maybe even better.

I blinked, trying to determine whether I was biased because I tended to find musicians sexy . . . Nope. Even when I mentally stripped him of his bass guitar, he was still hot as hell, and I admired every inch of him. The stubble on his face and the way his shaggy black hair swooped across his forehead. He was wearing tight washed-out jeans and sneakers, and a white collared shirt with the top button undone. His biceps bulged beneath the material every time he moved, and I wanted to lunge out and bite those lips as he sang backup and got up close to the microphone.

The band finished playing a Bollywood hit classic and immediately went into a Lenny Kravitz cover. The bass guitarist perked up, and by the renewed energy beaming off him, I could tell this song was his element.

I licked my lips. Was my mouth literally watering? I surreptitiously touched my face to check for drool. Thankfully, I was in the clear.

I tried to look away from him, but honest to god, I couldn't. I was hypnotized. He had the confident aura of a lead singer. Chris Martin. Prince. Patti Smith. The rawness and ruggedness of a drummer like Travis from Blink-182.

And the aloof, *sexy* swagger of a bass guitarist.

Mesmerized, I watched him. Exactly how his body moved or his hands ran over the guitar. His fingers seemed lazy on the strings, almost asleep in the deep rhythm, but a beat later, they were on fire as he launched into a solo Paul McCartney or Louis Johnson style. Or—gulp—my all-time favorite, Flea from the Red Hot Chili Peppers.

His solo finished, and a moment later, I caught him looking in my direction. I was standing pretty far away, but it felt like our eyes locked, and a sweaty pulse of heat started coursing through me.

Hey, girl.

I batted my eyelashes in return, starstruck.

Wow, you sure know your way around that bass guitar.

I know my way around a lot of things.

I swooned. In real life and in my imagination, as once again his eyes flashed my way.

What are you doing after the show?

I felt weak in the knees as I waited for his response to the imaginary flirtation we were having in my head.

Coming over. I know you want me to.

You'll have to be quiet. My friends' parents will be home . . .

He raised his eyebrows at me. Was it a wink? I was too far away to tell, and I blushed from daydreaming about what might happen if . . .

"The band is very good, *nah*?" Aasha Auntie asked, startling me. She cleared her throat as I turned to look at her.

"Yes," I answered, my face still flushed. "Very good."

She paused, a sly grin on her face. "Are you *sure* I can't introduce you to my son?"

Her eyes flicked to the stage, and my heart dropped into my stomach when I realized who her son was.

The bass guitarist I'd been trying to eye-bang in plain sight.

The handsome hunk of a man who clearly wasn't making eyes back at me but looking at his *mother*.

CHAPTER 9

The next five minutes were definitely among the top three most mortifying moments of my life. (The first being when my skirt fell down during my school production of *A Midsummer Night's Dream*, and the second occurring last year, when I accidentally screenshared my shopping cart at Victoria Secret during a Zoom meeting. Honestly, the fact that I was in the process of purchasing my very single self a grandmother-chic housecoat was more embarrassing than if it had been lingerie.)

But unlike my former classmates and coworkers, Aasha Auntie let me off the hook pretty easily. She obviously knew I'd been checking out her son but didn't press me on it, and politely hugged me goodbye when I made my escape and told her I'd better go find Diya.

My face was still hot with shame when I went outside. I'd been expecting fresh, cool air to greet me, but the night was heavy with humidity. I fanned myself with a napkin, grabbed a sparkling water from the bar, and then returned to Diya, Mihir, and their friends.

The whole group took up two tables at the far end of the terrace, and for a while, I tried to put my embarrassing moment behind me and join in the conversation. Mihir was in the middle of telling everyone a story about his bachelor party, which I'd already heard about from Diya, and I'd almost put the bass guitarist out of my mind when I noticed him outside.

I straightened my shoulders, watching him. He'd changed out of his jeans and tight collared shirt, but he looked even more handsome in the light-colored *sherwani* he'd put on. I tried not to watch him work the crowd, mingling and smiling and shaking hands and generally being a total hottie, but I couldn't help it. My eyes kept involuntarily leaving my hands, my drink, or whomever in the group was talking, and wandering back to *him*.

"Sam!"

My body contorted awkwardly when I saw Diya stand up from her chair and wave at him. I silently prayed he wouldn't come over, but within ten seconds, he'd wrapped up his conversation and was coming toward our group full steam.

I sank down in my chair, mortified. Had he seen me staring at him? All of a sudden, I felt like I was in my high school cafeteria again, like a total nerd lusting after our basketball team's starting point guard. (Raymond, by the way, never even knew my name, while thirteen years later I still knew his middle name was Andre and that he ordered his chicken burger without mayo from the lunch lady.)

Luckily, *Sam* made his way to the other end of our table. He didn't look my way while he chatted to Diya and the others, but still, I could feel myself sweating through my sari every time he glanced in my direction. His accent was both British and Indian—oh god, he even *sounded* like Riz Ahmed—and by the way he was talking to everyone, it seemed that Sam wasn't just the bass guitarist but a friend of Diya's.

"Where are my manners," Diya said after a few minutes. "Sam, have you been introduced to Niki?"

"Niki?" he repeated, giving me a look. I couldn't tell what it meant and was really, really trying not to care, and so I coolly waved in return.

"No," he said, holding my gaze from across the table. "I don't think we met . . . officially."

Officially?

Oh god. He definitely caught me gawking at him.

"Hey," I croaked, unsuccessfully attempting to come across as casual. "Great show tonight."

"He is so talented, right?" Diya chimed in, turning back to Sam. "You know, Niki is a musician also. One time in college she—"

"Had a short-lived rock-and-roll phase," I said, interrupting her. "Just the music. Not the lifestyle."

Diya and the others laughed, including *Sam*, and she started telling everyone about the time we unsuccessfully tried to use fake IDs to get into a jazz club. I was stiff, hyperaware that everyone was listening to a story about me. I tried to keep my gaze away from Sam, but yet, I couldn't control myself. I chanced a look at him. And this time, he definitely wasn't looking at his mother.

His eyes were squarely on me.

"Do you hear that?" one of the bridesmaids said after the story was over. "It's 'Gangnam Style'—what a throwback!"

"The DJ is on?" Diya sprouted up from her chair. "Should we go dance?"

"Oh sure," Sam joked, "now that I'm done with my set, everyone's in the mood for a dance."

"Sorry, sweetie." Diya pinched Sam's cheek as she rushed by him. "We just can't dance to your music!"

I downed my sparkling water in preparation for the dance floor, but when I jostled my chair backward, the tail of my sari caught beneath the leg, and I nearly fell over. Luckily, I didn't and was eventually able to break free without looking completely foolish. Still, it took me a while, and when I finally detangled myself, everyone had gone inside.

Everyone, that is, except Sam.

He was staring at me like I had food on my face. I stepped toward him, quickly wiping my lips to double-check. No crumbs. *Good*. But—oh god—had I just smeared my lipstick?

"I'm curious about this rock-and-roll phase you claimed not to have had," he said. "Because I can picture it, clearly."

Sam sauntered toward me, his hands deep in his pockets. My stomach lurched as his eyes ever so briefly dropped to my lips.

"Do you like Soundgarden? Your long hair is a dead ringer for the lead singer's."

"You think so?"

"His name is Chris Cornell—"

"I know who the lead singer of Soundgarden is," I interrupted playfully, crossing my arms. "Seattle *is* the birthplace of grunge."

Sam raised an eyebrow at me.

"And if I'm like any of those guys, it's clearly Kurt Cobain."

"Why is that?"

I shrugged. "Because I'm the best."

Sam's face split open into a grin, and my stomach somersaulted as it occurred to me that he was flirting with me. And OMG, I had successfully flirted back!

"Now I understand why my mother volunteered to set us up," Sam continued, stepping toward me. "What I don't understand is why you turned her down."

"I . . ." I stammered, my cheeks reddening. He was standing much too close to me.

"How could you reject me? We hadn't even met."

"I'm so sorry—"

Sam waved me off. "This is really bad for my self-esteem, Niki."

I was about to apologize again, but then his mouth quivered, and it was enough to clue me in. He was *teasing* me.

"I'm hurt, you know. *Really* hurt."

I pursed my lips to keep from smiling. Sam knew how to dish it out. But he happened to be messing with the younger sister of Jasmine the Torturer, who made it her life's mission to screw with me, so I knew exactly how to throw it right back.

"I'm so sorry, Sam," I said earnestly. "I did reject you. You're handsome and all, and I really liked your band, but the truth is, I'm in love with someone else."

This didn't seem to be the answer he was expecting. Sam furrowed his brows at me, but I cut him off when he opened his mouth to speak.

"Are you going to be OK?" I asked earnestly. I linked arms with him, steering him to the edge of the terrace. I rested my elbows on the guardrail and stared out into the distance, sighing dramatically. "Can I tell you a secret?"

I gazed up at Sam, deadpan. I could tell he thought this conversation had made a turn toward la-la land, and he wanted to get as far away from me as possible. He looked uncomfortable, his hands fighting through the fabric of his pockets. Lightly, I clutched my chest.

"It's Mihir."

Sam squinted at me, and a beat later, his face went dark. "Mihir *Gaur*? As in, you are in love with *Diya's* fiancé?"

I nodded. "I've come to break up the wedding. If Bollywood has taught me anything, it's that I need to follow my heart. Right?"

I leaned my right hip against the guardrail, facing him. Our eyes locked, and my pulse pounded as we waited for the other to break.

One. Two. Three. Four . . .

I cracked a smile.

"You were having me on." Sam ran his hands over his face. "Shit. You had me worried."

"*Good.*"

"Like, what was I supposed to do? Go tell my good friend that *her* good friend from America was about to ruin the wedding?"

"It's crazy how that sort of thing is glamorized in movies,

right?" I asked. "Isn't that the whole premise to *My Best Friend's Wedding*?"

I wasn't sure Sam would get the reference, but he did. And when he smiled, I forgot that we were two normal people joking around and remembered what a spicy dish he was. Like extra hot mango *aachar*.

It felt good to have maintained my composure around him and to know that I could still be myself around a cute guy, unlike when I was younger. We talked for a few minutes about problematic rom-coms, and then Sam started asking me about myself. I didn't know if it was because he was a good actor or not, but he did *seem* genuinely curious, and very briefly, I told him about my family and how my parents had both left India independently and had met, married, and had children in the US.

"Are you in finance, like Diya?"

I shook my head. "Tech."

"Oh, so you're like that hacker in *The Girl with the Dragon Tattoo*?" he teased.

"More like . . . *The Girl Who Lived in One of the Tech Capitals of the World*." I shrugged. "And I was always good with computers, so it seemed like the practical thing to do."

"I didn't have you pegged as the type of girl to make practical choices," Sam said. "You're Diya's friend. I assumed you were a wild card like her."

"A wild card?" I laughed. "No. Not even close."

"From what I hear, you did plan a trip to India on about a day's notice—"

"That sort of impulsiveness was a one-time thing."

"And why is that?" he asked softly.

I breathed in, the muggy air filling my lungs. I should have known this follow-up question was coming, and although I wasn't proud of the fact I was no longer employed, I wasn't going to lie about it.

"I had a change of circumstances."

Sam's eyes opened wide. "As in . . ."

"As in I was let go."

"Oh." His face darkened. "Sorry. Didn't mean to drag that out of you."

I waved him off. "No, it's fine. I'm happy to talk about it." I swallowed hard. "I liked my job well enough, but I wasn't exactly passionate about the company I worked for. Its products arguably add no value to this world, and the board must have realized it, because they didn't approve next year's budget." I shrugged. "A bunch of us got laid off."

"Still. I can tell you would have put a lot of yourself into that job. It must be hard to leave behind." Sam paused, his gaze so intense I felt a shiver. "But do you reckon everything happens for a reason?"

I squirmed. "You mean, do I believe in fate?"

"Serendipity. *Kismat*. Destiny. There are many words for it."

"No," I answered. "I don't."

"So, you don't think you were meant to lose that job?" Sam whispered. He moved in closer to me, his elbows resting against the guardrail. "That it was the universe's way of forcing you to look for one you will love even more?"

"If I wanted to make myself feel better, *sure* . . ."

"You don't think you were *meant* to come to Diya's wedding?"

My mouth twitched. The thought had crossed my mind, but only fleetingly.

"No," I replied.

"Really, no?" Sam persisted. He drew in even closer, and when our forearms touched, my face flushed red. "You don't think all of that happened so you could end up right *here*? Standing here with *me*?"

At some point, he'd gone from serious to teasing me again. I laughed, taking a giant step away from him. Sam's physical proximity, the heat of his forearm, the potent scent of his aftershave—it was starting to get overwhelming. The fireworks boomed in my ear, and I pressed my hand to my temple, wondering if I should go find Diya. It was getting late. I hadn't had a good night's sleep since . . . I couldn't even remember when. And while it felt good to be flirting with a hot bass guitarist when I was on vacation, I knew full well it didn't mean anything.

"So, tell me about you," I said suddenly. Now that he'd listened to my story, it would be impolite not to ask him questions about himself. I figured about five more minutes of this would suffice, and then I could bail and track down Diya.

"What about me?" He flashed a grin. "You know the basics. I'm Sam from the Band."

"So, Sam from the Band"—I crossed my arms, facing him fully—"tell me about your band."

"Well, these guys here"—he gestured toward the stage back inside—"we just muck around and play for parties when I'm in town. My band is back in London, where I live right now."

Right now. So he was one of those guys. Not only a musician but a wanderlust. I was both jealous and impressed, and even more convinced than before that he was a player.

"What kind of band is it?" I asked.

"Have you heard of shoegaze?"

"Have *I* heard of the Verve? My Bloody Valentine?" I rolled my eyes. "Should I continue?"

"Sorry." He raised his hands in surrender, grinning. "I forgot for a moment I was speaking with an expert."

"Right." I laughed. "Anyway, what's your band called?"

"Why do you ask?" Sam asked, bumping my shoulder with his. "Are you planning to stalk us online so you can stare at me again?"

I opened my mouth to fire back at him but froze up. I was caught. Outed. He'd seen me gawking like a groupie.

"I was just . . . admiring your musicianship," I stammered. The spot where his shoulder had touched me was on fire.

"Rubbish."

"I wasn't! I love music. *All* the music. Even yours."

"That's too bad, then," he said. "Because I couldn't stop staring at you."

Heat pooled in my core, drifting south as he held my gaze. His eyes sparkled at me, and I felt like a moth summoned to a flame as instinctively I leaned into him.

Damn, he was good.

"You weren't looking at your mom?" My voice was squeaky and weird, and I cleared my throat and detached myself from his stare.

"My mother is a beautiful woman"—Sam laughed—"but no, I wasn't looking at her."

He seemed shy suddenly, a rosy blush to his cheeks.

"You had her on her toes tonight," he said. "Most people can't keep up."

I smiled, thinking of Aasha Auntie. "Well, your mom is *cool*."

"I know. Never challenge her at beer pong."

"I wouldn't dream of it."

"She mentioned she really liked you, you know." Sam was fidgeting, like he was nervous, but players didn't get nervous, so that didn't make any sense. "Like, as a person generally, but also . . ."

As a potential match for Sam? He didn't say it, but I knew that's what he was getting at.

"Oh, and how does a guy like you react to having his mother pick out his girlfriend?"

"I'm not sure, honestly," he said. "She's never offered to do it before."

I furrowed my eyebrows, wondering if he was just trying to flatter me. *Surely*, that's all it was. But from the way he spoke about her, I could tell they were close, and I doubted he was the kind of guy who would tell a bold-faced lie about his mother.

"She was an actor, you know. Did she tell you?"

My eyes brightened. "She was?"

"When she was nineteen, she defied her family's wishes and started acting in Tollywood." Sam must have noticed my blank expression, because he went on to explain that it was the nick-name for the Bengali-language movie industry in the city's Tolly-gunge neighborhood.

"That's so badass," I said afterward.

"You have no idea. Anyway, she had small roles in at least a dozen movies, and *then* she met my father."

I smiled, ready for an epic love story.

"He's a film producer here in Mumbai." Sam shrugged. "In the end, she gave up on her dream to follow him here."

"Oh." That wasn't nearly as romantic as I'd hoped. Sam had glossed over all the good parts. "Well, couldn't she act here in Bollywood?"

"Sure. She speaks Hindi perfectly, but I suppose she pre-ferred to stay home with us." Sam went on to tell me about his sister, Leena, who worked in LA, and his brother, Prem, who lived here in Mumbai, both of whom were much older and had high-powered jobs, spouses, and families.

"Has your mom thought about going back to work?" I asked, still fascinated by Aasha Auntie's other life. "Now that you guys are grown up."

He shook his head. "You have no idea how many times my sister and I have tried to convince her. She could play someone's mum or auntie."

"Sam, she could be the leading role!" When he didn't say anything, I continued. "Anyway, I'd love to watch her movies sometime."

"She still had her maiden name back then. Google 'Aasha Bhaduri' and you'll find her."

"And your dad's movies?"

"Dad's movies," Sam said quickly, "you don't need to watch. He's not in them, after all."

"Where is he, by the way?"

"Working."

"On location?" I asked.

"No, at home in his office." Sam scratched his jaw. "Niki, would you like to go upstairs?"

He switched topics so suddenly it took me a moment to register what he was asking. I laughed, throwing him the side-eye.

"No. Not like *that*." He grinned. "I'd forgotten you don't know this hotel. There's a roof upstairs. With a *pool*."

"A pool," I repeated.

"Indeed."

"Perfect," I said, gesturing at my sari. "I'm already in my swimsuit."

Five minutes had come and gone. I had reciprocated polite conversation and showed equal interest in Sam's life, and now I was free to go grab Diya and get out of here.

I knew I shouldn't let myself be flattered by his charms. The smart thing—the *right* thing to do—would be to detach myself from this moment, appreciate it for what it was, and walk away.

But I didn't want to. My body ached just being near him, and I gripped the guardrail hard, as if latching on to it would keep me from following him upstairs.

His eyes scalded me as they landed on my lips, but the look was different this time. If I had smeared my lipstick earlier, he didn't care. That's not why he was looking.

"Will you come?" he whispered.

I thought about all the times I'd said no instead of yes, all the moments I'd never let happen. I thought about all the fun Jasmine said I'd never had.

I thought—

You know what? I was thinking too much. I was about to let this moment slip by, too. And so when Sam from the Band offered me his hand, I switched off my brain and I took it.

CHAPTER 10

*S*am and I slipped away from the party, and I followed him
to a bank of elevators at the opposite end of the hotel. When we
got out on the top floor, he pressed his forefinger to his lips and
beckoned me to follow. I hadn't realized we needed to sneak onto
the roof, which was only meant for paying guests, and a shot of
adrenaline coursed through me as we tiptoed around a group of
security guards playing cards and up a few flights of stairs to
the roof.

We were the only ones up here, pool hours long over, and at
the top of the building, we had a near panoramic view of the
city. There were fireworks going off in every direction, and down
below, the city was humming, music and laughter and celebration all playing in vivid harmony. My cheeks hurt from smiling
as Sam and I walked a lap around the roof, taking everything in,
and every so often, I felt the weight of his eyes on me. Weird, I

also thought I could hear Rihanna's "We Found Love" pulsing somewhere in the background.

"Happy Diwali," I whispered, after we'd gone completely around.

"Happy Diwali."

We stopped walking and he turned to face me. His chin was in my eye line, but I couldn't look up; I was afraid of what would happen.

Shine a light through an open door . . .

"So, why do we really celebrate Diwali, anyway?" I blurted, trying to drown out the song. I walked toward the pool, hiking up my sari. I sat down on the edge and dangled my feet in the warm water. Sam joined me a beat later.

"Do you know I've asked four different people about the holiday, and each one gave me a different answer?"

"That's not surprising."

"Well, what's your answer?"

"The explanation is really quite simple," he replied. "It's a Hindu Halloween."

My mouth dropped open, and then I smacked him on the shoulder. "O-M-F-*G*, Sam!"

"Ow!" He laughed, rubbing where I'd hit him. "I'm taking the piss. And I'm quoting *The Office*. The American version. Did you watch the Diwali episode?"

"Oh . . ." I nodded vaguely in recognition, smiling despite myself at the memory of Steve Carell's obtuse (and rather racist) one-liner about the holiday.

"Yeah. Wow." I shook my head. "Man, why haven't any of my favorite shows aged well?"

Sam shrugged, swinging his feet in the warm water. A beat later, his right foot rested against my calf.

"The explanation really is simple," he continued, and I tried not to think about the fact we were touching. "Everyone may have different rituals and traditions, many of them forgotten, but Diwali is essentially about celebrating the victory of good, or *light,* over evil."

"Really. It's that simple?" I gestured to the city around us. "Good has triumphed? When there's so much pain and suffering and poverty in this world? Good has already won?"

The comment had just slipped out, and I didn't know how someone like Sam—who grew up in India relatively privileged—would respond. I didn't share deep thoughts with many people—I was usually awkward about it and worried that our politics wouldn't align—but talking with Sam, who was sincere and earnest but lighthearted, too, it felt natural. It felt like I was talking to someone I'd known my whole life who, despite our varied experiences and backgrounds, understood the world on the very same level.

I wasn't sure how long we sat like that, but afterward, I felt both drained and completely filled up, like I'd just woken up from the deepest of sleeps. Without thinking, I moved my hand onto his knee, and he grabbed it. Our fingers interlocked, and I reveled in the touch. The heat.

The familiarity.

"Should we go back down?" I asked after a while, wondering if Diya would be looking for me.

"If you want to." He paused. "This party always goes quite late. And after the dancing comes the gambling."

I nodded. At Diwali parties back home, the uncles in particular took to card games as soon as dinner was over, especially *thine pathi*, which I'd never been able to master.

Sam withdrew his hand, and a beat later, a shiver shot down my spine when I felt it on my cheek. I turned to face him. His mouth was parted, but I could barely hear his breathing over my own. His fingers traced the outline of my jaw, and as they fell to my chin, ever so lightly he tugged. Instinctively, I leaned toward him, his thumb curling gently around my bottom lip.

My mind was blank, my body on fire.

"Wow," I said, trying not to pant. "You're good."

"Good at?"

I hesitated. "Just good . . ."

"I'm not following."

I cleared my throat and forced myself to withdraw from him. To rid myself of his . . . *spell*. My whole body felt weak and tingly, and I pulled my feet out of the water.

"Niki . . ."

I stood up, fixing my sari. He was just a good actor. He knew how to weave this tangly, magical web, and catch girls like me in a moment of weakness.

"*Niki.*"

Sam was still sitting, his feet dangling in the pool, his arms bent backward as he stared up at me.

"Yes?"

"Are you running away?"

"Yes." I swallowed hard. "As a matter of fact, I am."

Our eyes locked, and he reached out his hand and grabbed my palm.

"Don't."

I tried to wriggle free, but Sam held tight. I laughed. "Sam, you're going to make me fall in."

"Should I let that happen?"

My face flushed. He was smiling with his eyes, that beauti-ful, frustratingly kissable mouth. A mouth I needed to get very far away from.

"I dare you," I said sarcastically, and in response, Sam tight-ened his grip on me. I was facing away from the pool and squint-ing at him ever so slightly, I leaned backward.

He was holding on to me tight, and after a moment, I dipped farther backward. Our eyes were locked in a gaze, and Sam low-ered me down one more inch, and another inch after that. I was at a dangerously acute angle with the water's edge, and if Sam let go, it was utter certainty that I'd fall in. But he knew I would pull him in with me if we fell, and we stayed like that for a mo-ment longer, locked together, hovering at the precipice of some-thing wide and very deep.

"If this was a Bollywood movie," I said, "you'd let me fall in."

"What about Tollywood?"

"Same thing."

Sam loosened his grip on me by a fraction. "And then?"

"And then I'd dance around for you in my wet sari."

"Of course. I should have known." He lowered me down another inch. "It would be raining, too."

"And we'd throw flowers at each other."

"Sounds romantic as hell."

He lowered me down even farther, so far that I had to clench my abs to keep myself from falling in.

I licked my lips, challenging him. "You're playing with fire."

Sam grinned. "You mean water."

"No," I said. "I mean *fire*."

I had goose bumps all over. Our sexy banter wasn't just happening in my head but IRL. I knew the tail of my sari had fallen into the pool, but I didn't care, and I didn't know what would happen if suddenly Sam yanked me and I was in his arms, near those lips . . .

"Oy!" someone hollered. "What are you doing?"

Startled, we both turned to look, and just as we caught sight of a security guard and I went into panic mode, Sam's grip . . . *slipped*.

And I fell. Just me. In my mother's beautiful canary yellow sari, tumbling ass first into the pool.

CHAPTER 11

*S*o. The rest of the night was awkward. The security guard reamed us out in a mixture of Hindi and English for about ten minutes, although he did stop to laugh at me as Sam helped me out of the pool and I did my best to wring out my sari.

Ha. So funny.

Eventually, the security guard let us go, and Sam led me to the back exit, where there were fewer witnesses. My phone, my purse, everything was in Diya's glovebox, so he texted her on my behalf and told her he was taking me home.

In the car, Sam kept apologizing over and over for letting go of my hand, but I just laughed it off and kept changing the subject to anything humdrum I could think of, utterly embarrassed. Not for being a sopping wet mess during a fancy party. But for letting myself get close to him, for nearly . . . I shook my head. I wasn't going to go there again.

Outside Diya's apartment building, we said our goodbyes without much fanfare, and once upstairs, I tiptoed past Auntie and Uncle Jo's bedroom door, behind which they were snoring soundly, and into the guest room.

I let out a huge sigh. It felt like I hadn't breathed any oxygen for hours, and I was ready to put the evening behind me and fall straight into bed. But it took me hours to fall asleep, and even though I kept telling myself not to, I kept reliving the whole night over and over. How talented Sam was with his bass guitar and how his gaze seemed to hit me like a shock wave every time he looked at me. The way I felt just being near him.

The way I nearly let him kiss me.

I had done the right thing by putting an end to it. Right? We would have kissed, and yes, it would have been soul crushing and breathtaking, like in a Rihanna music video, but it also would have been a fling. Sam lived in a different country, and even though he was *Indian*, that didn't mean he was the kind of guy you could take home to your parents. What kind of Indian parents wanted their daughter to end up with a sexy London rock star?

I tossed and turned for what felt like forever, but I must have fallen asleep because suddenly I was being shaken awake by Diya. She was in a bathrobe, a towel wrapped around her head, and I moved over so she could crawl in next to me.

"What time is it?" I asked groggily.

"Noon. No stress. I just woke up also." She slid into the sheets, tossing my phone and evening bag onto the covers. "Raj texted you."

I shrugged, grabbing my phone. Raj had indeed replied to my message overnight, a few texts asking about my trip and then telling me about his week so far. Strangely, it kind of read like a work-related e-mail.

"You should reply now," Diya prompted. "With the time difference, he might have already gone to sleep."

"I will." I set the phone on the bedside table. "Soon. So, how was your night?"

"Oh. *My* night was perfectly fine." Diya rolled toward me. "How was *your* night?"

"What . . . what do you mean?" I stammered, avoiding eye contact. "Oh, you're talking about Sam. Nothing happened—"

"You are a *terrible* liar. If nothing happened, then why did you leave with him?"

To clear my name, I was forced to tell Diya about the pool incident and then explain the reason we were up there in the first place.

"But honestly, we didn't even *kiss*," I said, crossing my finger over my heart. I left out the part that we very nearly did kiss and that my bottom lip still throbbed from the anticipation.

"Who knew my Niki was such a player," Diya teased. "You have Raj on the go and now *Sam*."

I let out an exasperated sigh as Diya giggled. Her towel had unraveled, and her wet hair spilled out onto the pillow. I glanced toward the windowsill, expecting to find my wet sari where I'd laid it overnight. I furrowed my eyebrows when I realized it was gone.

"For the record, I am one hundred percent Team Raj," I heard

Diya say, and I looked back at her. "My vote is you go home and make passionate love to that handsome bearded man, and call me and tell me everything about it."

"Consider it done," I said blandly.

"But Sam." Diya clicked her tongue. "He is a good distraction. Cute, *nah*?"

My face flushed.

"And you do have a lot in common." Diya sat up, her eyes searching. "Wait. Maybe I am Team Sam . . ."

"Diya." I whacked her with my pillow. "If anyone's a player, it's clearly Sam."

"Why do you say that?" Diya nodded, waving me off before I could say anything. "Oh. Because he is extremely good-looking. Yeah. Sure. But he was a late bloomer. Sam was kind of a dork until, like, very recently."

I rolled my eyes. Everyone claimed to be a late bloomer, which annoyed true late bloomers like me.

"I will prove it to you." Diya dug into her robe pocket, fishing out her own phone. After a minute of scrolling through pictures, she pressed the screen toward my face. "See? See what a little weirdo he was?"

I blinked, scanning the photo. It was taken in the living room just outside the door. Diya was with her friends, and everyone looked like they were in high school, fifteen or so. It took me a moment to spot Sam. He had the same piercing eyes and soft lips, but he was much shorter, rounder, too. And his haircut didn't do him any favors. I squinted.

"Wait," I hesitated, vaguely recognizing the youthful face. "Sam is your good friend *Sameer* Mukherji?"

"Yeah," Diya nodded enthusiastically. "Of *course*. Now that he thinks he is Tom Hiddleston, we call him Sam, but he is still the same adorable little boy."

I cleared my throat. Diya may have never spoken about her hot friend Sam, but back in college, I had heard all about Sameer, and I felt flustered trying to merge the two versions of the man together.

Sameer and Diya had known each other since they were babies. Their parents were close and sent them to the same school, where they had the same teachers and groups of friends, their lives only diverging when Diya moved to Seattle and Sameer picked a college farther down the West Coast, UCLA. Back then, she used to talk about him all the time, and suddenly I remembered random stories about them together, and me once asking her point-blank that if she liked him so much, why hadn't they ever dated. She'd told me that, in fact, they had gone out for three weeks in the sixth grade, mutually calling it off when they kissed for the first time, and both agreed that it felt like making out with a relative.

"Do you know Sam cut himself off financially from his parents?" Diya said after a few minutes had passed. "Like *properly* cut off."

I shook my head, trying to feign disinterest. "No. Didn't come up."

Diya went on to tell me all about how Sam/Sameer had gone

to business school because his father refused to pay for a music degree. But after graduation, instead of going home and getting a secure job in Mumbai, he moved in with his sister in Los Angeles, and then later to Berlin, working in pubs while forming a band with musicians he met at gigs. They started touring around Europe, Diya said, small venues in basements and warehouses and opening for more well-known groups, and eventually, everyone relocated to London. They had the biggest fan base in the UK, which made sense, as it was the birthplace of the shoegazing subgenre.

"How does he support himself?" I asked Diya afterward. I couldn't help asking. The lack of salary and stability in music for those who weren't certifiable geniuses was the reason I'd never even considered going down that path.

"The band does well from what I understand." She shrugged. "But he does odd jobs also. He can be extremely private, so I am not really sure."

I pulled the covers up to my chin. From our conversation the night before, I could tell something was off with Sam and his dad, but I wondered how Aasha Auntie felt about his life. I wanted to ask Diya, but it was personal and decided not to pry any further.

My stomach somersaulted. I was hungry, my insides confused by my body's new schedule, plus the information Diya had just dumped on me.

It was easy to believe that what had happened last night was some run-of-the-mill move by Sam, the player. The sexy bass guitarist. But now that Sameer was in the picture, the sweet guy Diya had told me all about? Who she'd vouch for? Well, now I didn't know what last night meant. Probably nothing.

It was Diwali after all, and in the spirit of the moment, we'd just gotten carried away.

CHAPTER 12

*D*iya was officially off work now that the first wedding event was only one week away, and as we drank chai together in bed, I devoted my time and my services to her one hundred percent to help with whatever she needed.

She told me to chill out and that nearly everything was handled, and so we spent the afternoon together a short drive north of her building, drinking coconut water straight from the shell and lounging in the sun on Juhu Beach.

It was her last day of rest, because the very next day, Auntie and Uncle Jo awoke Diya from her nonchalant, prewedding slumber, and the apartment turned into a zoo. One with wedding planners coming and going, vendors and suppliers, a hustle and bustle that seemed to go most smoothly when I simply stayed out of everyone's way.

I assisted where I could, but after a few hours of contributing, everyone kept shooing me away, telling me to make the most of my time and see the city. I tried not to bow to the pressure, but they insisted, pushing me out the door, along with their cook, Pinky, whom they'd asked to be my tour guide.

Even though I understood before I arrived that domestic help was much more prevalent in India, it was unsettling at first to have so much attention and help. But Pinky and I got on like a house on fire, and pretty soon, it felt natural to be hanging out with her. She was probably in her late thirties and wasn't old enough for me to address as Auntie, so I started referring to her as *didi* during our afternoons out, which was the respectful term for elder sister. (Pinky also admitted to me that she had been the one who'd rescued my sari from my bedroom the morning after the Diwali party and had found a specialist dry cleaner to save it from ruin. I hugged her so hard in thanks she teased me that I'd broken one of her ribs.)

Auntie and Uncle Jo's driver, Manish, took us everywhere over the next few days. We checked out the architecture of Old Mumbai and the Gateway of India, and shopped at the Colaba Causeway, as well as other stores Pinky told me were popular on Linking Road. We took a day trip east of the city to the Elephanta Caves and, another day, saw the Hanging Gardens and the Nehru Science Centre. Manish even let me drive the car for a bit on Marine Drive. Mumbai traffic was frightening to me, but I stayed in the slow lane closest to the waterfront and summoned Uncle Jo's proverb about successful driving in India.

Good brakes. Good horn. Good luck!

But my favorite excursion *had* to be our final day of sightseeing, when we went on a food crawl. Although Pinky and Manish had been instructed to steer me clear of street food to be safe, Auntie Jo had given us a list of restaurants that served the dishes Mumbai was famous for, like *pani puri*, *pav bhaji*, *mango fadooda*, and the best *paprdi chaat* I'd ever tasted. Everything was delicious, and I took selfies of Pinky, Manish, and me devouring everything, and then sent them immediately to my family group chat, where everyone was understandably jealous. The best pictures I also posted on Instagram, and Diya, who wasn't able to join us again because she and Mihir were meeting with the pundit officiating their wedding, commented within five minutes.

As you would say, Niki, I am experiencing serious FOMO.

Afterward, Manish dropped me off at the apartment. Nobody was home, and I slumped into the couch, stuffed and pleasantly fatigued. I scrolled mindlessly on Instagram for a few minutes and, when I got bored of that, clicked on my message thread with Raj.

Our exchange was pretty dull to be honest, but it was difficult to force a conversation with someone I didn't know that well yet—especially with the twelve-hour time difference. I thought about sending him a few more pictures from our food crawl but decided against it in favor of something more productive: job hunting.

I wasn't in the mood to switch off vacation mode, which I was enjoying immensely, but I knew it was time for me to start considering what I would do with myself when I got home from India. Opening Google, I searched "data analytics jobs Seattle," and luckily, there were quite a few roles posted—even if none of the companies looked all that interesting.

I hadn't brought my laptop to India, and so I grabbed Diya's from her bedroom. Her password was still, adorably and disgustingly, DiyaAndMihirForever, and I minimized the dozens of wedding-related websites she had open and logged in to my e-mail.

My CV was already in good shape, and so I got to work on the cover letter, amending it slightly for each job. I fired off four applications and was working on a fifth when I heard the front door click shut and then the familiar pattering of Diya's heels across the floor.

"Niki?"

"In here!"

A beat later, Diya limped into the room, looking absolutely exhausted. Her hair, which she'd styled that morning into an elegant topknot, had come undone and was hanging limply by her face.

"If you ever decide to get married," she said, collapsing next to me on the couch, "elope."

"That bad, huh?"

"I don't want to talk about it." Diya pulled her feet up, glancing at the computer. "Tell me, are you watching porn on my computer?"

I blushed. Even as a joke, why did everyone think I watched porn? Did I look *that* horny?

"My nani uses that computer," Diya whined.

"Should I bookmark the page, then?" I deadpanned. "Do you think she'll like threesomes better—"

"Gross! I can't think of her like that."

"FYI, Diya, women her age can be *extremely* sexually active—"

"OK, you shut up now." She kneed me in the stomach, laughing. "Tell me. What were you really doing?"

"Uploading my audition for the casting couch."

"And you used my *parents'* couch?"

She glared at me until the giggles burst out from both of us. After they'd subsided, I finally told Diya about the roles I'd applied for, and even though she was shaking with fatigue, I could tell she was trying to act supportive.

"I am going for a quick bath," Diya said after I'd finished babbling. "Join me for a drink on the balcony afterward? Whiskey sours?"

"Are you up for it?"

"I am getting married, Niki, not *dying*." She peeled herself off the couch, as if in slow motion. "I am always up for a drink."

I laughed. "It's a date, then."

Diya started to walk away, but halfway to her bedroom turned around and stared at me.

"Yes?"

"Something fairly odd happened today." Diya paused for like a good ten seconds. "Sam asked me for your phone number."

A weird, snotty wheeze came involuntarily from my throat, but I played it cool and pretended that it was a standard cough.

"Oh yeah?" I managed to say.

"*Yeaah.*" Diya took another step toward me, lovingly mocking the North American way I elongated my consonants. "I said no. I told him you were unavailable."

She told him *no*?

I kicked myself. Wait. That *definitely* is what I would have wanted her to do, and I avoided her searing gaze and nodded with more vigor than usual.

"That's what you would have told me to say, yeah?" Diya crossed her arms. "Because of Raj—"

"*Raj!* Yes, of course I'm unavailable. I'm practically engaged," I joked.

"Because if you *are* interested in Sam—"

"I'm not," I cut Diya off, trying to keep my voice steady and convincing.

"OK, *good.*" A wide grin spread across her face. "I'm not sure I could handle if two of my *best* friends ended up hooking up. I would be too *damn* excited, *yaar*, and force you to marry."

Diya disappeared into the bathroom, and I pulled my legs up onto the couch, shaky and exhilarated and, honestly, a little terrified. I didn't understand why this was affecting me so much. It was clear on Diwali that he'd felt the attraction, too, but the fact that he wanted to get in touch was throwing me for a loop.

When I heard the shower go on, I opened a private web browser on Diya's laptop. (No, I did *not* want to look at porn.) But in a moment of weakness, I keyed in Sam's name. All week I'd managed to withstand creeping him online, but right now I couldn't resist. And I wasn't sure if I wanted to.

It didn't take me long to find out the name of his band (Perihelion) or that they'd been going strong for more than five years and were practically celebrities of the underground music scene in London, regulars at the coolest venues in Brixton, Hackney, and Camden. And from what I read online, it was Sam's talent that caught the attention of a small record label in London and prompted them to sign Perihelion. He wasn't the lead singer, but he wrote all the songs and was clearly the front man, his original bass lines being the thing that gave them their distinctive sound.

I scrolled faster and dove in deeper, fully committing to the online stalking of Sam from the Band. It seemed that Perihelion had released three albums so far, their biggest hit being "Guess the Star," which charted for a few months in the UK and got them invited to open for the British leg of a popular rock band's tour. I was smiling ear to ear, impressed. I clicked on the "Upcoming Shows" tab of Perihelion's website, but there were no shows posted from the last year; their website must have not been kept up to date. I snuck a look toward the bathroom. I could hear Diya drying her hair, and so I opened YouTube and started watching the first video on Perihelion's channel.

It was a performance of "Guess the Star" at a club in London from two years earlier. The lead singer reminded me vaguely of Jasmine's boyfriend, Brian, but blonder and slightly better looking, and just when I wondered where Sam was, he appeared from the shadows.

On Diwali, Sam had performed covers of popular songs I knew well. But even though I'd never heard this song before, it felt familiar. Like I'd been listening to it my whole life. The bass was like a heartbeat, loud and accelerating and tearing right through me. I felt like I was there in the crowd, looking up, sweaty and out of breath and pumping my fist as Perihelion took control of me, of everyone else on the floor. Because there was something about music, wasn't there? A good song or beat or rhythm. It could take you anywhere, jog an old memory you didn't even know you had. Make you feel something you didn't know you were capable of.

The song was over all too quickly. My finger hovered on the trackpad of the laptop, and I was tempted to play the next song. Let myself go just a little bit further.

But I didn't. I closed the laptop, and a few minutes later, Diya wandered out in her pajamas, and we made cocktails to enjoy on the balcony.

A moment of weakness was just that, a *moment*, and I didn't want to entertain a crush on a guy whom I would never see again. My feelings and the memories we shared together would ultimately be nothing more than a cheap plastic souvenir.

CHAPTER 13

The next two days were crunch time, and the Joshi family finally accepted my offers of help with the hundreds and thousands of things that needed to be done, vetted, approved, carted, mapped, uploaded, double-checked, and/or managed ahead of the wedding. It was pandemonium, but I was very happy to do anything that would lighten their load. (Not to mention, staying busy was a great distraction from stalking Sam on social media. Aasha Auntie, too. I'd already watched clips of half the Bengali-language films she was in. Needless to say, she was brilliant.)

One of the tasks Diya delegated to me was finalizing details for their group honeymoon at a resort in Goa, an hour's flight away. Diya and Mihir, who insisted they'd already taken enough couple trips together, had invited their close friends along and tried to convince me to come, too, but I didn't want to crash a holiday with their tight-knit group of friends that seemed to be all couples. Besides, my family in Punjab was expecting me. My flight to Amritsar, where most of my relatives lived, was scheduled for the morning after the wedding.

On the Friday morning of the *sangeet*, I bade farewell to Diya's family, and Manish drove me to my hotel in Andheri West, where all the wedding festivities were taking place.

I had some time to kill in the afternoon before I needed to get ready, and so I decided to explore the area by foot and make my way to the Infiniti Mall, which the hotel clerk had said was one of the biggest shopping plazas in the city. Manish or Diya had driven me around the whole time I'd been in Mumbai, and only ten minutes into my walk, I realized how hot and sweaty I got without frequent access to air-conditioning. I also realized how different it felt to be wandering around on the streets alone.

Most of the time, the shift was subtle, something that happened to women all the time back in the US. An unnecessarily long stare by a passerby, a quick up and down, even an under-the-breath mumble you're not quite sure was meant for you.

But sometimes, like when I passed through a construction site and crossed paths with four young men beneath a tunnel of scaffolding, it was more obvious. Even frightening.

At first, they tried to talk to me in Hindi and then in English. When I smiled politely and kept going, they turned around and started to follow me. I picked up my speed, my heart racing until I was back out in the sunlight and around other pedestrians, but still, they stayed right on my heels, calling out to me. One even tried to touch me.

I bit my lip hard, spun on my heel, and shouted at them until they left. We were in broad daylight with witnesses everywhere; what would they have done if they'd been protected under the dark of night? If they had found me all alone?

I clearly remembered watching the news that fateful day in 2012 when the whole world learned about the student who was brutally raped and murdered on a New Delhi bus. The incident sparked international outrage and shone a light on the widespread and horrifying sexual violence against women and girls in India, leading to certain legal reforms and more media coverage on other attacks. But from what I understood, not much had really changed. Rape culture and sexual harassment in India may be less taboo to discuss, but the threat of violence still hung precariously above every step and choice a woman made.

I finally arrived at the mall. I felt hot and weak, and I sat down on a free bench to catch my breath. I hated that I was so naive; it hadn't even occurred to me that I would catch a glimpse of it here in one of Mumbai's wealthiest neighborhoods. I hated that we women had to make ourselves smaller to stay safe— make detours and compromises never expected of *men*. I fanned myself, boiling to a rage. And as I glanced around at all the stores, at the glitz and unfairness of it all, the last thing I wanted to do was shop.

I was one of the lucky ones. I'd only been followed, and in broad daylight at that, and I had the privilege and the means to order myself a ride back to the hotel, to pay for accommodation, where I could fall asleep feeling safe.

What about all the women and girls who didn't have that option? And not just here in India, but even in the US and the rest of this whole damn world? My head spun, thinking about all of them. Wondering if the world would ever fucking change.

I wasn't in the mood to go to a party, but when I got back to my hotel room, I changed into the midnight blue *lengha* I'd brought for the *sangeet* and threw on a bit of makeup. The wedding itself would be religious, so tonight's party would be the equivalent of a reception, and it was the event Diya was most looking forward to. It would be a chance for all of us to drink and celebrate, as well as to enjoy performances by musicians and dance groups.

I felt a bit better after arriving at the seaside venue and finding Pinky, and then later, Diya and Mihir and their families. I didn't want to monopolize the couple, and so after a few minutes, I wandered aimlessly until I spotted a few of the bridesmaids, groomsmen, and their spouses near the bar. I knew I wouldn't be able to avoid Sam all night, and sure enough, when I got close, I spotted him among the group. Even though Sam was wearing a standard Western suit like most of the other men here, he stood out like a red herring.

At least, he stood out to me.

Our eyes met as I approached, as if I'd called out his name. In a panic, I grabbed a samosa from a passing waiter. It was only after I shoved the whole thing into my mouth that I realized the samosa was extremely hot, in both temperature and spice level.

"Niki!" Sam turned away from the conversation, stepping toward me. "It's lovely to see you."

"*Hahgh.*"

I'd been trying to say hi, but my mouth seemed to have a mind of its own.

"Do you require a napkin?" Sam asked.

I shook my head, *aloo* crumbling out of the samosa singeing a hole in my mouth. My face red, I pressed my hands over my lips.

"Is that a yes?"

Without waiting for me to respond, Sam disappeared, and a beat later, he was back with a napkin. I whipped around to deal with the situation. After I'd finished chewing and wiped my face clean of debris, I turned back to him.

I smiled sheepishly. "Uh, thanks."

"Anytime," he said, clearly trying not to laugh at me. "How is your sari—did I ruin it?"

"No." I smiled. "Don't worry. Pinky was able to save it."

"Good." Sam hesitated. "Look, I just wanted to say again that I'm so sorry—"

"Stop it," I interrupted. "It's not your fault. I was . . ."

What *was* I doing? I'd been dangling myself precariously over a pool to what, mess with him? Taunt him?

Entice him?

"I was being stupid," I said finally. "It's my fault I fell in. *And* the security guard's."

Sam laughed, and it changed his whole face. I'd forgotten how gorgeous it was. Blinding, too, like turning on a lamp in the dead of night.

"I still feel like I owe you a drink." He cleared his throat. "Or something, at least . . ."

"Isn't it an open bar tonight?"

"Yes, well. I was thinking about a different night, actually."
Sam leaned in. "How about dinner, once the wedding is over?
How long are you in town?"

"Sam," I said, trying to maintain composure. "You don't owe
me anything."

"All right. Then how about, I'd *like* to have dinner with you.
I'd really like it, actually."

My gut wrenched. This was the moment I'd been afraid of
tonight but also, annoyingly, been longing for. Sam from the
Band was asking me out on a date.

"Look, Diya told me you weren't available." Sam paused,
rubbing his neck. "But I'd kick myself if I didn't ask anyway. Diwali was . . ."

His gaze tore through me, ripping me to pieces. Saying so
much more than his words.

"Not a typical night," Sam said finally.

"No." Even though it was hot outside, I was shivering. I
rubbed the goose bumps on my forearms. "I suppose it wasn't."

"You thought so, too?"

I nodded, stepping closer to him as I bit my bottom lip. "It's
not every night a stranger throws me in a pool."

CHAPTER 14

*H*is face didn't crack a smile, like I thought it might, and we stood there staring at each other for what felt like hours.

"You tease me, Niki Randhawa."

"I'm not a tease," I said, wondering if Diya had told him my last name or if he'd similarly gone online and looked me up.

"You think I'm a tease, I expect." Sam looked pained. "From my conversation with Diya the other day, well, I have the feeling you think I wasn't being genuine."

"Is that so?"

"She might have used the word 'player' . . . "

I laughed and made a mental note to whack Diya with a pillow at some point in the future. She was a good friend, and I knew she hadn't meant to sell me out, but she was about as subtle as a rock.

"Is that what you think about me?"

"I don't know what I think about you, Sam from the Band." I gave him a look. "Why *did* you change your name?"

"I didn't. I abbreviated my name."

"Sameer is beautiful, though—"

"Sameer doesn't sound like the bass guitarist of a trendy band you'd pay good money to see live, does it?"

I crossed my arms, wondering where that was coming from.

"Anyway, it doesn't matter," said Sam. "The point I was trying to make was . . ."

He squinted at me, and I laughed.

"I forgot my point."

"It must not have been important, then." I faked a yawn. The *kathak* dancers finished up their set, and everyone burst into a round of applause.

"We almost met once before, you know," I heard Sam say after we'd stopped clapping. I turned back to him, hating and loving in equal measure how fiercely he was looking at me.

"Have we?"

"I came up to Seattle for the weekend. Diya invited me to hang out with her 'crew.' I imagine you were part of that?"

I smiled, thinking of our tight-knit group of friends from college, Diya being the glue that held everyone together.

"Well, why didn't I meet you then?" I asked. "Did you stand us up?

"In fact, I did." Sam blushed, his fair cheeks lighting up like a billboard. "I was with my college girlfriend, and she didn't really like Diya. I know"—he paused, reading my face—"it's hard to imagine anyone not loving her instantly. Well, that was the problem. Amanda was jealous of our friendship."

"You *did* date for three weeks in the sixth grade," I said mildly.

Sam scratched his jaw, smiling at me. "Diya told you?"

I nodded.

"What else did she say?"

"You kissed once, with *tongue*." I shook my head at him. "You might as well have proposed."

"I did propose," Sam said. "I believe our friends married us behind the school. We never did file for divorce, mind you."

"Well"—I glanced at my watch—"you have about three days to get that sorted out."

Out of the corner of my eye, I noted the *kathak* dancers leaving the stage and Auntie Jo walking up to the microphone. I tilted my chin for a better view. It looked like she had started speaking, but the crowd was too noisy for me to hear what she was saying.

"Were we supposed to go hiking in Discovery Park?" I asked Sam, a vague memory popping into my head. "During our senior year?"

"I believe so." He nodded. "You remember?"

"Unfortunately, I do." I shrugged sheepishly. "You see, I *also* stood Diya up that day. Whoops."

"Wow, we're such amazing friends."

"I know, right? She was *so* pissed at you. She'd planned a whole day out because you'd never been to Seattle." I laughed. "And she was pissed at *me* because I bailed to . . ."

I trailed off, my face heating up.

"To?" Sam prompted

"To drive my ex-boyfriend somewhere," I said, rushing my words. "Anyway, if you and I both bailed, I guess it wasn't meant to be."

Just as Sam opened his mouth to speak, Auntie Jo loudly shushed the crowd, chastising everyone for not listening to her speech. I chuckled softly, turning away from Sam, and listened to Auntie Jo as she thanked everyone for coming and then announced the order of the festivities for the rest of the night—dance performances by the bridesmaids, another by a few of Mihir's sisters and cousins, and then a professional *bhangra* group as the finale.

As the dancing started, the crowd pressed closer to the stage. I was standing in front of Sam, and even though I couldn't see him, I was aware of every inch of his body.

"Fancy another drink?" I heard him ask while everyone was applauding the first group of dancers. He'd stepped forward and was standing so close to me we were nearly touching.

"No, thank you."

He placed his hand on my waist. "Sure?"

"I'm sure," I whispered.

I looked back toward the stage. The next dance started, and I thought Sam would move his hand away, but he didn't. He lingered, his fingers light on the waistband of my *lengha*. My body shivered when his thumb found the slit between the skirt and the top, and he pressed it against my bare skin.

"Tell me," he whispered. "Where were you driving your ex-boyfriend?"

"I can't remember—"

"Yes, you can. Tell me, Niki."

Sam's voice was soft, yet urgent. I vaguely wondered if he was jealous, but that would be crazy, and so I dismissed the thought immediately.

"Niki . . ." Sam goaded. "Come on."

I sighed. I knew Sam wouldn't let up until I told him, so I did.

"A StarCraft tournament," I said finally, dicing up my syllables.

"You're joking."

I didn't respond, my mouth twitching at the memory of my ex. Of myself, when we were together.

"You're *not* joking." Sam laughed when I shook my head stiffly. "Wow. I suddenly have a very clear mental picture of your ex."

"Yeah, yeah . . ." I muttered.

"Are all your exes so debonair?"

"There's only been the one," I said. "Let me guess. Amanda was . . . lucky ex-girlfriend number thirteen?" I noted the tenor of jealousy in my own voice and cleared my throat. "Well, maybe twelve," I said blandly. "Excluding Diya."

"Excluding Diya," Sam said, "I've only had the one."

I tilted my head, and Sam's profile came into view. My pulse quickened as he looked over and caught my gaze.

"Really?" I asked, unsure why I was pressing the subject. "*One* girlfriend? You?"

"Just Amanda," he said. "Is that so hard to believe?"

"Is it hard to believe that Sam from the Band doesn't have

girls throwing themselves at him in jolly old London?" I asked, imitating his Britishisms.

"Now why would they do that, I wonder?"

"I have no idea."

Sam cracked a smile, his fingers tickling my waist slightly as he moved. I shivered. I hoped to god he didn't notice.

"So why, then?" I asked again. I was strangely curious, desperately so, and couldn't stop myself from asking. "Why only Amanda?"

"It wasn't intentional, but we were together five years, nearly." He nodded, his eyes somewhere else. "It knocked the wind right out of me. And after something like that, I suppose, it takes a very long time to catch your breath."

Sam turned to me, our eyes locking together. My heart was racing so fast it felt like I was about to spin out of control.

"Do you know what I mean?"

I nodded, slowly. I knew exactly what he meant.

Sam's face was close to mine. Too close. There were people everywhere, and if anyone was paying attention, they would have been able to see the way we were looking at each other. His hand still on my waist. The way he tightened his grip and tugged me gently into him.

"You're playing with fire again," I said softly. My heart was pounding louder than the music.

"Do you want me to stop?"

No.

"Yes," I said instead, and he immediately withdrew his hand. My waist felt cold without his touch, his heat, and I was almost thankful as more guests joined the crowd, forcing us closer and closer together. My back was flat against him, and I didn't know who I watched dance and to which song, or how much time even passed as we stood there, as our hands found each other and refused to let go.

"This isn't going to happen," I whispered.

"If you say so."

His thumb was like a beating heart on my palm, tapping out the rhythm of the music.

"One dinner."

I shook my head.

"Give me one good reason—"

"I don't do flings, Sam."

"Neither do I." He paused. "If you don't believe me, believe Diya. I'm not some play—"

"Our zip codes, then," I interrupted, scrambling for an answer. "That's a good reason."

"Is it?"

I felt his breath hot on my neck. My body was roaring. I was not myself. I was not Niki the good Indian girl who obeyed her parents, whose life revolved around her career, who never let herself get carried away. I didn't know where the hell she'd gone, but without her, I felt lost and free in equal measure.

The dance ended, and my pulse dropped to a normal rate as our bodies were forced apart in the crowd. The bridesmaids returned from the stage, and in a panic, I left Sam's side to go congratulate them on their performance.

. . .

*M*y phone buzzed later that evening, when I was halfway through dinner, wedged between Masooma and one of the other bridesmaids.

Dinner? Please? ☹

The text was sent by a +44 number, and I'd watched enough British television to know that was the UK country code.

How did you get my phone number?

I spotted Sam down the table just in time to see him glance down at his phone screen. The edges of his lips curled upward.

Diya tasked me with guarding her purse this evening. She's had the same passcode since high school.

I laughed, covering my face with my hand. Masooma and the others sitting in my vicinity were discussing their upcoming trip to Goa. I angled my chair away from them, texting Sam back.

Thief . . .

I was thinking about what to say next when Sam texted again.

You'll LMK about dinner, right? Think about it.

A beat later, he texted again.

Diya mentioned you liked acronyms.

I grinned despite myself.

"LOL." I guess that's true . . .

I looked up to find Sam staring at me again, his eyes boring into me like a rocket. The music was loud, and the party was noisy, but in that moment, it was if the whole room fell silent. My senses overloaded as my lips parted, and I imagined what it would be like to kiss him.

I have another acronym for you.

I looked down as he texted me, my breath baited as I waited for Sam's next message.

YOLO

At some point during the evening, my mood had turned for the better. I'd left the weight of the day behind me and immersed myself in the spirit of celebration. The party. The present.

But what *was* the present? Why allow myself to get carried away with something that could never last into the future?

You only live once.

I thought about saying yes to the date, and then I thought about saying no. And then I thought about making a joke that, actually, according to both of our religions, we *didn't* only live once; we could be reincarnated.

Before I'd made up my mind one way or another, the group finished up dinner, and I was whisked away to the bar, the dance floor, and then to attend to Diya, who had gotten overwhelmed by the attention and drunk a little too much. At the end of the night, when it was only the younger guests left at the party, I found Sam lingering in the foyer, waiting for me. I froze midstep, my stomach dropping at the sight of him.

"Niki!"

I tore my eyes away from Sam and toward Mihir's best man, who had called out my name. He and his wife were piling into a taxi.

"Aren't we staying at the same hotel?"

I bit my lip, nodding. I remembered seeing them in the lobby.

"Then we'll take you back!" his wife exclaimed. "Are you ready to go?"

I shifted my weight between my heels. My feet hurt, and my head was starting to pound from lack of water or sleep or maybe both. I didn't know if I was ready for a date with Sam, and what that would mean, but I knew that I was in no state to decide.

I smiled in thanks, walking toward the taxi, and right before I stepped inside, I turned around.

Sam had disappeared.

CHAPTER 15

When I got back to the hotel, I threw myself on the bed, too lazy to take off my *lengha* first. I opened the message app on my phone. Sam hadn't texted me again, and it was no wonder. He'd asked me on a date, and not only did I not give him an answer; he'd seen me leave without trying to say goodbye.

I wasn't an experienced dater, but I was proficient enough to know the ball was firmly in my court. If I wanted to go on that date, I needed to make the next move.

I rolled onto my back, stuffing a pillow beneath my head. In my very sheltered love life, I'd never made a "move" on anyone, and as I thought about what to do, I realized I needed an outside perspective. From someone with *lots* of dating experience.

"Go for Jasmine!"

My sister answered the video call on the first ring. She was at her tiny kitchen table, where she sat when working from home, and still in her pajamas. She grinned at the sight of me.

"Are you wearing *makeup*?"

"I just got home from the *sangeet*." I laughed.

"Well, you look nice. Let me see your full outfit."

I complied, holding my phone out to show her.

"Is that *mine*?"

I shook my head, just as I realized that it was indeed hers. *Right*. Jasmine had bought it to wear to the Sharma wedding over the summer. Not me. I'd worn the silvery green thing that went out of fashion like two days later.

"It's fine," she said blandly. "Just give *me* Mom's yellow sari when you get home, OK? Brian's work Christmas party is black tie this year, so I gotta dress up."

I nodded, trying not to roll my eyes. *Brian*. Ugh.

"So," Jasmine said, pressing a mug of coffee to her lips. "What's up?"

"Well, I wanted to take you up on your offer." I paused. "To *talk*—"

"About that doctor?"

I squirmed. "No . . ."

I got nervous and started stalling, and thank god Jasmine didn't have any pressing deadlines that morning, because it took her a good half hour to drag it out of me. Not just what was and wasn't going on with Sam, but the full backstory, too. How I'd gotten drunk with Raj on our first date, and even though I hadn't heard from him in a while, he'd said he wanted to see me when I got back to Seattle. How I'd literally fallen (in a pool) meeting the hottest, sweetest, and most charming *musician*, Sam from the Band, a guy I could have literally copied and pasted from my wildest fantasy.

How I couldn't stop thinking about him and was very tempted to text him right now and tell him as much.

The conversation made me want to dunk my head under cold water, but I think Jasmine really enjoyed me coming to her for once with a problem, something that I didn't already have the answer for. She listened to me patiently, tapping a ballpoint pen against her laminate table. After I was done babbling, she took a deep breath and leaned toward the screen.

"Niki," she said tentatively. "The answer is very simple."

I held my breath, ready for her version of the answer.

"Yeah?"

"I think you should walk away from Sam."

Wait, *what*? Jasmine wanted me to . . . walk away?

"Not because of Raj. You don't owe him anything . . . His family is probably setting him up with other girls, too, you know."

Jasmine droned on as my stomach bottomed out at the thought of saying no to Sam. At the realization that her advice wasn't what I wanted to hear.

"You've only been on one date," continued Jasmine. "And you said it yourself—he's been too busy to text you back—"

"This isn't about Raj," I interrupted. "This is about Sam. And I *like* him, Jasmine. So why exactly should I walk away from him?"

Jasmine smirked. "You called me hoping I would encourage

you to go have dinner with Sam, didn't you? Have a fling on your little 'break'?"

"No," I insisted. "I—"

"You totally did!" She laughed. "It's fine. I get it. Sure, maybe *I'm* the type to have a fling on vacation, but you aren't, Niki. You're going to catch feelings."

"I *am* not!"

"You've already caught them. You're *sick* about him." She pointed at me. "I can see it all over your face."

"It's been a long time, Jasmine. Maybe I'm just horny!"

Laughing, Jasmine grabbed her blue-light glasses from off-screen, pushed them up her nose. Suddenly, I was irritated and desperate to end this conversation as soon as possible.

Fun, giggly Jasmine thought she could go around doing whatever she wanted her whole life, and then tell *me* not to? How was that fair?

*J*asmine's stupid voice telling me to "walk away" wouldn't get out of my head. I heard it while taking off my makeup. While I organized my suitcase and watched reruns of *Indian Idol*. As I tossed and turned trying to fall asleep, debating whether or not to go on a date with Sam.

In the end, I didn't text him back. Jasmine planted a seed of doubt, and overnight, it bloomed.

I *tried* not to think about Sam over the next two days. At Diya's *mehndi* party, which was for women and girls only, and

where we applied henna to our hands and feet. And then the following day at the *haldi*, the *pooja* done ahead of the wedding to
purify and bless the happy couple.

I knew Sam was invited to the *haldi*, and so I mentally prepared myself to see him. He might have lost interest in me after I
blew him off, but on the chance he didn't, what would I say to
him? What if he asked me on another date?

I took a seat at the back and watched the ceremony, as Diya
and Mihir's loved ones took turns marking their faces, limbs,
and clothing with the potent turmeric paste. It started off serious, but by the end, some of their friends were getting creative
with the application, and Diya and Mihir started shrieking in
protest—worried that the yellow would stain their skin.

Even though I enjoyed the celebration, my eyes kept involuntarily leaving the happy couple in search of Sam. Sometimes I
thought I felt him staring at me, but when I turned to look, it was
never him.

Where was he? As one of Diya's closest friends, he should be
here. It was strange that he wasn't.

I stayed until the very end, and when Sam still didn't show
up, I went back to my hotel room, deflated. I had the whole evening free. Had I been planning to say *yes* to him in person? To
"make a move" and whisk him away for an impromptu dinner
date?

Stretching on the floor of my hotel room, I channel surfed
until I landed on a Bollywood movie from the early 2000s, one of
my favorites, with snowflakes and moonlit walks, featuring Kajol
and Shah Rukh Khan. It was romantic and cheesy, and watching

it, I physically *ached* for Sam. For something I would now never get the chance to see through.

Tomorrow was the wedding, and with more than fifteen hundred guests, and the venue as large as Diya had described, I might not even see Sam. And the morning after, bright and early, I was leaving for Amritsar.

CHAPTER 16

𝓣he big day finally arrived. I put on some bold eye shadow, a gold *lengha* that also technically belonged to Jasmine, and my best I-do-not-care-about-Sam smile. I was determined to not allow my lusty little crush to distract me from enjoying Diya's wedding day.

While Diya and her family got ready, the bridesmaids and I sat around in their hotel suite reminiscing and trading Diya stories. Today was the traditional Hindu wedding ceremony, and so they didn't have a formal role, nor were they wearing matching outfits. Even though it was superficial, the fact that I wasn't left out finally made me feel like a real bridesmaid, too, and I even teared up a bit when Diya instructed the photographer to include me in all the bridal party photos.

The wedding was at an outdoor venue with an expansive lawn and gardens, the *mandap* a glittering sun at its center. As modern as Diya was, she'd opted for more traditional decorations, choosing saffron, white, red, and golden marigold garlands, which cascaded over every inch of the wedding altar.

She looked like a princess up there in her rose gold *lengha*, a heavy bridal *dupatta* pinned to her head. Mihir looked handsome, too, but I couldn't take my eyes off her. I stood up near the front with the wedding party. The pundit spoke in Sanskrit, and even the Hindus among the group didn't understand the ancient language, but I'd been to enough weddings to understand the intent behind most of the rituals he performed. It was spiritual and beautiful, and as the sky turned to dusk, I felt like I'd been transported into another world.

The ceremony was absolutely magical, and I was so, so happy for my Diya.

After the ceremony, ushers passed out baskets of flower petals to shower the couple with blessings. There were guests everywhere, and by the time I'd lined up and offered my blessings, I had lost track of the rest of the wedding party. I scanned the crowd for a few minutes, and when I couldn't find any familiar faces, I helped myself to the dinner buffet on the other side of the venue and found an empty seat at a table.

My eating companions were one Dr. Raman Mehta and her husband, Mr. Akshay Mehta; Henry Asquith III, self-proclaimed savant and business partner of Raj's parents; a stuffy trio of aunties, who smiled at no one and spoke only among themselves; and Mihir's mother's new yoga instructor, Blake. A white guy who was wearing a *kurta pajama* so thin I could see his nipples through it, flip-flops, and a man bun.

Seriously.

Blake dominated the table conversation (for those participating) and told us all about his spiritual journey through Bali, Thailand, and now India, where he'd been living for six months.

He had wise eyes and a voice like a warm bath, so incredibly calming it was as if the words he was actually saying didn't matter. Which was true. Because Blake—or Yogi Blake, as he requested we call him—was completely full of shit.

I had my spiritual awakening illegally paddle boarding through a nature reserve?

I always do my sun salutations after the sun goes down. Magic mushroom shakes really limber you up . . . ?

Like, *what?*

"So, how does one train to be a *yogi?*" I asked after devouring my dinner and having had enough of his crap.

Yogi Blake's eyes bulged, but he didn't answer.

"I'm very curious—"

"So, where are you from, Niki?" he interrupted. "Where has your journey taken you?"

"It's taken me here," I said stiffly. "All the stars must have aligned."

"Do you believe in astrology?"

"Do yogis?"

Blake, sorry, *Yogi* Blake, smiled at me surreptitiously and then glanced up at the sky. "There is so much to see and to learn, to absorb, and we must take it upon ourselves to reflect . . ."

Here we go . . .

". . . and to balance the ancient wisdom with the knowledge of today's modern world."

I smiled at him, pleasantly surprised by the left turn in conversation.

"Like, with science? I agree—"

"Yes, *science*. Sure. Whatever you want to call it." Yogi Blake sat forward, his eyes simultaneously piercing and glazed over. "Do you have a telescope?"

I hesitated. "No."

He stretched his hand toward the sky, as if reaching for something. "I keep mine on the terrace. I go out there every night."

"Isn't there too much light pollution in Mumbai to see anything?"

"It depends on what you're looking for."

"With a telescope, don't you look for . . . *stars*?"

"Can you keep a secret?" he whispered, so the others couldn't hear. "It's not all stars up there, Niki."

I braced myself but still wasn't fully prepared for the next thing that fell out of his mouth.

"There are UFOs."

"As in . . . unidentified—"

"Flying objects. Yes. They're everywhere." Yogi Blake leaned in, one eyebrow a caterpillar crawling down the side of his face. "They're *watching* us—"

"*There* you are, love."

I froze hearing Sam's voice just behind me. A beat later, I felt his hand on my shoulder.

"Shall we go fetch the kids?"

"Yes!" I looked up at him, grinning. "Yes, *please*."

"You have children?" Yogi Blake exclaimed. "That's wonderful. I've been thinking about writing a parenting book."

"Oh, yeah?" I asked, standing up. "How many kids do you have?"

"None," he answered. "But I was a child once."

I glanced at Sam, who looked both amused and shocked, and without another word to the "yogi," I led him away to a different, unoccupied table.

"Thank you," I said laughing, as we took our seats. "How long were you standing there?"

Sam set down two glass bottles of Limca, which I just noticed he'd been carrying. "Long enough to hear that aliens are watching us."

"They *are* watching us, Sam."

"Oh, I know." Sam pointed at a group of aunties gawking at us. "See?"

I grinned so hard my face hurt. "Do you know them?"

"No," he said blandly. "But I'm Aasha's youngest son. So they know me."

"It sounds like you have a reputation around here."

Sam shook his head. "It's Mom who has the reputation."

I watched Sam's strong hands twist off the caps to the Limca bottles, and when he handed me one of them, I took a long, refreshing swig. I didn't *want* to feel excited that he'd come looking for me, but I couldn't help it. My heart was thundering away like a drum line.

"So," I said, trying to act casual. "Where were you yesterday?"

"Why? Did you miss me?"

"You didn't skip Diya's *haldi* to play hard to get, did you?"

"And what if I did?"

I raised my eyebrows, unable to tell if he was joking. "But you just couldn't stay away . . ."

"I could have, but I felt bad you were trapped chatting to that *gora*." Sam nodded at the bottles of Limca. "Plus, you looked rather thirsty."

I laughed, squinting at him. "Did you just tell me I look thirsty?"

Sam picked up the bottle nearest him and sipped from it. "Yes?"

"That's very rude."

"How, might I ask?"

"Thirsty means . . . *desperate*." I lowered my voice. "Like, I'm *thirsty* for some action."

"Are you?"

"No!"

Sam grinned, pulling his chair close to me. "You do realize that by sitting here with me, we're having dinner together."

"I already ate dinner. With Yogi Blake. Have you eaten?"

"Yes. But I'll take what I can get."

"So maybe you're the thirsty one."

Sam held my gaze as he brought his bottle of Limca to his lips. He tilted his head back ever so slightly, the cold lemon-lime liquid falling out of the bottle.

"*So* thirsty." I shook my head as I watched him drink. I didn't mention that I was feeling, uh, a bit parched myself. That he looked so damn good tonight I was mentally relieving him of his clothing.

"I've prepared a few talking points," Sam said, setting down the bottle. "In case conversation during the big date went awry."

"It's gone awry," I said mildly. "What's the first topic?"

"You, of course." Sam smiled. "And the fact that you're a musician."

My jaw stiffened. Sam had tried to probe the subject a few times on Diwali, but I'd steered the conversation away because I was embarrassed. I used to spend every free hour practicing the piano or loitering in the aisles of HMV or listening to any new-to-me music I could get my hands on. But somewhere along the line, I'd gotten too busy studying or working or bingeing Netflix. I'd let my passion slip away.

"Niki?" Sam said, prompting me. "Tell me, please? What's your instrument of choice?"

I glanced down at the cutlery. "A butter knife."

"Niki . . ."

"The gong, then."

"Come on, love." Sam bit his bottom lip. God, he was sexy. "What's the harm in talking about it?"

"Piano," I said finally. "But I'm not a rock star like you, or anything. I played classical music."

"Brilliant. What period?"

"Um . . ." I shrugged. "A bit of everything. I competed quite a bit. My teacher convinced me to play a lot of baroque pieces, but I loved the romantic composers. Schubert. Chopin. De—"

"Debussy?"

I beamed, nodding. "He's my favorite."

"Mine, too. Will you play for me?"

Sam's eyes locked onto me, and dear god, he was turning me on. There was no other way to say it.

"Sure," I said, averting my gaze. "Right after you play 'Guess the Star' . . . "

"You looked me up?" he asked a beat later.

My cheeks burned. "Diya told me—"

"One. I don't believe you. Two." He touched my knee. "Stop changing the subject."

I glanced over to where his hand was still touching me.

"So, will you play for me?"

"Now?"

"Yes."

I laughed. His hand was still on me, and my insides felt queasy. *"Here?"*

"Yes. We're at a massive wedding venue. Surely, there's a piano."

"No—"

"Please?"

Sam pouted, and damn he looked cute, so cute I was almost tempted to say yes.

My stomach was flip-flopping all over the place. We weren't sitting far away from each other, but it felt intimate, like it was just the two of us in the whole universe rather than two of fifteen hundred guests on a crowded lawn. Even though it was nighttime, I was suddenly hot and bothered, but mostly hot, as beads of sweat pooled at my temples.

"Anyway, the second talking point?" I asked Sam, clearing my throat. "On a first date, I always like to ask about one's expectations on foreplay."

Sam laughed, a bemused look on his face. We both seemed surprised by the forwardness of my joke, but the truth is, I wasn't feeling like myself.

Actually, I wasn't feeling very good at all.

My insides squeezed again, and as a dull pain coursed through me, I knew it had nothing to do with my attraction for Sam.

"Sam?" I asked. I could barely hear myself, my voice so faint. "I . . ."

"Are you feeling all right?" he asked, as my words trailed off. He pressed the back of his hand onto my forehead. It felt like an ice cube.

"No." I swallowed hard, my stomach a roller coaster. "I . . ."

I closed my mouth. I was about to throw up, and as I frantically searched the lawn for a restroom, I realized I was not going to make it.

A beat later, I keeled over. And as Sam held back my hair and *dupatta*, I wretched as quietly as I could beneath the table.

CHAPTER 17

*J*hadn't been that sick since my junior year of college, when Jasmine poisoned me with her first attempt at homemade sushi.

Back at my hotel, I sat on the floor of the bathroom, my forehead resting on the toilet seat. The porcelain was warm, and I sat up straight opening my eyes, but the movement was too sudden and another wave of nausea rocked me to my core.

"Sam?" My voice croaked.

"I'm right behind you, love."

I felt his hand on the back of neck, and suddenly, the pressure of it made the world stop spinning the wrong way.

"Shall we try a bit of water again?"

I caught a look at myself in the shower reflection as I sipped from a cold bottle of water. My wedding outfit had been discarded at some point, and I was wearing blue pinstripe pajamas, which I'd owned since high school. The cloth clung to my skin, slick with sweat. I wanted to take a shower but didn't have the energy to stand up.

"What time is it?" I whispered.

"Nearly midnight."

"You should go. I'm fine." My stomach growled out in pain, protesting. "You're missing the wedding. You should—"

"Abandon Cinderella? Don't be daft, Niki."

"That's rude," I mumbled.

"Yes, I'm very rude." He gripped the bottle of water around my hand, lifting it up toward my mouth. "A few more sips?"

I obeyed him, but after another gulp, the pains in my stomach took on a life of their own, and the next thing I knew, I was vomiting again. And again. Until there was nothing left, and I was dry heaving and crying out in pain.

I don't know how long I was on the floor like that, but Sam didn't leave my side. Not once. So I had no idea when he called his mother.

Aasha Auntie was still dressed up from the wedding, a vision in cream and gold, and when she bent down to cup my face in her palms and kissed me on the forehead, it felt like my own mom was there taking care of me.

Vaguely, I became aware of her instructing Sam to help me into bed, to have me try liquids again in the morning. I could hear myself mumbling an apology to them both as I climbed under the covers.

"Don't feel bad, dear," she said, sitting next to me. "All my foreign friends fall ill at least once in India. There is a cost to eating such tasty food!"

I smiled up at her, dazed.

"Sam, she needs *adarak*. Go ask reception—"

"I have some," I whispered. My eyes were already closed, reality spinning away from me.

"*Hah?* Where."

"My sister's plane pack." I almost laughed thinking about it, but I felt too weak. I gestured at my backpack on the floor, and a little while later, felt Aasha Auntie coax a soft ginger chew into my mouth. She made me stay awake long enough not to choke on it, and as the ginger dissolved in my mouth, it sent me off to sleep in a sweet, soothing wave.

*I*t was daylight when I awoke. My stomach didn't hurt anymore, although my temples were pounding. I blinked, taking in the room. The curtains were drawn back, the city bustling behind the window. I tilted my chin downward.

Sam was still here. I smiled at the sight of him.

"Sleeping Beauty awakes."

I rolled over to get a better view and was surprised by how weak I felt. Sam was on the bed, too, lying head to toe on top of the covers. He'd taken off his fancy wedding *kurta* and was wearing only the *pajamas* of the outfit, his bare chest and shoulders covered by a bath towel.

"I thought I was Cinderella."

He sat up, the towel slipping down from his broad shoulders, and I laid my head back down as a wave of dizziness washed over me.

"How are you feeling?"

"Like a princess." I pressed my hands over my eyelids, pressing hard as I remembered how much of a burden I'd been. "I'm so sorry. I ruined your night. Your mom's, too."

"Don't give yourself so much credit," I heard Sam say. "The wedding was practically over by the time you—"

"Vomited in a crowd of fifteen hundred people?"

He laughed.

"Did anyone see me like that?"

"Only a few. But you really needn't worry, Niki. Everyone just thought you were the drunk American."

"Sam," I groaned, rolling onto my back. "Really?"

"*Not* really, no. There was no alcohol served yesterday. Remember?"

I shrugged, opening my eyes. Sam had moved and was now sitting right next to me, his back against the headboard. He'd brought the towel with him, draping it over his body like a blanket. I chuckled, running my fingers over the fiber of the towel. He caught my hand with his own and squeezed twice.

"You're so modest."

"Mom left strict instructions," Sam said, changing the subject, although I thought I detected the faintest quiver in his voice. "Today you're only allowed water, mint or ginger tea, and if you're up for it, *kicherdee*."

I nodded. Although I wasn't hungry, my stomach definitely felt better than it had the evening before.

"I'm up for it."

Sam let go of my hand and immediately became strictly business as he called down for room service. I slipped away to brush my teeth and shower. I moved slowly, my limbs heavy, and after I was done, wrapped a plush bath towel around my body. I'd forgotten to bring clean clothes into the bathroom.

"Feel better?" Sam asked, as I came out. He had changed back into his *kurta*, made the bed, and was now tidying up my room. My pulse quickened in an odd, fluttery way as he took my pajamas from me and started folding them.

"Like a princess."

I thought I would be uncomfortable, self-conscious that I was wearing nothing but a towel in front of a man I'd only met the week before. By the way he was looking at my neck and shoulders. The way he bit his lip as his gaze darted south, along the curves of my waist and hips.

But I wasn't. I wanted him to look. I wanted to close the space between us, let the towel drop to the floor. I wanted . . .

"You should sit down," he said sternly. "You're wavering."

"Am I?" I asked, just as a wave of dizziness crashed over me.

"You're severely dehydrated. I don't want you to pass out. Here—" Suddenly, Sam's arms were around me, and I sighed in relief as he helped me into bed. It felt good to be horizontal again, the sheets warm and soft against my bare skin. "The *kicherdee* will arrive soon. Rest until then, OK?"

"OK." Sleepily, I smiled up at him, worried that he would leave. But he didn't. Instead, he combed my wet hair with his fingers. I could have lain like that forever.

"Sam," I said, a few minutes later. "Thank you."

"For?"

"For everything. For taking care of me. For calling your mom—"

"It was nothing, Niki."

It wasn't nothing. Sam's actions were kinder and sweeter than I—in my limited dating experience—had ever experienced. I was overwhelmed by his presence, how much he seemed to care about me. Was I still unwell? Was it nausea that was making me feel so completely unguarded, so unlike myself?

A few minutes later, Sam bent down and kissed my forehead. It was gentle, his lips barely grazing my skin, as if a butterfly had landed but for a second. I reached up and caught his chin with my palm, scratched his stubble with my fingers. His face was so close I could feel his breath on my neck, and I trembled as he bent lower and kissed me again, this time on my shoulder.

"Sam," I said, trying not to moan at his touch. He sat up, and when I saw the vacant look on his face, I knew in my heart that he felt the same way. That if I wasn't sick right now, the barrier of bath towels and duvet wouldn't last for long.

"Yes?"

"Dinner last night . . ." I smiled. "It didn't count."

"It didn't?"

I shook my head. "I threw it up, remember?"

Sam grinned, pressing the back of his hand on my cheek. "Of course."

"Should we . . ." I hesitated, not used to being so forward. "Should we plan another?"

"Sure. Shall I call ahead and make us a reservation at the local hospital's cafeteria?" he asked. "I hear they serve red Jell-O."

"Sam." I laughed.

"Or how about chicken noodle soup? Bit risqué for a dinner date—"

I cut him off by pressing my hand over his mouth. I could feel him laughing against my palm.

"How about we go out when I can eat *solid* foods again," I continued, my voice stern. "But I'm buying. After everything you did for me last night, I think I'm the one who owes you dinner."

Sam cupped my palm in his, sliding it down to his neck. "You don't owe me anything, Niki."

"I know." I smiled at him sheepishly. "But what if I want to have dinner with you?"

Sam beamed down at me, overpowering the sun streaming in through the window. "I have a place in mind. It's called Frank's Café. It's posher than the name suggests."

"Sounds perfect." I snuggled closer to him on the bed.

"Although the restaurant is a bit of a trek." He paused. "It's in Goa."

I scanned his face, searching for signs that he was joking. But there were none. And my heart stopped as the fog lifted, and I remembered I was supposed to have left for Punjab early that morning.

"Shit." I laughed as I told Sam about missing my flight to Amritsar.

"I guess this was meant to be." Color flushed his cheeks. "Goa, I mean. You were meant to come to Goa."

"I take it you're going on the group honeymoon?" I propped my head on my elbow, facing him.

"Sort of. Well, I'll hang out with them during the day, but I'm not staying at the resort. My parents have an apartment nearby."

"I can't go," I replied, fumbling for words. "My family is expecting me. And besides, I didn't book a hotel room at the resort . . ."

"You could . . ." Sam trailed off.

"I could what?"

"You could delay your trip to Punjab by a few days. And as far as the hotel—well—why don't you stay at *mine*?"

I giggled. "Could I, now? That's an awfully presumptuous dinner—"

"Mom's already back there," he said quickly. "She left this morning. She lives there half the time, practically. And we have guest rooms. Two guest rooms, *and* a dog's bed—but you'll have to fight Scooby for it."

I laughed and suddenly felt shaky all over. Sam seemed nervous, and I was enjoying it more than I cared to admit out loud. The idea that I might have been driving Sam from the Band as crazy as he'd been making me was . . . exhilarating. Heartwarming. All sorts of words that I didn't typically use in real life, but only in my silly little fantasies.

"So, what do you say?" Sam asked me again. "Will you have dinner with me?"

This time, I didn't hesitate. I nodded, and then I did something I hadn't known I was capable of doing. I reached up and I kissed him.

Sam seized up in surprise. I giggled against his lips, and a beat later, I felt him soften and kiss me back. He was warm and gentle, and I wanted more. I needed more. I pressed my palms against his cheek, scratching down the sides of his neck as I drew him closer. He gasped, our tongues prodding, and I felt weak and winded as he wrapped me in his arms and pushed me down against the bed.

I loved his weight on top of me. I loved the way he kissed me. The way his fingers danced against my bare skin.

I couldn't stop myself, but when my towel started to unravel, Sam grunted and rolled away from me. My chest heaved as I wrapped myself tighter, overwhelmed by the gentleman that Sam was proving to be.

"Sorry," he mumbled.

I grinned, listening to him catch his breath.

Was I still asleep? Was I living in a dream?

I didn't care. And it didn't matter where or when or in what state I would wake up. I was going to make the most of this dream while it lasted.

CHAPTER 18

*G*oa!" Mom echoed, after I told my family over video chat that I had delayed my trip to Amritsar. She looked over at Dad, lovingly smacking him on the shoulder. "Who is that lovely Goan family who used to live across the hall? Niki can go visit them—"

"Mom," Jasmine snapped from off camera. "She's with friends. She won't want to visit some random auntie and uncle!"

"And how do you know?" Mom clapped back.

"Ask her." Jasmine appeared in view, her chin and left cheek only just visible behind Mom and Dad. "Niki, do you want to spend your precious holiday time going to visit people you've never met—and whose *names* Mom can't even remember?"

"I can remember their names, if you give me a minute," Mom grumbled. "If I didn't have a daughter driving me crazy."

I laughed, watching them together. After another good night's sleep and Aasha Auntie's strict diet of *kicherdee* and tea, I felt nearly back to normal. I felt prepared for my trip to Goa with Sam—at least, as prepared as I'd ever be.

"So tell us everything," Dad said brightly. He wrapped an arm around Mom's shoulders. "Where will you be staying?"

"A hotel," I mumbled quickly. "I forget the name. I'll e-mail you—"

"Be very careful," Dad said gravely. "There are drinking clubs in India now; do you know this?"

I pressed my lips together to keep them from curling upward.

"Clubs, in *India*?" Jasmine deadpanned. "Really, Dad? I thought the country only had temples."

"*Chup*," Mom said, although she was smiling, too.

"Niki, you must not go anywhere alone at night," Dad continued. He had totally missed the joke and still looked very serious. "Who is your hotel room partner? Do you have buddy?"

"Buddy," Jasmine snorted.

"Do you, Niki?" Mom repeated. "Diya will be on honeymoon. You will not stay alone, you promise us? It can be dangerous."

I nodded, promising them I'd be careful. After I'd been harassed in broad daylight here in Mumbai, I had no intention of making myself any more vulnerable.

"*Aacha*." Dad nodded. "Who is your buddy? Do we know her?"

Blood rushed to my head as I began to panic.

"She's one of Diya's friends," I said vaguely. When Mom and Dad continued to stare at me expectantly, I sighed. "Her name is Sam."

It was strange how easily the lie slipped off my tongue, how

I managed to hold it together even when Jasmine threw me one of her knowing looks. I'd told the family small lies before to protect feelings so they wouldn't worry; I wondered if I could count this as one of them.

"You don't know her," I continued, trying not to feel too guilty. "But she's great. Anyway . . ."

I spent a few more minutes assuring Mom and Dad that I would eat more carefully and stay hydrated in Goa, and that I'd contacted our relatives to let them know I'd be delaying my visit by a few days. Afterward, Jasmine stole the phone from them and went upstairs.

"Where's Brian?" I asked, watching her settle onto my bed. Her old room was now our parents' study.

"He's running late. We might start dinner without him." She shifted the pillow beneath her. "So you decided to have that fling, huh?"

"Why would you say that?"

"*Sam* from the Band?" Jasmine smiled. "Come *on*. You should have told Mom and Dad that Sam's a guy, Niki. They wouldn't have cared—"

"As if they wouldn't have cared," I interrupted. *As if my Indian parents wouldn't care that I was staying with some guy I'd known for little more than a week.*

"You're twenty-nine, sis," Jasmine continued. "You don't owe them an explanation. You don't owe them anything . . ."

My jaw clenched, and I forced air out through my nostrils. Maybe she didn't feel like she owed Mom and Dad, but I did. I still lived under their roof. Everything I had was because of their sacrifices, and if they wanted me to be their good Indian daughter, I needed to be.

At least, I needed them to believe it.

Jasmine continued, her lecture grating on me. "If we live to make them happy, no one wins—"

"Stop it," I said icily, cutting her off. She'd been going off on me for a few minutes already, and I was so over this conversation. "That's enough."

"Fine," she said, after a moment had passed. "Let's agree to disagree." Her smile brightened. "So, have you slept with him?"

I rolled my eyes, although inside I was still fuming.

"You *have*, you little minx . . ."

"Jas!" I said sharply. Our house was small, and her loud-ass voice carried. "Keep it down. And no. I haven't."

Half-heartedly, I quickly told her about where I was really staying in Goa and that I was planning to sleep in the guest room.

"So you're basically going on a family holiday . . ." Jasmine said, after I'd told her the part where Sam's mother would be around, too. "Sounds like a fun fling, Niki."

Jasmine's words rung unpleasantly in my ear, like I was standing too close to a speaker. I didn't like that word as much as I had a few days earlier.

"You're in dangerous territory." She paused. "Are you thinking this through?"

I bit down on my lip, hard. I was tired and still a little shaky from my bout of food poisoning, and I was sick of Jasmine getting to have all the fun. I was sick of her lectures.

"Are you *sure*—"

"I'm sure!" I snapped. "I can handle myself, OK, Jasmine? I can handle a . . . *fling*."

"Niki," Jasmine pressed. "Be careful. You don't know what you're getting yourself into—"

"Because I'm such a fucking nerd, right?" I yelled.

My voice echoed on the other side of the line. Jasmine looked taken aback, but I wasn't having any of this anymore. I was fuming.

"It's not fair. You've had your fun." I paused, my words hard around the edges. "Now leave me in peace while, for *once*, I have mine—"

"But—"

"And he lives in London, OK?" I laughed spitefully. "So, it's not like you need to worry about *me* shacking up with some random fling . . ."

I bit my tongue, watching Jasmine's face. Shit. I hadn't meant to say that out loud.

The silence hung between us for a moment as I tried to figure out a way to walk this back. To apologize. But I was still angry— at Jasmine or myself, I wasn't quite sure—and I wasn't able to find the words.

"That's what you think about my relationship with Brian?" Her voice wavered. "I shacked up with some random *fling*?"

I didn't respond, and my hands clenched, fingernails digging into flesh.

"You don't like him, do you."

No. I didn't. And Jasmine had never asked me this question

point-blank before. But maybe that's because she already knew my answer.

"It's been three years, Niki, and you never told me?" She was shaking, visibly. "You're my *sister*. I can't fucking believe you!"

"And how would you have reacted if I told you the truth, huh?" I fired back. "You do the opposite of whatever people advise you to do. If I told you the truth, if any of us had, you would have hated us and dated him anyway."

"How do you know that?"

I scoffed. We both knew I was right. Brian was a dud. A toxic, moody, only-charismatic-when-he's-had-a-few *dud*. And just two weeks after what was meant to be Jasmine's one-off rebound after her last ex, she'd brought Brian home for dinner and forced him into our lives, like she did all of her decisions.

At least they know who I really am, Jasmine would say, justifying every time she kicked up a fuss, referring to the plethora of our South Asian friends who just did whatever they wanted and lied to their parents about it.

But maybe Jasmine should have lied, for all our sakes. Because what she didn't see was what happened to Mom and Dad after she slammed the door and took off without bothering to tell anyone where she was going, without caring about how much she made them worry. Yes, they accepted her. Yes, they loved her and they always would. But that didn't mean she didn't put them through hell. Jasmine had made them cry harder than she'd ever know, their bedroom door shut, their voices only audible to me when I pressed my ear hard against the wall.

So of course I had to be the good daughter. Live my life the way *they* wanted. I didn't want to cause my parents that sort of pain. I had to think carefully about how not to make those same mistakes, to be the calm in the storm rather than the hot, dizzying puff of air that caused it.

"I'm going to hook up with Sam," I said decidedly. It wasn't fair that Jasmine got to have all the fun out of the two of us. I was on vacation. I was on a *break*. It was my goddamn turn.

"Go ahead," she said. "But you're going to get your heart broken."

I fumed. "Jas—"

"And I'm telling you this *now*, even though you're mad, because I'm a *good* sister." She stared at me with cold eyes. "Unlike you."

"*I'm* the bad sister?" I scoffed.

I was the sister that listened to Mom and Dad and did everything they ever wanted from both of us. I was the sister that picked up the pieces, that made the responsible choices, that did everything right—everything *good*.

"You know what, Jas?" I was shaking, unable to look at her or feel anything at all but anger, red and hot. I opened my mouth, ready to swallow it all. Ready to be the bigger person—the better sister—and apologize.

But I'd already lost my cool.

And I told my big sister to go fuck herself.

CHAPTER 19

*Y*ou're so quiet this afternoon," Sam said as we rolled our suitcases through the apartment complex.

"I'm taking it all in."

"Sure?"

My shoulder bag was slipping off my arm. I hiked it up, nodding. "I'm sure."

The hour-and-a-half drive from Goa International Airport to his family's apartment near Mandrem Beach had been utterly breathtaking. Scenic, sprawling beaches more gorgeous than the ones I'd come across on Instagram. Picturesque towns and buildings that seemed almost European with their architecture and Catholic churches, remnants of the Portuguese colony everywhere you looked. Even here, a maze of walkways leading up to the apartment building was lush with greenery and flowers, an archway of coconut trees hanging overtop.

I was in awe. But I was also really bummed out. Jasmine hadn't texted me back since our fight earlier this morning, even though I'd sent her about fifty apology messages. But she had a right to be angry with me. We used all kinds of terrible language to refer to other people—*usually* in jest—but Jasmine and I never aimed it at each other. Without a doubt, I'd crossed a huge line.

But was I in the wrong for hiding my true feelings about her boyfriend? *Did* that make me a bad sister? All these years, I'd thought I was doing the right thing by keeping my mouth shut about Brian, but now I wasn't sure what was the bigger betrayal. If I should have been honest with her, like she'd been with me today, even if it meant she'd be mad at me for it.

I looked over at Sam walking beside me. His eyes were on the ground, as if he were worried about tripping over his laces. He'd been nervous around me all day and had even spilled his coffee on his khaki shorts while we were waiting to board. To my great amusement, for about a half hour he looked like he'd wet himself.

Sam caught me staring, and I realized I'd been holding my breath. There was no doubt about it. I was majorly crushing on Sam, and I wondered fleetingly if there was a grain of truth to what Jasmine had said to me.

No. I felt my ears redden just thinking about her. About her lack of faith in me. Who was she to go around doing whatever the hell she wanted, and then tell *me* I wasn't capable of this? Keeping my feelings in check while having a fling?

"What are you thinking about, Niki?" Sam asked me suddenly.

"I'm thinking we should go to the beach." I nudged Jasmine's voice out of my head and decided not to let her ruin my vacation. "How far away is it?"

"Walking distance." Sam stopped short, and then looked upward, using his hand to shield out the sun. I followed with my eyes and found Aasha Auntie waving down at us from a balcony one level up, a vision in stylish linen pants and a loose *kurta*, her short, salt-and-pepper hair slicked back behind her ears.

"Yoo-hoo!" she called down, beckoning us to come more quickly. "Hello, my sweets!"

Even though I was happy to see her, I grimaced as Jasmine's annoying voice popped into my head. No, this was certainly not a family holiday.

This was definitely just a *fling*.

*W*hen we got upstairs, Aasha Auntie hugged me with such warmth and familiarity it was honestly a bit overwhelming. I wasn't sure why I got emotional—I pulled away when it became too much.

I gave Auntie a box of Mom's *pinni*, and smiling in thanks, she popped a piece into her mouth before setting off for the tour. I was thankful Mom had packed so many boxes for me. I'd also given one each to Pinky and Manish before leaving the Joshis' apartment for the hotel, as well as one to the friendly woman at the concierge when I'd checked out of my Mumbai hotel. I still had several left over for my relatives when I got to Punjab.

The apartment was spread over two floors. The kitchen, the

living room area, a bedroom, and a bathroom were on the bottom floor, and upstairs, there were three more bedrooms and another bathroom. Halfway through the tour, their dog Scooby woke up from his slumber and started following me around. After one scruff on the back of his neck, the adorable little thing wouldn't let me out of his sight.

"Your face is shining again." Aasha Auntie stopped outside a door partially ajar, leading to what I assumed would be my bedroom for the next few days. Or however long I ended up staying. (Sam and I actually hadn't discussed when I'd leave for Punjab, although my flight back to Seattle was booked for twelve days from now.)

"You look healthy once more," Aasha Auntie continued.

"Thank you," I stammered, getting stupidly overwhelmed again. "For letting me stay with you and for taking care of me that night—"

"Oh, honey. I didn't come for *you*. Sam was managing just fine." She smiled. "Poor boy. He was *so* worried about you. I thought *he* might get ill."

Sam appeared at the top of the stairs just in time for me to see his face go beet red. I stifled a laugh.

"Anyway, you can sleep here." Aasha Auntie pushed open the door, and the room wasn't what I was expecting. The walls were lined with bookshelves, and there were several guitars and a keyboard next to the bed.

"It still looks like a teenager's room!" Her laugh rang out, and my head swiveled very slowly in her direction. She was star-

ing vaguely into space, and it occurred to me that she was showing me Sam's room.

Hold the phone. She wanted me to sleep with *him*?

I threw Sam a pleading look. "Um."

"Niki will stay with you," Aasha Auntie said to him. "Yes?"

Sam's eyes bulged.

"It's fine, *beta*."

"Yeah," Sam grunted, "but—"

"Why so much drama?" She batted her eyelashes innocently,
turning to me. "You will stay with Sam, *nah*?"

Uh . . . *Nah*, I wouldn't. Yes, I was on an adventurous kick,
and the thought of cuddling up next to Sam all night got my mojo
flowing, but this had *bad idea* written all over it.

1. Aasha Auntie would be just down the hall.
2. Aasha Auntie was—let's spell it out—an *auntie*!

I was panicking, alarm bells going off everywhere.

I'd never ever met a brown parent who would not only be
OK with their child shacking up under their roof but actually *en-
courage* it. Mom and Dad were among the chiller parents of our
South Asian community, and even they made Brian sleep in a
different bedroom on a different floor of the house when he and
Jasmine stayed over during the holidays. (I mean, fair enough.
Brian had never bothered to learn the golden rule for dating a
South Asian girl: *do not fucking touch them in front of the parents.*
He once attempted to kiss Jasmine—on the *mouth*—during a

family gathering, and Dad got so flustered he excused himself to the restroom and didn't come back for an hour.)

"Auntie," I said, sweating buckets. "If it's not too much trouble, I'll stay in a different bedroom."

"And what if I told you it *was* a lot of trouble?" Aasha Auntie turned to me, her eyes sparkling. "This room is already made up, *beti*."

I swallowed hard. "Then I guess I'll take the dog's bed?"

Sam choked just as Auntie rolled her eyes, barking out a laugh. "Scooby is very possessive. That's fine. You can sleep downstairs."

My face and neck were on fire as she disappeared, leaving Sam to get me settled in the bedroom downstairs. I was still hot and weirded out, and as soon as Sam closed the door, I collapsed onto the bed.

"Sorry about that," Sam said, sitting down next to me. "She's quite the character."

"Was that a test?" I asked, nervous. "Did she want me to prove I was a good girl or something and make me ask for my own room?"

Sam grinned. "She'll love that you thought that, but no. Honestly, she's very relaxed about those things. Very *modern*, as her gossipy friends like to say."

"No kidding."

"I suppose she made some assumptions because we . . ." Sam trailed off and I eyed him.

"Because we . . ." I echoed, grinning. "Did you tell your mom we *kissed*?"

His face contorted, giving him away.

"Oh my god. You're a little mama's boy, aren't you?"

"I am not!"

"You *are*. I bet you're the favorite."

"I'm the youngest, so she babies me, but my brother, Prem, is the favorite. *Her* favorite."

"And your dad's?"

Sam hesitated, and just as I kicked myself for prying into their family affairs, he spoke up.

"My sister. Leena." He smiled. "She's the best. You'll love her. Everyone does."

I gestured to the pink frilly curtains and pillow shams. "Is this her room?"

"She hasn't visited in a while, but yeah. Leena has three young kids, so we usually go to them in LA."

"Does Prem have kids, too?"

"A baby boy, and another is on the way."

Sam pulled out his phone and started showing me family photos—everyone gathered in Prem and his wife's apartment in Mumbai or here in Goa or on the boardwalk in LA. Sam looked very much like his siblings; they were all spitting images of Aasha Auntie, although Sam and Leena had their father's eyes. Their dad was in only two of the photos.

"You're close with Prem and Leena. I can tell." I handed Sam back his phone. "That's really nice."

"It is." Sam nodded. "It's hard with the three of us each on a different continent, but we're there for each other as much as we can be. Like you and Jasmine, I expect."

I hesitated. At some point during our time together, I'd told Sam all about my complicated big sister, but I hadn't told him about our fight earlier that day. After all, he *was* just going to be a fling and didn't need to know all the details.

"Exactly," I said finally. "Just like me and Jasmine."

CHAPTER 20

*W*e didn't have time to go to the beach in the end. It was getting late, and we'd promised to meet up with the group at their resort in Bardez, which Sam told me was the party capital of Goa, with its nightclubs, bars, music festivals, and beach parties. Luckily, Diya was several years past her bar star phase and wanted to have a low-key night.

After tea with Aasha Auntie, Sam and I took a taxi over to the hotel. It was only a twenty-minute drive, but it felt like an eternity because Sam and I still weren't saying much to each other. He was acting all nervous again, which was putting me back on edge. I wondered if he was second-guessing his decision to invite me to Goa. We hadn't kissed or so much as held hands since yesterday, when he left me to sleep off the rest of my food poisoning back in Mumbai. A few times during tea, he looked at me like he wanted to, but Aasha Auntie was around, and I didn't let myself get within a foot of him.

"There you are!"

Diya was waiting for us in the lobby, and she raced over to us, her heels smacking the marble floor. If I had to describe this hotel in one word—well, it was very *Diya*.

She hugged Sam first and then me, studying our faces as she pulled away. "Hi!"

"We could have met you in the restaurant," Sam said. "Shall we head in? I'm starving."

"Not so fast," Diya said. "I needed to speak with you both alone."

Her voice was serious and my stomach dropped.

"So, you decided to come," she continued, looking at me. "*This* was unexpected. Are you good?"

"I'm good."

Diya narrowed her eyes, flicking them toward Sam. "Are *you* good?"

"I'm swell, mate."

"Brilliant." She gripped each of us with one hand. "Now. Listen up. I love you both. *Equally*. But you must think of me as Switzerland, OK?"

"So, you'll hide all of our blood money?"

Sam grinned while Diya smacked me.

"Pay attention, Niki."

I nodded and mimed zipping my mouth shut.

"I'm Switzerland. Do you understand?" She was visibly

shaking with excitement. What had she told me back in Mumbai when discussing whether she'd give Sam my phone number? That if we got together, she'd have to force us to get married?

"Don't tell me anything," she warned. "And I will try my best not to ask."

*D*iya had somehow managed to score a table for fourteen people at the trendy restaurant on the roof of the resort. The view was amazing, the ocean literally sparkling back at us as dusk turned to night. Diya would feel terrible if she knew I got food poisoning at her wedding, and so I had sworn Sam and Aasha Auntie to secrecy. Thankfully, Sam and I were seated at the other end of the table, and so she didn't see me order conservatively— opting for Limca instead of wine and a mild vegetarian curry instead of my usual order of the spiciest thing on the menu.

It felt strange sitting there, Sam on one side of me and Masooma on the other, seven pairs made up of six couples and whatever the hell Sam and I were. I could feel some of the others in the wedding party gawking at me and Sam curiously, making comments with their eyes, but I chose to ignore them. Luckily, Masooma, whom I once again spent much of the evening talk to, didn't ask me about him once.

"I'm so glad to have met you," she said while we pulled out our phones and followed each other on Instagram. I wasn't sure I liked all of Diya and Mihir's friends, but Masooma was just lovely.

"I'm going to be in Seattle next month for a conference," Masooma said, handing me back my phone. "We should grab dinner."

"Absolutely," I beamed, trying to think of what restaurant to take her to.

"Will you be home by then?"

I nodded. "I'm flying back via Delhi in twelve days."

"What are your plans for the rest of your holiday?"

I popped a mouthful of creamy curry, delaying. In my peripheral vision, I could see Sam listening to our conversation, and it occurred to me that we hadn't actually discussed how long I was going to be a houseguest or when he himself would be flying back to London.

"All done, ma'am?" The waiter arrived, saving me from having to answer Masooma. I shook my head, smiling. The curry was delicious, and I wanted to finish every last drop. He turned to the bridesmaids sitting across from us, who gestured for their plates to be taken away.

"That was really disappointing," one said loudly to the other. "I almost threw up."

My mouth dropped. *What?* I was stunned, and I inadvertently made eye contact with the waiter and threw him an apologetic look. His face didn't give anything away.

"I had four bites and left the rest," the second one said, huffy. "*I* cook better than this."

"When was the last time you were in a kitchen?"

"When our last cook didn't show up for work—her daughter was in labor or something."

"She didn't show up?" the other snapped. "Did you *fire* her?"

"Wanted to. Mummy said no. It doesn't matter; she's quit since. Who knows where she landed."

I squirmed in my seat, my eyes still locked with the waiter's as he cleared our dishes. The two bridesmaids' lack of compassion and awareness over their own privilege was nothing short of astounding. Not everyone could afford to holiday at beachside resorts and eat out at restaurants. Until recently, they were luxuries my own family wasn't able to afford.

"I think I remember that cook," the second bridesmaid continued. I looked up and watched her sucking on the straw of her cocktail. I wanted to dump it all over her head.

"She made very tasty *aloo tikki, aacha*?"

"She ate too many *aloo tikki*," the other said, puffing out her cheeks. "She was so heavy. *Yaar*, do you remember—"

"Do you know what I remembered?" I interrupted, unable to bite my tongue any longer. The bridesmaids turned to look, as did Masooma, Sam, and the others in our vicinity. I waited a beat, holding their gaze.

"My manners."

CHAPTER 21

Eighteen years ago

*J*s everything OK—"

"Shh!" Mom interrupted me, setting her hand firmly on the table.

From the chair opposite, Jasmine threw me a wry look. Mom was eavesdropping on Dad, who had answered the phone in the other room ten minutes earlier and had been speaking Punjabi in a low voice ever since.

"What is he saying?" I mouthed to Jasmine, who just shrugged and spooned *aloo* to her lips. We were both nearly finished with our dinner, while our parents' plates were still practically untouched. Mom kept dunking the same piece of *roti* into her *daal*, but then her ears would perk up, and she'd forget to eat it.

I let my mind wander away from the table, from whatever was being said to Dad on the telephone. Today had been typically dull, except for the fleeting high I'd felt after getting an A on my math test. I smiled. I also had that small win during the lunch hour, when my "friend" Tiffany tried to swap juice boxes—mixed berry for *apple*—and I finally stood up to her and refused.

Suddenly, Dad appeared in the kitchen, and I held my breath as he slouched into his seat next to me. He still had the cordless phone in his hand, extended out in his palm. It was as if he didn't know what to do with it.

"What happened?" Mom asked him. She took the phone and then pressed her hand into his. "Is she all right?"

Dad sighed, and when he shook his head, my tummy began to feel funny. "Dadima broke her hip."

The table fell silent. Mom pressed her palm over her mouth. I didn't know what to say, and so I stayed quiet.

Dadima was my only grandparent left. Mom's parents were long gone, and Dad's father, who we called Dadaji, had a fatal heart attack when I was still in diapers. I was too young to remember the summer he visited America, but Jasmine claimed to. She always told me that he smelled like ginger snaps.

"Will she need a cast?" I managed, remembering the cast the doctors put on my wrist after I fell Rollerblading.

Mom smiled at me sadly. "It's more complicated than that, *beti*. I suspect she'll need surgery."

Dad nodded. "It's scheduled for Friday. It will cost . . ."

He trailed off, and I stared down at my empty plate, too uncomfortable to look anywhere else.

I never used to think about money, but over the last few months, I'd started to notice how stressful a subject it was for my family. How frequently it was the topic of Mom and Dad's conversations and arguments. They worked long hours and as hard as the other parents at school, but for whatever reason, our family never seemed to have enough. For groceries, rent, and bills—*yes*—but not for all the other things my friends seemed to have. Our presents on Christmas morning were minimal, our school supplies the generic brand, our extracurricular activities limited to those freely available through the community center or local Y.

"How much will it cost?" Mom prompted, and a beat later, Dad replied in Punjabi.

"That's OK." Mom rubbed his forearm, smiling. "Your sister needn't worry. We'll cover it—"

"But—"

"No arguments, *hah*?" Mom said brightly. "After dinner, we'll call her back and tell her not to worry."

"So she's going to be OK," Jasmine said as a statement and not a question. I looked over at her. Jasmine was now a teenager and miraculously had the ability to convey multiple emotions in the blink of an eye. Right now, she somehow looked worried, sad, and bored. Although these days, Jasmine always looked a bit bored.

"Your Dadima will be fine," Dad answered flatly. "But it will take a while to heal." He paused, glanced over at Mom. "She won't be able to come visit us this summer. I think I'll go—"

"Of course," Mom said. "We'll both go to India. I can take leave from work, too."

Jasmine stiffened, her fork rattling down on the plate as she dropped it. I flinched.

"Sorry," Jasmine muttered.

"Is there something you'd like to say?" Mom asked stiffly.

"It's not important—"

"You can still go to Camp Juniper," Dad said, "if that's what you're asking."

Mom inhaled sharply. In Punjabi, she started to say something, but Dad cut her off.

"It's *OK*," he said softly. "We'll manage."

Jasmine's smile stretched wide across her face. She'd been on a monthslong campaign to convince our parents to send her to the all-girls sleepaway summer camp everyone who was *anyone* seemed to attend. As legend had it, it was two weeks of canoeing and swimming, hiking and campfires.

Two weeks without parental supervision.

Jasmine and I weren't even allowed to sleep over at our friends' houses, but somehow, she'd managed to convince Mom and Dad by keeping her grades up and a PowerPoint presentation on the mental health benefits of nature, athletics, and group activities; it even contained testimonials from parents who had sent their daughters to the camp and lived to tell the tale.

"Niki can come, too, right?" Jasmine asked.

I squirmed in my seat. Although Jasmine outright ignored me when we crossed paths at school, surprisingly, the campaign was for both of us to go.

"Oh—" Dad's eyes widened, and I witnessed something I wasn't used to seeing on my father.

Fear.

"Um . . ." He shoveled some *aloo* into his mouth, stalling, suddenly invested in his uneaten dinner.

I shuffled my sock feet against the floor, the static building. I wanted to go to Camp Juniper, too. I wanted to go *badly*. But lately, I was learning to read between the lines. After two years of being bullied, I now understood that a compliment from Tiffany at school wasn't always a compliment, and that adults said a lot more with their eyes than their mouths.

"I can't go this year," I blurted. "I don't want to."

Mom, Dad, and Jasmine all turned to look, and my face heated up.

"Tiffany's birthday party is the same week. She'll be so mad if I'm not there."

"You're going to miss camp for *her* birthday?" Jasmine asked skeptically. "She sucks, Niki."

"She doesn't *suck*," I stammered. "Besides. Her parents are taking all of us to that water park—"

"Wild Waves?" Jasmine interrupted, and I nodded.

A moment later, I felt Dad's hand on my back, a comforting pat that was his way of expressing affection. He wasn't a hugger; he was barely a handshaker.

"This party is important to you?" he asked vaguely.

"Totally," I exclaimed. "I have—uh—*friends*. Unlike Jasmine." I couldn't resist the jab, even if it wasn't true. Between the two of us, Jasmine was the popular one. "I don't need to go to camp."

"As *if*," Jasmine fumed. "I—"

"*Bus*," Dad warned, although he was smiling, so I knew I

wasn't really in trouble for squabbling. It was the first smile he'd cracked all evening.

"Are you sure you don't want to go to camp with Jasmine?" Mom's voice was small, and I could tell she didn't believe me. "It would be only fair . . ."

Mom and Dad had taught us never to lie, but lately, I was also starting to learn that they didn't always follow their own rules. Like before dinner, when Mom asked Dad if there was too much *mircha* in the *aloo* and Dad said no, even though the food was *way* too spicy. Or the week before, when I asked my family if they noticed the new patch of acne on my chin, and everyone insisted they couldn't, even though it was practically visible from outer space.

Or just now. When Dad had said, "We'll manage."

"I'm *very* sure," I said, smiling widely so everyone would believe me.

I was eleven. I was a *kid*. But I was old enough to have learned that sometimes lies—very small ones—weren't wrong. They were important. Sometimes lies were what held a family together.

CHAPTER 22

*I*s your mom asleep?" I asked Sam, as we tiptoed into the apartment.

"Doesn't look like it." Sam kicked off his shoes. "She must be out."

It was hot inside, and I took off my cardigan, nervous about suddenly being alone with Sam. Before arriving in Goa, I'd imagined a fling would go from zero to sixty in a flash, but we'd somehow plateaued around ten miles per hour.

"What do you want to do?" I asked, following him into the sitting room. We still hadn't been to the beach, and I wondered if it would be safe to go at night.

He turned around slowly, studying me with those intense eyes of his. After, he extended his hand, pulling me forward as I took it. It was the most physical contact we'd made all night.

"Come with me."

He led me to his room, but I knew he wasn't taking me to bed; he sat me down at his keyboard.

"Play for me," he whispered, settling in beside me. We were thigh to thigh on the bench, his khaki pants flush against my bare legs.

"What should I play?"

"Anything you want."

I flexed my hands, nervous energy practically sparking from the tips of my fingers. It had been a long time, too long, and my hands shook as I set them on the keys. After a minute, I started to breathe. Then my fingers started to play.

The start was soft and slow, and it wasn't perfect, but it came to me clearly, as if the sheet music were right in front of my eyes. I could feel my heart beating, the rhythm taking shape around it as chords on the keys.

I stumbled partway through the movement as the tempo picked up. Breathing hard, I forced myself through, letting the muscle memory take over. My hands glided over the keys, and I forgot where I was, or even who I was, until it was all over, and I felt Sam's arm fold in around me.

"That was beautiful," he whispered, lightly kissing my shoulder. I shivered, reveling in the touch of him.

"I'm . . . speechless, Niki."

"Thanks." I cleared my throat, trying to keep it together. I hadn't expected to get emotional; after all, it was just the piano.

"*Clair de Lune*," Sam said. "Right?"

I nodded. Debussy. I knew he'd recognize it.

"Do you ever write your own songs?"

I withdrew my hands from the keys and tucked them on my lap. Sam leaned his head against my neck. I could feel him laughing softly in my ear.

"You do, don't you?"

"Maybe."

"Can I hear one?"

"No. Absolutely not." I turned to him, smiling. "No one's ever heard them . . . They're silly."

"So?"

"No, Sam," I said evenly. "They're *silly*. Do you ever watch people from afar and imagine their life and their backstories and all that?" From his blank expression, I could tell Sam had no idea what I was talking about, so as quickly as I could, I told him about Romeo and Juliet back home. How sometimes I got carried away when people-watching and imagined what their love story might sound like as a song.

Sam thought this was hilarious, and he tickled me—nay, *tortured* me—until I agreed to sing my Romeo and Juliet song for him. I wasn't much of a singer, but luckily, my lyrics were in the alto vocal range, and I'd composed it to the tune of a certain song.

A certain popular, uh, Taylor Swift song.

"That was glorious," Sam said afterward, loyally. I could see him trying not to laugh, and I nudged him hard in the ribs.

"Yeah, yeah—"

"It was cute. Really cute, Niki." He grinned, wiggling his eyebrows. "Do Romeo and Juliet ever get together?"

"I hope so," I said. "Maybe one day."

"But will they ride away together on a magical coffee cart?" he said, mocking the lyrics I'd just "sung" for him.

"I told you it was silly," I pouted.

"Aww," Sam said, eyes glinting. "It's adorable. And frankly—well, rather *shocking*." He leaned in closer. "Niki, you're a romantic. I had no idea."

I was about to protest, but then he gently pressed his fingers against my lips.

"I won't tell anyone." His thumb parted my lips. "It will be our little secret."

Sam's gaze was too intense, and as heat coursed through my body, I shot up from the bench. "So, what kind of guitars do you have?" I squeaked.

I gave myself a mental pep talk, half listening as Sam told me about his Fender and vintage acoustic. I knew he wanted to kiss me, and even though I wanted that, too, my nerves were taking over my bodily functions. A thousand contradictory thoughts and questions ran through my head, a mile a minute, many of them in Jasmine's holier-than-thou voice.

OMG. You are in a cute boy's bedroom!

Do you even remember how to have sex?

You're going to get hurt.

Niki, just go for it, you sex positive goddess!

"Niki?"

I snapped my head toward Sam. I had no idea what he'd been saying a moment earlier, nor had I noticed him lie down on the bed.

"Sorry," I blushed, taking a step backward. "What did you say?"

He smiled up at me and tucked his hands under his head. "I asked you why you didn't give music a go as a career."

I didn't feel like talking about Jasmine just yet—our fight was still too raw—and so I didn't tell Sam that majoring in music after Jasmine picked art would have been too hard on my parents.

"You think it would have been fanciful," Sam said before I could think of a reply. "Ridiculous, even."

I opened my mouth to speak, sitting down at the edge of the bed. I didn't want to offend Sam and his decision to chase after his dreams, but I was also reluctant to lie to him.

"You and my father both," Sam mumbled.

Sam turned his head away from me, toward the window.

We hadn't spent a lot of time together, and he hadn't shared many details about his life, nothing someone snooping couldn't find on Instagram. He had two siblings. He was close with his mother. He'd spent his first five years in London sharing a house with his bandmates in a neighborhood called Peckham, although now he shared a "flat" with an accountant and his cat, Tipsy.

I scanned his face, trying to decide how much to probe. I wasn't Sam's friend or his girlfriend. If he didn't want to tell me about his relationship with his father, then I knew I shouldn't ask.

"Hey," I said, squeezing his hand. "Let's do something fun. Beach?"

Sam tilted his chin, gazing up at me. "Tomorrow. I promise.

Diya says the whole crew is going to come up to see us tomorrow. Mandrem Beach is her favorite, too."

"Great." I smiled.

"By the way, I overheard Smita and Priti being pricks to our waiter. I'm sorry about that. They can be rather rude."

After I told them off at the restaurant, Masooma had also apologized for their behavior, sending me a DM over Instagram beneath the table. Apparently, everyone in the group thought they'd become too uppity in recent years, but no one had yet found the courage to tell them off.

"Don't worry," I said dismissively. "I don't judge you guys for being friends with them."

"You should judge us a little." Sam smiled. "But the thing is—we've known each other for so long, at this point, they're basically family." He paused. "You take it or you leave it."

"I get that." I shrugged. I was still feeling weird about dinner, and I couldn't find the words I was looking for. "I just . . ."

Sam squeezed my hand, prompting me. "What is it, love?"

"Our waiter tonight . . ." I trailed off again, breathing hard. "When I looked at him, I didn't just see some waiter, you know? I saw myself. *My* family."

"What do you mean?" Sam asked quietly.

"We come from humble farming communities. Most of my family isn't well off." I paused. "A lot of them work in service roles for people like your friends. For people like you, Sam."

"That might be the case," he said quietly. "But not everyone—"

"I know not everyone is like Smita and Priti. I know people

can have money and also be *kind* and *good*, but that doesn't mean it's fair. Why do some people get everything and others . . . *don't*? Why did *I* get to grow up in America, and my cousins here . . ."

"You feel guilty," he said plainly.

Rationally, I knew I shouldn't feel guilty. My parents had worked for the life they built in the US for their daughters' futures, but I wasn't feeling all that rational these days.

"I don't know how I feel."

"Are you looking forward to Punjab?" Sam asked. "To meeting your family?"

"Sort of . . ."

Sam reached for my hand and interlocked our fingers. I had meant to steer clear of serious subjects, like my relationship with Jasmine or Sam's father. Somehow, we still ended up talking about a different, tenderer one. *Me.*

"I guess I'm afraid," I said quietly.

"What are you afraid of?"

"I've had a better life than them, and I'm scared of seeing something *hard*." I looked down at our palms. "That's terrible, right?"

"Who are you to say that you've had a better life than them, huh?" Sam pinched me playfully on the nose with his free hand. "You sound like an American."

I laughed, leaning my weight into him. "I do. But guess what?"

"What?" he whispered.

"I *am* an American." I threw my hands up. "Or Indian-American. Or whatever you want to call it."

"Here in India," Sam said, "some might call you an NRI. A nonresident Indian."

"A nonresident Indian," I repeated, considering the label. Growing up, I'd always wondered what to call myself. Punjabi-American. Indian-Sikh. *Jat*. Desi. Brown Girl. I hadn't heard the term "NRI" before, and as I considered it, I started to wonder out loud why these labels even mattered so much to me. What should matter is how I thought about myself.

I felt lighter as we talked, the way I had on Diwali, and a weight lifted from my chest as it became clear to me that Sam was right. As I figured out a way to articulate feelings that I hadn't ever said out loud.

I didn't have a better life than my cousins who grew up here in India. I had a different life. And it wasn't for me to say who was right and what was wrong, or to carry the weight of what was so fucked up about the world on my shoulders, like a would-be savior.

All we can do is stand up for what we believe in, be a good person, and do our best not to harm anyone in the process.

"I love Punjab," Sam said, smiling at me as our conversation veered back to the subject of my family trip. He tucked my hair behind my ears. "I think you'll love it, too."

"You've been to Amritsar?"

"Twice. The first time, I was too young to remember. It was a family trip." Ever so briefly, Sam's face went dark. "But I went back a few years ago with friends. It's a beautiful city."

"I'm looking forward to it." I didn't want to think about parting ways already, but my family was expecting me, and we needed to plan for it. "What day should I leave?"

"That's up to you. There's still time to decide."

"But when will you be going back to London?" I paused, weary of prying, of disrupting Sam's plans. "Do you have any shows coming up?"

"Not imminently," he said vaguely. "And I'm not quite sure yet. I might wait and see how long this cute girl I know sticks around."

"She's cute, huh?"

"Rather dorky. But a bit cute, yeah—"

I grabbed a pillow and smacked him in the face. Laughing, Sam wrestled it from me and then pinned me down on the bed, his left hand gently pressed around both my wrists.

His face was only inches away as he hovered above me, most of his weight balanced on his arms. Without thinking, I arched my hips upward and practically groaned as he lowered himself onto me, our stomach and thighs pressed together.

"Am I squishing you?"

"Yes." I closed my eyes and played dead, letting my tongue loll to the side. "You've killed me."

"Still cute," Sam said quietly. "Even dead."

I opened my eyes to find him staring down at me, and my heart literally skipped a beat. God, he was hot. I was so nervous before that I'd almost forgotten about the way his eyes sparkled when he looked at me. The way his lips naturally pouted in a sexy sort of smirk, which I was beginning to think wasn't so much aloof as it was thoughtful. The way he looked at me, his eyelids heavy, and somehow still managed to see everything.

Sam lowered his face a fraction, those dangerously kissable

lips close enough for me to pounce. I licked my lips, trembling, and when Sam kissed me, my mind went blank. Every thought and question and doubt slipped away, and all I could feel were his lips pressing against me.

My heart raced as he released my wrists, and I wrapped my arms around his back, pulling him closer. I could feel him pulsing against me as we kissed more deeply, his hand finding the small of my waist, grazing upward from my ribs.

I was melting. I was hot and desperate for more, writhing aimlessly as his lips traced the soft skin of my neck, landing in a gentle kiss on my collarbone.

"Sam," I moaned. He looked up at me in a daze.

I opened my mouth, panting, ready to throw caution to the wind, to Jasmine's words of warning, and jump headfirst into a pool of unknown depth and proportion.

"Niki?" he whispered. He rested his chin lightly against my chest, breathing hard and fast, and just then, something . . . clicked.

Not us.

A freaking *doorknob*.

In a flash, Sam and I were off the bed, and I tugged my shirt down as we raced over to the keyboard, footsteps echoing on the stairs just outside.

"I'm home!" Aasha Auntie called. "Are you decent?"

"Yes," Sam barked, a half laugh, half-mortified yelp.

I ran my hands through my hair just as she appeared in the doorway, her hip cocked to one side.

"How was your night?" Sam croaked. I wasn't sure how he

was speaking. My heart was pounding so fast I could barely breathe.

"Such fun!" Auntie took one step into the room, her purse swinging at her side. "Niki, I have a ladies group here—all of our children have left home, and so we cook for each other."

"Sounds lovely," I managed. I didn't sound like myself, but at least they were words.

"Niki was just playing for me," Sam said. "She's very good."

"I am not surprised. Will you play for me, too?"

"I uh . . ."

"*Later*, Mom." Sam smiled at her, and Auntie started nodding profusely, taking the hint.

"*Aacha.* You kids have fun." She turned around, hips swaying as she left. "These walls are soundproof, Niki, in case you were curious."

As soon as Auntie closed the door behind her, my face collapsed into my hands. "Well," I groaned, my palms muffling the sound. "*That* was mortifying."

Sam pressed his face against my cheek, kissing me. "That was close. It's like high school all over again, huh?"

"I didn't sneak around with guys in high school, Sam."

"Oh yeah, I forgot. You were a little dork."

I swatted him away, but he just pulled me closer.

"Did you have sex in high school?" I asked teasingly.

"Lots."

I guffawed, and Sam squeezed me accusingly.

"Indian people have sex, you know." He pressed his hands

together in namaste and thickened his accent. "You Americans—you think we are all so pious?"

"I meant it's surprising that *you* had sex in high school," I fired back. "I've seen pictures . . ."

I teasingly pinched his cheek, thinking about that adorable, chubby little boy Diya grew up with. He'd grown up into a straight-up hottie.

A hottie who, for the first time in my life, made me feel completely out of control.

CHAPTER 23

$\mathcal{I}$ woke up to bird songs and the low hum of the generator. Smiling, I threw the covers off, grabbed my phone, and headed into the kitchen. It was just shy of seven in the morning, and so I quietly rummaged around the pantry until I found everything I needed to make a big pot of Punjabi tea—cardamom, cinnamon, black pepper, sugar, fennel, cloves, and Mom's secret ingredient, ginger.

I set the water to boil and then sat down at the kitchen table, scrolling through my phone. Jasmine still hadn't replied, although I knew she was alive because she'd checked in on our family group chat. I fired off a quick text in there myself and then logged into my e-mail.

My pulse quickened as two new messages appeared. Overnight, two of the companies I'd applied to had gotten back to me: they wanted me to come in and interview.

A few days earlier, these e-mails would have had me popping the metaphorical champagne and blaring Beyoncé in celebration, and so the knot of uncertainty in my stomach was a surprising one. Wasn't this *good* news? I was unemployed. I needed something solid to step on, a foothold to get back on track.

And here, right *here* in my hand, could be the answer.

I glanced up when I heard footsteps running down the stairs. A moment later, Sam shot around the corner.

"Good morn—"

He interrupted me with a kiss, his hands cupping my face in his palms, and a beat later, he pulled away.

"What was that for?" I asked, breathless.

"Mom's up." Sam kissed me on the nose, then whispered, "She's right behind me—"

"Yoo-hoo," she called, thundering down the stairs. "No funny business, *aacha*? Your Aasha Auntie is *here*!"

She entered the kitchen giggling at her own joke, while Sam rolled his eyes and I tried not to die.

"Oh, *beti*. What is this tasty smell?"

"*Cha*." I hopped off the chair, still embarrassed that she yet again nearly caught me macking on her son. "I hope it's OK that I helped myself in the pantry?"

"Be my guest! Punjabis make the *best* tea."

Aasha Auntie and I finished off the *cha* while Sam prepared breakfast, cutting up mangoes, papayas, and melons into a large ceramic bowl. I watched him, kind of in awe, especially when he returned from the pantry and started adding spices to the mixture.

"This is Sam's specialty. Masala fruit salad."

I leaned over the bowl and took a big whiff of the spicy-sweet aroma. "Smells great."

"Are you veg or non-veg, Niki?" Auntie asked me.

"Non-veg," I answered. "I'll eat *anything*."

"Perfect. Sam cooks delicious chicken curry I am most eager to try again." She looked over at him curiously. "Tonight, *beta*? I will call the butcher."

"Sure." Sam sprinkled a bit of salt over the fruit salad. "Do we have *aloo*?"

"We are running short. I will also call the vegetable *waala*."

"You can cook," I said to Sam. It was more of a question, but I said it like a statement.

"A bit."

"He is *very* accomplished chef—so modest, Sam." Aasha Auntie handed me the tea strainer. "When did you learn, *beta*? I am forgetting."

"When I left for college," Sam answered, as he peeled another mango, "I had to. I missed your cooking too much, Mom."

My chest felt all light and fluttery as I admired his domestic prowess, the way he prepared the fruit salad and hashed out a meal plan with his mother. Traditional South Asian mothers tended to dote on their sons. And while pampering was one thing, spoiling them rotten was entirely different. And I'd met my fair share of Indian boys, *one* in particular, who were barely capable of tying their own shoelaces, practically debilitated by the pedestal on which they were placed.

After breakfast, Auntie Aasha volunteered to drop off Sam

and me at Mandrem Beach, as it was on her way out. I was desperate to sneak in another kiss, but Diya, Mihir, and the others had already arrived, and Sam and I didn't have a moment alone together.

We found a pristine stretch of sand that fit the whole group, and I laid my beach towel out next to Diya and Masooma. Mihir had brought a cooler full of coconut water and beer, and a Bluetooth speaker, and we spent the rest of the morning basking in the sun, cooling down in the ocean, and listening to everything from Benny Benassi to Dr. Dre to Bollywood classics like "Bole Chudiyan."

By midday, we were on our third dunk in the ocean. I stayed back when the group went ashore, enjoying the swell and dip of the waves. Curious, I searched for Sam and wasn't at all surprised to see that he'd stayed behind, too. My stomach lurched as he swam toward me in an effortless front stroke, his muscly arms rising in and out of the water. All morning, we seemed to have had an unspoken agreement not to inflict PDA on the group, although I'm not sure whether it was for the sake of modesty or to avoid prying questions. Luckily, I remembered to bring sunglasses, and I could discreetly ogle him as much as I pleased.

"This is quite a spot," I said once he was close. "How long has your family been coming here?"

"Years," Sam said. "Since I was a teenager, at least."

"Must have been quite the babe magnet."

"The girls created a rota. There were queues down the pavement, Niki. They all wanted—"

"All right, all right," I said, splashing back in the water.

"I'm kidding." He threw water right back at me. "As you

pointed out yesterday, girls didn't pay much attention to me when I was younger." He paused. "I only ever brought Amanda."

Oh yes, *Amanda*.

I lay flat on my back, floating on the waves. I didn't know her, and it sounded like she and Sam had been over for years, but I couldn't help but feel jealous. I knew I shouldn't. It didn't matter. But the feeling washed over me like one of these damn waves that kept flinging seawater into my mouth.

"Tell me about her," I said, staring up at the sky. The sun was bright and I closed my eyes. "Was she American?"

"We studied together at UCLA."

"A California girl." I paused, licking the salty water from my lips. "Did she like it here?"

"Not really," he said. "She said she liked the food, but that was about it. The beaches, the culture, the nightlife—she thought LA had it better."

I scoffed. Goa felt like paradise, and LA—well . . . OK, fine. LA was pretty great, too. If there was one other city I could see myself living in besides Seattle, it was LA.

"Tell me about your ex," Sam said after a moment.

I stood up, my head spinning as I shook water out of my ear. We were treading in dangerous territory again. Ex-boyfriends and-girlfriends definitely counted as a serious subject best avoided with a fling.

"I mean, besides the fact that he competed in StarCraft tournaments," Sam continued.

I laughed, stalling, dancing my arms around in the water. "Are you jealous?"

"Extremely."

I rolled my eyes.

"Where did you guys meet?"

I dug my heels into the sand, hesitating. Exfoliating. "Same as you and Amanda. In college." I paused. "At the library, to be specific."

"Naturally," Sam grinned. "So why did you split up? He didn't cheat on you, did he?"

"No, not at all." I paused, wondering why Sam had assumed that. "He couldn't multitask to save his life—juggling girlfriends would have been too much for him."

"Then?"

"Sam . . ." I was uncomfortable, both annoyed and pleased but more so *annoyed* that Sam was pressing this subject when both of us should have steered clear.

"Come on—"

"He broke up with me," I said quickly. "I don't know why. I guess I wasn't what he wanted."

"It's hard to believe that you're not what everybody wants."

Sam edged in closer and put his hands around my waist. I bit my lip, trying not to smile.

"Should we join the others?" I pulled my bathing suit strap to the side. We'd been in the sun for only a few hours, and my tan lines were noticeable. "I'm getting dark," I joked.

Sam sighed and groaned into my neck, pulling the strap back up.

"I like your skin. I like you however you are."

"What a line." I laughed, glancing toward the beach. The

group was far back on the sand, toweling off and not paying attention to how close we were standing.

"You don't actually care about tanning, do you?" His eyes were searching my face, but I was trying to avoid them. "Your skin is beautiful, Niki. You know that, right?"

"When I was young, some of the aunties at the *gurdwara* used to give Jasmine and I a hard time in the summer when we played in the sun." A wave crashed into my face. I spit out the salt water and then continued. "They told us we'd never find husbands if we got too dark. But I'm over it."

"Are you?"

I caught his gaze, shaking my head when the realization hit me that Aasha Auntie must have mentioned the incident with the sour-faced auntie in the restroom.

"Your mom told you."

"Sorry," Sam mumbled. "Is that OK? We tell each other everything."

"Did you tell her about our *second* kiss last night?"

"Every detail," he deadpanned.

I splashed him in the face, and in turn, he pulled me in even closer. My heart raced as I pressed against him, wrapped my legs tightly around his hips. I could feel my heart pounding in my chest, or maybe it was Sam's. Maybe it was both of ours.

"I'm mostly over it," I whispered, quickly kissing him on the cheek. There were still people nearby in the water—*Indian* people—and I wasn't comfortable taking this any further.

"Which auntie do I need to take down?" Sam asked me, his hands gripping my back.

"Basically, every auntie who's ever been told to buy Fair and Lovely."

"Haven't you heard? Colorism has been dismantled," Sam joked. "It's called Glow and Lovely now."

I laughed out loud, as if changing the name of the skin lightening cream made a single bit of difference. As if people of color all over the world, particularly women, weren't still made to feel inferior for having a healthy dose of melanin.

I glanced up at the beach, and I could just make out Diya and Mihir staring at us. We were too far away, but I could almost see the shit-eating grins on their faces.

"We have an audience," I said, tearing myself away from Sam, and suddenly out of his arms, the water felt cold.

Too cold.

So. I got out of the water, with Sam following me, and did my best not to think about how good it felt to be held by him.

CHAPTER 24

*O*f *course* I thought about it.

It was impossible not to, the way Sam kept *looking* at me like I was his favorite flavor of ice cream, and he had a hankering for mint chocolate chip. The way he . . . Christ. Just *everything* about him.

Sam was making my heart palpitate in a way that would have Jasmine screaming "I told you so"—that is, if Jasmine were speaking to me. So, as we packed up our stuff and joined Diya and the others at a nearby café, I instructed myself to get my shit together. To talk myself down from the ledge.

So what if I heard the lyrics to "Take My Breath Away" by Berlin every time our knees touched underneath the table? So *what* if I found him sexy beyond measure, even when he was stuffing his face with nachos?

It was a fling. An F-L-I-N-G.

After lunch, while everyone returned to dozing on the beach, I replied to the two e-mails burning a hole in my inbox and booked both job interviews for the week after I arrived back in Seattle. At some point, I needed to get back to my real life, and this—lounging here in paradise—was not reality. It was a vacation. A *break*. And whether I stayed in Goa only one more day or the full ten until my flight home, Sam and I would come to an end.

*S*am cooked a delicious meal for Aasha Auntie and me that evening, and the following morning, we woke up early to join Diya and the others for a full day of sightseeing in the gorgeous historic town of Old Goa.

The next day, Sam and I took a taxi into Bardez bright and early. Diya had finagled us guest passes for their resort, and I was more than happy to go along with her plan of relaxing by the pool and drinking overly sweet cocktails. It was another gorgeous, sunny day, as I sprawled out on a patio chair in literal paradise.

There was only one problem. Sam and I barely got a moment alone together.

At the apartment, Aasha Auntie was always around, and even though she went to great lengths to "give us space" and remind us the walls were soundproof (ugh!), I didn't feel comfortable doing anything rated higher than PG-13 with her in the next room. And during the day, we were always with the honeymooners—talking, eating, swimming, sightseeing, and everything in between as one large group.

I was having a great time—don't get me wrong—but I was starting to feel uneasy. Sam and I still hadn't discussed when I should leave for Amritsar, and I wanted to turn the notch up on what would be my only vacation fling ever before it came to an end. Hand-holding and secretly making out a bit were great and all, but I was desperate to be with Sam.

As Sam would say, I was thirsty.

By late afternoon, I was extremely hot and bothered, both from the weather and the view from my deck chair, which featured Sam shirtless, floating on a pool lounger a mere twenty feet away from me. Luckily, Diya came to my rescue. She needed to grab her meds and asked if I wanted a walk. Her allergies must have been acting up again; she'd been unusually quiet all day.

As soon as we got to her room, Diya flopped tummy-first onto the king-size bed. I searched for her signature gold-and-white medicine bag, rummaging through the bathroom and then her suitcase, which was mostly empty as clothes, shoes, and swimsuits were strewn all over the room. I loved Diya, but for the sake of our friendship, thank god we never lived together. Diya's college roommates were probably the only people on this planet who despised her.

"I can't find your meds," I said, after I'd checked the wardrobe. "Where are they?"

"Tote bag."

I crossed my arms. "You mean the tote bag that's on your arm?"

"That's the one."

Laughing, I cannonballed onto the bed. "You just wanted me alone, didn't you?"

"Maybe," she squealed, rolling away from me. "Is that a crime?"

We'd ended up on our sides face-to-face, and I smiled at Diya as she brushed my hair out of her eyes. Sam wasn't the only one who I couldn't get alone; Diya and I hadn't been together one-on-one since before the wedding.

"This bed is so comfortable," I said, wriggling farther into the spongy mattress. "You must be having one hell of a honeymoon."

"You and Sam can use it if you want."

"*Diya*." I laughed. So she *had* been eavesdropping that morning when I'd told Masooma about Sam and me not having space to "escalate" the fling.

"Should we call him up? I'll distract Mihir—"

I muffled her with a pillow until she shrieked.

"Seriously, dude! *Someone* should use it . . ." My mouth fell open, and she continued. "Honestly. We haven't done anything since we arrived. Not a *thing*."

"But it's your honeymoon!" I sputtered, still not believing her. "If all the group stuff is too tiring, you guys should—"

Diya waved me off. "We're good. I'm literally not in the mood. Neither is Mihir. The wedding took a lot out of us."

I sat up and suddenly realized that Diya knew she had her allergy medicines with her the whole time. She'd brought me up here for a reason.

"What's going on, D?" I said quietly.

She pressed her palms over her eyes, pushing down harder than looked comfortable.

"Did something happen with you and Mihir?"

She sighed heavily and then shook her head. "He's great."

"Then?"

"Then . . ."

I only dragged it out of her because I could tell she wanted to talk. But I was completely unprepared for what she told me next: shortly after the engagement, their families had hired an astrologer to read Diya's and Mihir's birth charts, sign off on the marital union, and propose an auspicious day for the wedding.

Although many Hindus were ardent believers in astrology, no one in Diya's and Mihir's families could have cared less about the results. For them, it was just a ritual. A rubber stamp. A photo opportunity. So it came as a shock to everyone when the astrologer predicted the marriage would *not* be successful; he told Diya she would never be able to have Mihir's children.

"The astrologer used the word 'barren,'" Diya said, her voice shaking. "He seemed to think he was saving Mihir's family." Her eyes were watering, and I wiped them away from her cheeks. "It's been months now, and I had practically forgotten about it. But now that we're *married* . . ."

She trailed off, although I knew exactly what she was getting at. Now that they were married, pretty soon the pressure would ramp up on producing the next generation of Gaurs and Joshis, and the bogus premonition was haunting her.

"What did he expect us to do?" She laughed. "After more than a decade, did he really expect Mihir's family to call off the wedding?"

"That's so fucked up," I said, furious on her behalf.

"We know it's crap. Our families think so, too—"

"Then forget about—"

"But Niki . . ." Her voice wavered, and I could tell she was holding back, that this was affecting her even more than she was letting on. "What if the astrologer is right?"

I scooped her into a hug and whispered, "He's not right. None of us have any control over this sort of thing, even him—"

"But it's possible."

"Anything is possible, Diya. It doesn't make it statistically likely."

She pulled away from me, defeated. "Do you think I should freeze my eggs?"

"Do you want to?"

Diya shrugged. She'd already told me that she and Mihir were in no rush to have children; they both loved their jobs and wanted to focus on their careers for a while.

"Just promise me one thing, OK? If you freeze your eggs, do it because it's the right thing for you. Not because of some *sign* from an astrologer."

She squeezed my hand, her beautiful smile cascading up at me. I hated that this had crushed her spirits.

"Please do not repeat anything downstairs, OK? I have not told anyone else. Not even to Masooma and Sam."

I crossed my heart, and when she nuzzled into my shoulder, I wrapped my arm around her. "I'm sorry I didn't know. I wish I could have been there for you."

"It is a weird thing to explain over FaceTime." She smiled sleepily into my armpit. "This conversation required a hug."

"I would have FedExed you one of my sweaters," I joked. "And you could have worn it like a hug."

"Would you have sprayed it with Dior?"

I laughed, happy that she remembered my brand of perfume. "Absolutely."

We lay there for a while in a comfortable silence, the kind of silence you only get with a friend who really knows you. After a while, Diya unfolded herself from my limbs and looked at me searchingly.

"Tell me something happy."

"Like?"

She wiggled her eyebrows at me.

"Oh, *that*." I giggled just at the hint of Sam. "I thought you were Switzerland."

"I can't be involved in whatever is happening, but I still want to know." She petulantly tugged on my arm. "Spill!"

"There's not much to say." I tucked my hands behind my head, stalling. While I was tempted to update Diya on how things were going with Sam, it all felt rather unimportant after what she'd just experienced these past few months.

"Sam and I haven't really discussed what's going on," I said finally. "But it's a fling, I guess."

I guess. Thank god Jasmine wasn't here; she would crucify me with that sort of language. But what was I supposed to think?

Our chemistry was undeniable. We were like the coals of a campfire. With the right gust of wind, sure, we could burst into flames, but that wasn't going to happen when I lived in Seattle and Sam was going back to London. It was inevitable that we'd die right out.

Diya smirked. "A PG-13 fling, you mean."

"I know. I hope *somebody* is having sex on your honeymoon."

"There might still be time to—" She made a vulgar hand gesture, causing me to burst into a fit of coughs. "Will you stay longer? The rest of us are leaving in two days' time."

"Two days," I echoed, catching my breath. In some part of my brain, I knew that Diya and Mihir's group honeymoon was coming to an end, but I'd somehow forgotten. Feeling guilty about not yet confirming my arrival date with my family in Amritsar, I added, "Maybe I'll leave then, too."

"Luckily, you still have two full days left to—" Again, she made the gesture, and I pushed her hands away.

"Gross, D!"

"Just please be careful, *hah*?"

I held my breath, waiting for a lecture, wondering if she'd echo what Jasmine had said to me. "Sam is a *very* sweet guy. It would be wise to give someone like him your F-card."

I sighed in relief. I'd been planning to tell her about how Jasmine had thought it was a *bad* idea for me to have a fling, but I liked Diya's advice better and didn't want her to change her tune.

"F-card," Diya repeated. "Your fling card . . . Like a V-card?"

"Yes, Diya." I groaned at the pun. "*Hilarious*. Ha. Ha . . ."

"Maybe this time you will have a better experience." She shot me a knowing glance that made me grimace. Back in our senior year, Diya had been there for every agonizing step in the process of me losing my "V-card."

1. The anticipation after I'd first met my ex and he asked me to be his girlfriend.

2. The debate after a few months of dating (and pressure), and I kept finding excuses not to follow through with it.

3. The remorse after it happened, and I wondered if *that*—the anticlimactic awkwardness I felt for months—was all physical love was supposed to feel like.

4. The Cinderella stage, as Diya liked to call it, when I convinced myself that sex equaled love, and that meant we were going to get married.

5. And finally, back to remorse. After my ex dumped me out of the blue and I realized that the aforementioned steps had been for absolutely nothing.

CHAPTER 25

I could tell Diya was still feeling down about the astrologer's premonition, so while she was using the restroom, I called our circle of college friends on a group video chat. About half of them answered, and by the time Diya came out, I had four other friendly faces on my phone, eager to hear all about our trip and congratulate her on the wedding.

It cheered her up, especially because she hadn't seen some of them in a while, and by the time we went down to the pool, she was back to at least sixty-five percent classic Diya. It made me shake with anger thinking about what had happened. Sure, everyone was allowed to believe in what they wanted, but to tell a young woman that she would be barren with absolutely no scientific proof?

Disgusting.

Diya was exactly like her namesake. She was a light, a shining gift to the world. And I was determined to help wind her back up to the one hundred percent sparkly, optimistic, and love-fueled Diya she always was.

It was nearly dusk by the time we returned to the group. Sam had abandoned the pool for the lounge chair right next to mine, but instead of sitting down in it, I headed straight to the bar.

Although I'd opted out of most of our college group's big nights out, Diya had lived on campus and spent every weekend chugging beer from red plastic cups at some frat party, wrangling exclusive passes to a club opening downtown, simultaneously having a blast and holding her liquor a thousand times better than anyone else her size or age.

Getting a bit wild like the good old days might just be what she needed, and so when I got to the front of the line, I ordered a tray of shots to take back with me. (Tequila for those of us who drank and Limca for the others, so they could join in on the fun.)

After, I shuffled to the side to take a selfie for the group chat with our college friends. I was the notorious party pooper among the group, and I knew they'd find it hilarious.

I angled my phone far away, grinning wide, but I couldn't capture both my face and the gigantic tray. I looked up. The beardy man standing behind me in line was now ordering his drinks. He was probably close to my parents' age and had a friendly, familiar uncle vibe to him, and I waited until he'd put in his order to ask him for help.

"Excuse me?" I said, waving. He glanced in my direction.

"Hi, Uncle," I said in my sweetest voice. "I was wondering—"

"Yes," he said, cutting me off. "Of course."

Yes, of course, what exactly?

"You want a photo?"

"Oh." I nodded, beaming. "Yes, *please*."

I posed for the photograph, expecting him to take it from where he was standing two feet away. But then he closed the gap between us, put his arm around my shoulder, and took a selfie of the *both* of us.

"Does that suit you?" he asked afterward, showing it to me.

I raised my eyebrows. The frame captured both of our faces—Uncle smiling and me looking rather bewildered—the tray of shots nowhere in the frame.

"Um."

"Would you like another?"

I hesitated. "Is that OK?" I asked, feeling so awkward I'd started sweating through the armpits of the kimono-style beach cover-up. "I was hoping to take a photo of just me and the . . . shots."

Uncle's lips curled up into a smile, the ends hidden beneath the thick fur of his beard. Bemused was the only way to describe his facial expression, which was good. At least I hadn't inadvertently offended him.

Uncle took a giant step back, shot the photo, and then set the phone on the bar counter. "There," he said, smiling with his mouth and his eyes. It made him look rather handsome for an older gentleman. Like, *super* handsome, actually. "I hope those are not all for you."

"These?" I gestured at the shots, suddenly shy. "No, don't

worry. I'm on holiday for my friend's honeymoon." I pointed out the group, expecting them to be busy talking among themselves, swimming, and drinking. Weirdly, every single one of them was staring at us.

The uncle looked over and gave them a wave. "Big honeymoon."

"The bride has a big heart." Without giving too many details, I told him about how Diya needed some cheering up.

"And what about you, Uncle?" I asked afterward. "Are you vacationing in Goa?"

"I am here for work."

"What do you do?"

He smirked. "I have a job in the film industry."

"Oh really? That's so cool." I leaned forward, feeling rather chatty. "My friend—well, he's not really my friend. Or my boyfriend. Anyway, his mom used to be an actor in Tollywood. Amazing, right?"

"Absolutely amazing." He paused, thoughtfully sipping his beer. "So tell me. Why is this 'friend' of yours a friend only?"

"Um."

He looked genuinely curious, and I wondered how he'd react if I told him the truth, whether he was an old-school uncle who looked down their noses at "modern" women or was someone who had literally cheered on premarital relations, like Aasha Auntie.

"We live in different worlds," I said finally. I wasn't sure why I answered the way I did—more existential than factual—

but Uncle had asked the question, and that's how my brain chose to have me spit out an answer.

"How so?"

Again, I chewed on my words before replying. Sam and I lived in all sorts of different worlds. I was Sikh and he was Hindu. I belonged to a humble, immigrant, traditional family, and Sam grew up with the confidence and the means to live his life on his own terms, to pursue his hopes and his dreams. But most importantly, we lived in different worlds *literally*.

Like, geographically.

"He lives in London," I told Uncle. "And I'm in Seattle."

"That is not so far."

"It's, like, a twelve-hour flight."

"OK, that is quite far." Uncle laughed heartily. "Well, one of you can always move?"

"No," I said quickly, instinctively. "*Uncle*, I barely know the guy."

"I believe you do, *beti*. I think you know this 'friend' of yours very well."

I thanked him again for the photo and the chat, and then made my way back to the group. What did he mean "I believe you know him very well"? What had this uncle—a total stranger—allegedly seen in my eyes? Lust. That's what he'd seen. Surely, he'd just mistaken my physical infatuation with Sam for something straight out of a Bollywood movie.

I carefully maneuvered through the crowd, balancing the tray of shots on both my hands. I looked up just as I arrived at the group, rather shaky as I realized they were all still eerily silent, their arms crossed and wide eyes locked right on me.

"What's up?" I asked. "Tequila?"

"What do you mean, 'what's up?'" Diya exclaimed. "What is up with *you*?"

"Nothing?" Carefully, I sat down on the foot of her deck chair, setting the tray down beside me. "I thought we could get a bit wild . . ."

Diya looked utterly shocked, and I flicked my eyes toward Sam, then Masooma, then Mihir, and each member of the group in turn. Every single one of them looked equally dumbfounded.

"Should I take that as a no, or . . ."

"Do you know who you were talking to?" Diya shrieked.

A shiver shot down my spine as I looked back toward the bar. Uncle had gone back to his own table, to a small group of other uncles at the other side of the pool. Their heads were close together, talking animatedly over their drinks. I squinted.

"Do you really not know, Niki?" I heard Sam ask.

I shook my head, taking a few steps closer to the pool so I could get a better look. Was he someone that I should have recognized? His uncleness had seemed very familiar, and he did say he worked in the film industry. I didn't watch a ton of Bollywood movies, only the big hits. I wondered if I'd seen him in anything.

"She will get there," Mihir said behind me, laughing. "Give it a minute."

I set my hands on my hips, studying the uncle, trying to remember his features from when he was standing up close. OK, so he definitely had a movie-star quality now that I thought about it. His dark, brooding eyes. His suave, full beard. Not to mention he was, like, *super* fit for a man his age—late forties, early fifties maybe?—and he was objectively very handsome.

I took another step forward, nearing the edge of the pool, and just then, Uncle looked over at me.

A beat later he winked, and my heart fell into my stomach as it hit me.

"Oh. My. God." I clasped my hands over my mouth, and then wheeled around to the group. "OH. MY. GOD!"

Diya burst out laughing, then Sam, then the rest of them.

"Oh my god is *right*, Niki," Diya squealed. "And usually I am the stupid one."

"He doesn't have a beard, though!" I sputtered. "It can't be him."

"It is," Masooma giggled. "I heard he was in town filming."

"The beard must be for the role," Diya added.

I spun back around to gawk, foggy and delirious and *extremely* humiliated.

No wonder this random "uncle" had volunteered a selfie. No wonder during our entire conversation he'd looked downright *amused* at the fact that I had no idea who he was.

I had been speaking to the most famous person in Bollywood. The leading man of practically every major movie since the early 1990s.

The actor. The legend.

The Shah Rukh *fucking* Khan.

CHAPTER 26

*U*ncle. Shah Rukh. Mr. Khan. SRK. Whatever you wanted to call him. Well, he'd witnessed my come-to-Jesus moment from across the pool, and a few minutes afterward, he made his way around to reintroduce himself.

I was mortified and, now that I knew whom I was talking to, speechless. Diya had enough words for the both of us, thank *god*, and gushed to SRK for a good five minutes before Mihir interrupted her and asked him to take a photo with the group. It was rather surreal, being up close and personal with a celebrity worshiped by not millions but *billions* of people around the world, Bollywood sewn into the popular culture of every single continent. (Seriously. I'd bet good money that even scientists down in Antarctica download some of his movies for their long hauls.)

We made such a scene that the other hotel guests started realizing that SRK was here in the flesh. I felt a little bad that I'd blown his cover; up until I saw him at the bar, the beard had allowed him to go unnoticed. But SRK didn't seem to mind. He and his posse, at least two of which I now realized were bodyguards, slipped out the back exit, waving to us one last time before they left.

"Wow," Diya said, totally dumbfounded. She threw back a shot of tequila without so much as a wince, and then chased it with one more. "That was *epic* . . ."

As everyone launched into analysis mode on every detail that we'd learned about Shah Rukh Khan, I glanced over at Sam. He was reclining in his deck chair, still shirtless, his arms tucked behind him. I couldn't tell what he was thinking or even where he was looking; his sunglasses were covering his eyes.

I took one step toward him and gave him a half wave. He saw it. And when he waved back, I went over to him and sat down on the edge of his long chair.

"Hey."

He sat up, making room for me. *"Hey."*

"I think I'm still in shock."

"Me, too." Sam grinned. He gestured at Diya, who was taking a poll on whether SRK looked better as a young buck in *Kuch Kuch Hota Hai*, the villain in *Don*, or in his current state: full-on silver fox.

"Diya is in good form. Was something bothering her earlier?"

I smiled. Indeed, we were now experiencing one hundred ten percent Diya and rising. "It must have been the blues," I said vaguely. "The honeymoon is almost over."

"Of course." He paused, his voice quiet and swoony and making me think and feel things I shouldn't have been. "I suppose it is."

My hair had dried in bits and spurts after many dunks in the pool that day, pieces sticking out every which way. Sam reached for a strand, twirling it with his finger, and then tucked it behind my ear. His thumb grazed my ear, sending a hot shiver down my spine.

I cleared my throat, instinctively sitting upright. *Get it together, Niki.*

Get. It. Together.

This was not *your* honeymoon; it was Diya's. Sam was just a fling.

"I was thinking I'll leave when the others do," I said, rushing my words. "You said I can fly directly from here to Punjab?"

"Should do, yeah," he answered quietly. "Although I still haven't taken you to dinner at Frank's Café for a proper date." He paused. "How about Friday, then? It would be your last night in town."

Sam scooted closer to me, his hand finding the top of my thigh. I was suddenly very parched.

"Niki . . ." He trailed off. I'd been fixating on Sam's knee hairs, the way his fingers were skimming over my skin. Finally, I forced myself to look up. Immediately, I wished I hadn't. He looked pained, like he was holding something, biting his tongue when he really wanted to—*what*, exactly?

What wasn't he saying? What wasn't *I* saying?

"Pool?" I squeaked, desperate for a change in direction. The suggestion seemed to have distracted him, because he grinned.

"Do you trust me around a pool?"

"Do you trust me?" I fired back.

I shed my kimono cover-up and went to stand by the edge. Sam was next to me a beat later, stretching side to side with his arms overhead, as if he were preparing to dive in.

I wanted to get him back for dropping me in the pool on Diwali, so on an impulse, I lunged forward to push him, but Sam saw it coming and caught me in his arms.

"The lifeguard almost saw you," Sam whispered, laughing as he wrestled down my arms. His breath tickled my ear, his chest and arms hot and dry against my skin. "He'll kick you out if there's any *roughhousing*."

I bit my lip, shivering even though it was sweltering outside. Indeed, there were several large signs that threatened ejection for "roughhousing," and two couples earlier that day had been asked to leave for getting too combative during what started out as a harmless chicken fight.

I leaned back, but Sam kept his arms around me, dropping them from my shoulders to the small of my waist. I was wearing a mint green one-piece with a scoop back. His fingers found the edge of the material.

"Sam," I said, breathing heavily. "There's something really important I need to tell you."

I could feel him tense, his jaw locking as he looked me dead in the eye. I sighed theatrically.

"What is it, Niki?"

My heart was racing. I blinked at him, making big puppy dog eyes. I licked my lips, delaying, waiting for my moment. Out of the corner of my eye, I could see the lifeguard standing behind Sam's right shoulder, and the second he turned around, as hard as I could, I shoved Sam into the pool.

The momentum threw us both over the edge, and we surfaced gasping for air. I backed myself against the edge, coughing, my nostrils burning from the water that had gone up my nose. When I opened my eyes, Sam was right in front of me.

"You all right, love?"

I nodded, panting as I caught my breath.

"Good." He splashed me playfully. "Serves you right!"

I splashed him back, but then he held his hand out, warning me to stop. "No roughhousing, Niki."

"None at all?"

Sam caught the suggestion in the tone of my voice. He came even closer, pressing his hands against the pool's edge, trapping me between them. Pushing my back against the wall, I walked my feet up his shins and then to the tops of his thighs, my toes dangerously close to the edges of his swim shorts.

"Niki." He said my name like a grunt, flicking his eyes upward behind me to where the rest of the group was sitting.

"Are they watching us?" I whispered.

"No."

"Then kiss me—"

Sam didn't hesitate. He pressed his lips against mine, cupping my face in his hands as I wrapped my legs around his hips, pulling him closer. It lasted only a moment—one dizzying, aching moment—and then he released me from his grip and it was over.

"Oh boy," I said, better words failing me. I cleared my throat, unable to look Sam in the eye.

"Oh boy?"

"Do you want . . ."

I shut my mouth. I was hungry for Sam, for *this* to finally happen, but I wasn't good at propositioning someone. I'd never done anything like this before. My sexual adventures had been confined to the relationship with my ex—quietly, and only ever in his parents' basement.

"Did you know . . ." Sam ran his hand up my side. "Mom will be out tonight."

My heart raced.

"She actually made a point of telling me this morning that we'd have the apartment to ourselves."

I laughed, exhilarated at the idea. A little weirded out, too.

"Should we . . ." Sam bit his lip, and I was tempted to throw myself at him again. But not here. Not yet.

"We should," I whispered.

"Wouldn't you prefer to stay with Diya this evening?"

"I'm feeling a bit tired." I faked a yawn into my palm. "I think you should take me home."

*W*e spent one more hour by the pool, until it was dusk and about the time Sam guessed Aasha Auntie would be leaving for her dinner party. He told everyone we were "knackered"—another one of his Britishisms I found utterly adorable—but Diya and Masooma saw right through the charade. I think the whole group might have.

Back at the apartment complex, Sam held my hand as we made our way to the flat. I was on edge. On fire. And at the bottom of the staircase leading us to the inevitable, he pushed me up against the bannister.

My heart raced. "Yes?"

Under the cover of darkness, the coconut trees hanging over us, Sam kissed me like he'd never kissed me before, like it was the only one we'd ever get. I was breathless, trembling as I wound my hands through his hair, tugging him closer to me.

Sam's hands were all over me, my breasts, my hips, and a sweet, gentle ache flushed through me, starting at my heart and fluttering down below.

Minutes later, he pulled away, his eyes in a daze. "Well, then."

I laughed, rubbing my fingers against my chin. Sam hadn't shaved in a few days, and I loved the tingling graze of his stubble against my skin.

"Ready?" he asked.

Without answering, I raced him up the stairs two at a time. I reached the door first, but he had the key, and I teasingly used my body to block the entrance.

"You've got to pay the toll," I said, using my most serious voice. He kissed me on the tip of my nose, and I let him pass, hugging him from behind as he fished out his keys and pushed open the door.

"Niki, I—"

Sam stopped short in the doorway. The light was on, and when he stepped to the side, I saw that we were not alone.

Aasha Auntie was home, and Sam's dad was sitting there, too.

CHAPTER 27

*N*iki. *Sam.*" Aasha Auntie sprouted up from the couch. "How was your outing? Did you have a nice time?"

Sam's dad stood up slowly, his body stiff as he inspected me. Instinctively, I ran a hand through my hair—praying to god Sam's kiss hadn't messed it up too much—and then brought my hands together in front of my chest.

"*Namaste*, Uncle." I took a deep breath, painting a smile on my face. "It's so nice to meet you."

"Niki is Sam's friend," Aasha Auntie offered, her voice unusually high-pitched. "From America. She came for Diya's wedding."

"Niki." Uncle paused, his eyes flicking to Sam. "Welcome."

I swallowed hard, chancing a look at Sam myself. He was grinding his jaw, his eyes fixated on the ground in front of him. I'd walked into something. It was hanging in the air, so thick I could practically taste it, and I chewed my lip as I waited for somebody to speak. But after ten long, *painful* seconds, I realized that no one was planning on it.

"You have such a beautiful home," I volunteered, pointing indiscriminately at a turquoise vase on the windowsill. "It's so lovely of you to let me stay."

Uncle rubbed his palms together. "Really, this is my wife's home. I am not often invited."

"Do you really need an invitation to see us?" Aasha Auntie muttered.

"Mom, you *told* him to come?"

I looked from Sam to Aasha Auntie to Uncle. Pradeep Uncle, if I was remembering his name correctly. Oh great. I'd made it worse. He and Sam looked like they wanted to murder each other. The tension from when he first walked through the door had risen from a simmer to a raging boil.

"I am shocked that he agreed," Auntie answered flatly. "And that he gave us no warning. But yes. I thought he should come. I thought you should spend some time with him before you travel back to London."

"You thought wrong," Sam said icily.

I took a few steps backward as Aasha Auntie spoke to Sam in Bengali. Her tone was urgent, pleading, and Jasmine's words rang overtop like church bells.

It doesn't sound like a fling. It sounds like a family holiday.

Some family holiday. Apparently, Sam and his dad couldn't even stand to be in the same room together.

I was tempted to leave. It wasn't my place to be here right

now, and it would have been the right thing to do. I could have called a taxi and hightailed it back to Bardez, spent the night with Diya and Mihir in their hotel room. They wouldn't have minded. Diya happily wedged in the middle, it wouldn't have been the first time the three of us shared a bed.

I opened my mouth, ready to interrupt them and excuse myself, but when I caught sight of Sam, I *couldn't* leave him. And I didn't think he wanted me to.

When Pradeep Uncle joined in on the argument, I went into the galley kitchen and got started on a pot of *cha*. I could barely make out their voices over the sound of the water boiling. What were they saying to each other? I reminded myself it didn't matter, and I shouldn't get involved. After the tea, spices, and sugar had boiled for a few minutes, I added the milk using a tin mug to repeatedly scoop up the liquid and then dump it back out. Mom had taught me the technique when I was young; the milk thickened as it was exposed to the air.

As I stretched the milk, I texted our selfies with SRK to my family. My parents replied almost immediately, using a few of the choice expressions Jasmine and I had taught them over the years.

OMG you LUCKY girl!

Amazeballs!! Ask him if he has nephew for you??? ;)

Jasmine didn't reply even though she loved Shah Rukh's movies and she'd have woken up for work by now. I hated that we were fighting, but deep down, I knew it was temporary. Our fractured relationship was not nearly as wide as the rift that seemed to be between Sam and his father.

By the time the tea was ready, the arguing had stopped, and so I poured out four cups and returned to the sitting room. Sam had left. Only Auntie and Uncle were still there.

"*Cha?*" I asked brightly, setting down the tray on the coffee table.

Uncle smiled at me for the first time as he accepted the tea, and I saw a flash of Sam. A flash I liked.

"Ah. So tasty, *beti*," Aasha Auntie said, taking a cup. "Niki is Punjabi also—"

"A Punjabi girl, ah!" Uncle's face lit up. "Where is your family from?"

"All over," I said. "But a lot of them have left our villages and moved to Amritsar."

"We went there—do you remember?" Uncle looked over at his wife. Whatever had transpired, he looked softer now, less frightening. "In ninety-nine—"

"Ninety-*eight*." Aasha Auntie smiled but then frowned immediately afterward, as if she'd done it by accident. "Sam was very small."

Uncle was talkative without Sam around, and conversation flowed easily as we drank our tea. He wasn't as traditional or judgmental as he'd seemed when I first walked in. He showed interest in my life and was sympathetic about the layoff, ensuring me I'd find something better soon. I even found myself mentioning the job interviews I had lined up when I got back to Seattle. For some reason, I wanted to impress him.

After tea, Aasha Auntie and Pradeep Uncle left for their dinner party, and I went upstairs to find Sam. I'd expected to find him hunched over his keyboard with his earphones on or fiddling away on one of his guitars. But when I peered into his room, I found him sitting on the edge of the bed, as if he was waiting for me.

"You missed *cha*."

"Sorry." He smiled limply. "I shouldn't have left you down there. That wasn't cool of me."

I sat down on the keyboard bench, pulling it close so we were facing each other. "I still think you're pretty cool."

Sam sighed, his features softening. I couldn't read him. Did he want me to come up here? Did he want me to ask him about his dad? If it were Diya or Jasmine or any of my other friends, I would be over there in a heartbeat. I'd be saying the right things and making lists with color-coded action points, googling the right advice to impart if I didn't have it myself.

But Sam wasn't a friend. I didn't know what he was or wanted from me, or where either of us would stand if we let the wall come down.

"Are you OK?" I whispered.

"Yes."

His eyes locked onto mine, and I laughed. He was lying.

"Right."

"I am extremely OK."

"You're not. But . . ."

But, *what*? Should we both pretend that he was for the sake of a bit of fun?

"You don't have to talk about it—"

"You're leaving in two days, Niki. Fuck. I've ruined the whole night."

"It's not ruined." I poked him on the shin with my toe. "There's still time to cheer you up."

He suppressed a grin. "And how are you going to do that?"

I glanced down my body, suggestively tugging on my kimono until it fell down my shoulder. Sam laughed.

"And if that doesn't work . . ." I pointed to the keyboard behind me. "I'll play you one of my dorky songs."

"You'd do that for me?"

"I'd do anything for you."

The words had just sort of slipped out, and I rolled my eyes extra hard to try to convey that I'd been joking.

"How much has Diya told you about my father?" Sam asked me suddenly.

I pressed my lips together, searching Sam's face. I had promised myself that I wouldn't get involved, that I'd keep it light, and so I needed to say "nothing" and change the subject.

"She told me you cut yourself off financially," I said instead. "Sorry."

"It's OK. Everyone knows. It's not a secret."

"I'm so sorry you don't have his support. But you have to know—you are an incredible musician."

He scoffed.

"Sam, seriously. I've heard you play. And I've looked up your band on YouTube more than I'd care to admit. You're so talented—"

"Niki."

I pulled the bench closer toward him, waving him off. "You are. It doesn't matter what your dad says or doesn't say, OK? You're going to make it."

"No," Sam said evenly. "I'm not—"

"*Yes*—"

"I'm a failure, Niki. OK? *Just* like he predicted." Sam's voice was loud, startling me. "My band left me. We're *over*."

I shook my head, refusing to believe it. It *couldn't* be over, could it? I searched his face, looking for clues, and then realized they'd been there all along. The way Sam never wanted to really talk about his band or about his life in London, even anecdotally. The fact that Perihelion's website hadn't been updated. That all the videos of them on YouTube were more than a year old.

"A few moved home," Sam said, not looking at me. "The rest got proper jobs. The label didn't pick us up for another album, and everyone was happy to move on. Everyone except *me*."

Slowly, I stood up from the bench and took a seat next to him, offering him my hand. After a few seconds, he took it.

"You're not a failure."

"For the past six months, I've been working odd jobs as a sound technician for real musicians. I am a failure—"

"You followed your dreams, which is a hard thing to do. If it was easy, everyone would do it."

Sam brushed his thumb against my palm, rubbing slowly, and when he didn't protest, I continued.

"You'll find a new band. Or maybe your dream might have to

change a bit." I knocked my shoulder against his. "Maybe you'll have to become a solo star."

"Right."

"You're going to be *such* a heartthrob, Sam. Just you wait. People all over the world will have your poster above their bed, and I'll be jealous as hell."

Finally, Sam cracked a smile, and I got goose bumps when he looked over at me. "You're a sweetheart, Niki."

"I know."

"You know?"

I nodded, batting my eyelashes at him. "I know."

Sam turned to face me more, our knees still touching, our hands still intertwined.

"What's your dream?"

"My dream?" I shrugged. "I don't think I've really had one."

"No? You never wanted to be the next Mozart? Yanni?"

"I wasn't a prodigy like *some* people," I said, elbowing him. "No. I guess I just wanted to be happy. Well, I wanted to make my parents happy. My sister was such a loose cannon . . ."

This time when Sam asked me about Jasmine, I didn't hold back. I told him what it was like to grow up avoiding her shadow, always trying to be everything that she wasn't and focused on doing the right thing.

"I love her so much." I paused, thinking about how fiercely I missed her right now, how much I wished she'd forgive me. "But I resent her, too."

"For not believing in you?"

I shook my head, my cheeks flushing. He'd misinterpreted me.

Yes, I didn't want to disappoint my parents, but had I also been afraid of going after what I truly wanted?

"I wish I believed in myself the way Jasmine does. The way you do, Sam."

I wasn't sure how long we sat there. An hour at least, maybe two. And for a while, I forgot that Sam was only ever meant to be a fling, forgot that I was leaving in two days, and forgot myself entirely as we shared pieces of ourselves that so few people were able to find. A puzzle that fitted together in no apparent order. Because even though I didn't know Sam well, SRK was right; I already *knew* Sam. Inside and out.

Later, when there were no words left to say, Sam pressed a gentle kiss against my temple. His lips lingered, his breath sending a shiver down my spine, and my whole body trembled as they drifted down toward my mouth.

This kiss was different than the others. Softer yet more intense as he cradled my neck in his hands. I got lost in his touch, in the sweetness of his kiss, but all too soon, I wanted more. I wanted *him*.

I leaned back on the bed, my arms around Sam's back as I pulled him down with me. I craved his weight. His heat. I wrapped my legs around him, willing us closer as he kissed my neck, tugging my hair with his fist.

A soft moan escaped my lips as my kimono fell open and his hands found my waist, my breasts. Still, it wasn't enough. I reached up and pulled Sam's T-shirt over his head, throwing it on the floor next to us.

Sam smiled down at me, drinking me in.

"Did I cheer you up?"

I thought he'd fire something back, witty and stinging, but he just nodded. I pressed my hand against his cheek, grazing his stubble as he looked at me.

"What are you thinking about?" I asked him.

"I'm thinking about you, love."

"Good things?" I wiggled my eyebrows. "Or *bad* . . ."

Sam cut me off with a laugh, kissing my open mouth as I tried to finish my joke. Giggling, I eventually stopped, drowning in the pleasure of his body pressed against mine.

We dove farther, harder, and I felt myself opening up to him in a way I didn't know my body was capable of. Finally, I couldn't wait one more moment, and I sat up, panting. My hands trembled as I pulled down the kimono, but when I reached for the strap of my swimsuit, Sam caught my fingers with his palm.

I looked up. He was shaking his head, and fear prickled over me at the thought that he didn't want me the same way. But he did. I knew he did.

"Not tonight," he whispered. "We have time."

"We don't," I groaned in frustration. "Sam, this might be our only chance."

"What are you talking about?"

He closed his hand into a fist, trapping my fingers inside. My body trembled as he kissed my knuckles.

"Sam," I whispered, my voice shaky. "This isn't a fling, is it?"

"No." He laughed, his eyes brightening. "Did you really think it was?"

I'd wanted to. I'd convinced myself that I could keep my emotions at bay. But who was I kidding?

Jasmine was right. I'd caught feelings. I'd caught them bad. And lying there with Sam as he looked so deeply into my eyes it hurt, I knew that he'd caught them, too.

CHAPTER 28

*Y*ou'd think it would feel strange waking up alone in the guest bedroom the night after the new guy in your life essentially told you he wanted to be with you. That opening your eyes to an empty bed would water down the pure, utter ecstasy swishing around in your chest.

But it didn't. It felt absolutely right.

Sam and I didn't have sex in the end. And I didn't stay over in his room. Not because we didn't want to but because our relationship wasn't just a vacation fling. And it never was. The way we felt about each other—it *couldn't* be. Like Sam said. We had time.

I sat up from the bed, smiling so hard my cheeks hurt. It was another bright, sunny day, and the morning breeze from the window washed over my face like a cool cloth. Just outside the door, I could hear voices in the sitting room, and my balloon burst just a bit when I remembered Sam's dad would be around. Aasha Auntie had sent Sam a warning text when they were on their way home from dinner the night before, so both of us had gone to "sleep" in our own rooms before they got back. (In reality, we stayed up another two hours texting each other.)

I threw a sweatshirt on over my pajamas and slipped out of the room, ready to help diffuse the tension, but when I popped my head outside, it was only Sam and Aasha Auntie at the dining table. They were chopping fruit and buttering toast, happily chatting away about something or another in Bengali. Sam's face changed when he saw me, his lips curling into an even wider smile as I threw him a wink.

"Good morning, Niki."

Heat rushed through my body at the sound of him saying my name, and I remembered how close we'd come the night before. *Jesus, Niki. Get it together. His mother is sitting right there!*

"Morning," I said. "Aasha Auntie, good morning."

"Hello, *beti*," she said, not turning around. Her eyes were fixated on the mango she was dicing. "Sleep well?"

I took the seat beside her and opposite Sam, feeling for his foot beneath the table. "I did, thank you."

"Sam tells me you are leaving in two days only. This is a shame—we are having such fun with you around."

Sam caught my eye, but I couldn't read the look on his face. After last night, was it still the plan for me to leave in two days when Diya and the others flew back to Mumbai? Well, it was only a day and a half away now. As much as I wanted to see my family in Punjab, my stomach curdled at the thought of leaving

Sam so soon, of not making the most of the time we had together here in Goa.

"And when are you leaving me, *beta*?" Auntie asked Sam before I could think of how to answer. She melodramatically wiped a tear from her left eye, shaking out her hand as if it were sopping wet with her sadness. "When must I go into mourning?"

"What a drama queen." Sam popped a piece of pineapple into his mouth. "I'll leave a bit later, how about that? How would you like me for Christmas this year?"

"Christmas?" Aasha Auntie froze. "You will stay with us another month? What about your band?"

I bit my lip, watching Sam's face grow dark. No one in India knew about Perihelion having broken up, not even his own mother.

"I suppose we'll have to take an extralong break this year." He glanced my way, his features softening. "Because I might not go back to London straightaway . . ."

Aasha Auntie's face lit up as she, too, looked over at me, and my cheeks reddened under their gaze.

"What do you say," Sam said. "Should I come visit you in Seattle?"

I opened my mouth to speak, but before I could get any words out, Aasha Auntie lunged for me, smothering my cheeks and forehead with motherly kisses.

"I am *so* happy, *beti*." She squeezed me around the middle. "Sam told me about your discussion. And this *fills* my heart—"

"Mom," Sam groaned. "Stop it."

"Stop what?" Aasha Auntie planted one last kiss on me before releasing me. "Can I not be happy my son has found a decent girl? That—"

Sam fired something off in Bengali, and a beat later, Aasha Auntie calmed down and switched gears. He must have told her to cool it. Thank god. Sam and I had only just decided to be together and had a long list of logistics to sort out—like him apparently coming to visit me in Seattle, and what the hell was going to happen after that—and as lovely as she was, his mother being involved wasn't going to make it any easier.

"Niki, what would you like to do today?" Aasha Auntie handed me a bowl of fruit. "I have no social engagements. I am all yours."

I stole a look at Sam, who was trying not to laugh. Clearly, what both of us really would have *liked* to do didn't involve Aasha Auntie, but I didn't have the heart to tell her that.

"Where's Pradeep Uncle?" I asked, remembering Sam's dad. If he was tagging along, an activity that didn't involve much talking and largely took place in a public setting was probably the way to go.

"He left this morning," Sam said flatly.

"Already?"

Neither Sam nor Aasha Auntie said anything further, and as we ate breakfast and started planning the day, it was as if Sam's dad had never even been here.

A few hours later, Aasha Auntie took us to a local heritage home that had been converted into a boutique hotel and restaurant. It was absolutely gorgeous—a two-storied marvel of Goan and Portuguese architecture, or so said the brochure—and after a quick lunch on the outdoor terrace, we wandered around the grounds and rooms that were open to the public.

Everything had been renovated to look exactly like it would have when built four hundred years earlier, each surface, nook, and cranny either a bright color or crafted of stucco or vintage wood. The airy verandas were teaming with exotic plants and fruit trees, and when I spotted an empty love seat facing out toward the gardens, all I wanted to do was cozy up in it with Sam.

"Sorry about all of this," Sam whispered, coming up behind me. We were touring the second floor of the house, and Aasha Auntie had just disappeared around the corner.

"About colonialism?" I gestured down the grand hallway. "Not your fault."

Sam laughed. After, he planted a quick kiss on the nape of my neck that sent a shiver down my spine. "Right now, I'm more sorry we have to hang out in a colonizer's house with my mother."

I turned around, smiling. "I don't mind."

"At least my father isn't here, right?"

I grimaced, glancing down at my feet. I'd worn my best pair of strappy leather sandals, and I could just make out the tan lines from the flip-flops I'd been sporting all week.

"Niki?" I heard Sam say.

"Yes?"

"Why aren't you looking at me?"

I looked back up, slowly, bugging my eyes out in jest. "I am."

Sam grinned, wrapping his arm around me. "Spit it out, love. I know you. You want to know why Dad left. Right?"

I know you.

I smiled at the thought that Sam *did* know me.

"Mom apologized this morning for ambushing us," Sam continued. "She didn't think he would actually visit."

I studied Sam's face, finding his hand with my own.

"Dad and I had a big row last week. I was getting ready for Diya's *haldi* and he dropped by unexpectedly . . ." Sam's jaw stiffened. "I expect we haven't said that many words to each other since I told him I wasn't going to use my business degree."

I nodded, my stomach unsettled. "So that's why you missed the *haldi* . . ."

Sam went on to tell me about his parents' relationship, that while they claimed to still love each other, they were much happier living apart. His father stayed in Mumbai full time for work, while Aasha Auntie spent most of her time in Goa or in LA, with Leena and her family.

"When I graduated college and moved to Europe, I made everything worse. They fight about me a lot. Mom blames Dad for me not being around. I try to time my visits for when he's out of town, but I couldn't this time with Diya's wedding . . ."

"I'm so sorry, Sam," I said, unsure of what to say. I couldn't imagine not having a relationship with my father. "That must be so tough."

"Dad hasn't come to Goa in years. I don't know why she invited him here."

"You don't?"

Sam shrugged. "Mom thinks it's time we reconcile, I expect."

"And what do you think?" I asked.

"I think she should let sleeping dogs lie. We've been avoiding each other for seven years, and it's been perfectly all right."

I raised my left eyebrow, unbelieving.

"Plus," Sam said, lowering his voice, "now isn't the time. If he finds out my band's left me and I failed miserably, he'll never respect me."

"Sam, you didn't fail," I whispered, wishing he'd believe me. "You and Perihelion accomplished more than most musicians can even dream. Just be honest with your dad *and* mom. If you respect yourself, then he'll respect you—"

"Niki, I'm sorry, but you don't know my father."

I bit my tongue, embarrassed. Not only had I overstepped, but I was a hypocrite. I had shied away from the truth with my own parents; they currently thought I was staying with one of Diya's *girl*friends, a lie I had to further embellish every day when I texted the family group chat to check in and share pictures.

"Sorry," I said. My face was hot, and I turned to look at an oil painting.

"Don't be," I heard Sam say.

"It's none of my business."

"Isn't it?"

I turned to face him, butterflies rushing to my stomach.

"I bet your parents aren't so complicated," he said.

"If you're coming to Seattle, I guess you'll find out. Won't you?"

"I shouldn't have sprung the idea on you during breakfast." Sam blushed. "But what do you reckon? Should I come?"

I couldn't help but smile at the thought of touring Sam

around Seattle, showing him where I went to school and taking him to all my favorite spots and hangouts. Introducing him to my friends. Jasmine. My *parents*.

Would they like him?

I glanced at a nearby portrait of a stuffy-looking white man, who looked very rich but also incredibly bored.

Mom and my friends would love Sam within an hour of meeting him, although Dad and Jasmine would be tougher to please. Dad's eyes would bulge when finding out that Sam was a musician—a bona fide rock star—but surely he'd get over his hesitations when he saw how happy Sam made me. Meanwhile, Jasmine would grill him nonstop and ask probing questions trying to get him to trip up in order to protect me from getting my heart stomped on all over again. But Sam would hold his own. He'd give her all the right answers and eventually sweep her off her feet, too.

"Niki?" Sam prompted. I had zoned out and snapped my head back to look at him.

"Hmm?"

"So what do you say—shall I visit you?"

Suddenly, Aasha Auntie popped her head back into the hallway, eyeing us suspiciously. "Hurry up, lovebirds. I am feeling very parched. Next, let's order for *chaat* and a cold drink!"

"*Swell*," Sam deadpanned, tickling my waist as he turned around to face her. "We'll be right in."

Aasha Auntie winked at us before disappearing, playfully covering her eyes. I rolled my eyes, leaning against Sam.

"I should warn you," I said, weighing my words. "My mother isn't as relaxed as yours."

"Relaxed?"

"My parents are very traditional. Mom will definitely make you sleep in the guest room."

Sam stroked his jaw. His lips quivered, as if he was masking a smile. "So, I take that as a yes. Yes, you *do* want me to come visit."

I nodded, suddenly feeling shy.

"And your parents will—"

"They'll be fine," I said forcefully, trying not to think about how disappointed they'd be when they found out about the real "Sam." That I'd been lying to them.

"I know it's important to you that they're happy with your choices." Sam hesitated. "I wouldn't want to get in the way of anything."

"Honestly, it'll be OK." I smiled. "They might not love the idea of"—I gestured back and forth between us, as we still hadn't put a label on ourselves—"*this* at first, but they'll come around. I mean, they still love Jasmine after everything she's put them through."

"I would hate to drive a wedge—"

"You won't." I took a chance and quickly pecked him on the cheek. "So, how long will you be able to come?"

"Would a week be too long?"

I bit my lip. One and a half more days here in Goa. One *week* in Seattle. It wouldn't be too long. It wouldn't be long *enough*.

"Niki, I . . ." Sam trailed off, glancing back toward the door. Aasha Auntie had reappeared, evidently finished touring that room. He looked back to me. "I think we have a lot to talk about at dinner tomorrow."

*T*hat night, Diya, Mihir, Masooma, and her husband, Tahir, came over to the apartment. Although the rest of the crew had been invited, they still weren't back from a day trip to Palolem Beach in South Goa. I'd volunteered to cook, and so Aasha Auntie, Sam, and the others were my sous-chefs as we made a Punjabi-style feast—*aloo paratha, saag paneer*, and a simple *daal*, exactly the way my mom made it. Luckily, she had just woken up when I texted her for help with the recipes. Although I knew the general ingredients and the order everything went into the pots and pans, I'd never cooked Indian food without her help.

Dinner turned out better than I'd expected, and after a few bottles of wine to share and hilarious failed attempts at playing the card game *Bhabhi*, the night was over. Still, it took me hours to fall asleep. I couldn't stop smiling, and my head was swimming with memories from the day, flashes of Sam's smile, or a stolen glance across the dinner table. I was full up. With food and wine and laughter but, most of all, with Sam.

It had been twenty-four hours since I finally let it sink in that Sam and I were not a temporary fling, and the answer was becoming even clearer to me with each passing moment.

This was it. Sam was the one. My Matthew McConaughey.

My Romeo. And logistics like where we each lived and when we might see each other again felt entirely irrelevant.

My whole life I'd made practical decision after practical decision, and yes, my parents were happy with me, but I wasn't. I had a career I wasn't passionate about and an older sister I was jealous of and an addiction to romantic comedies that I lived through vicariously, and that was it.

I had a choice to make. The options, obstacles, and scenarios bounced around my head as I tossed and turned in bed, but as soon as I'd made the decision, everything came together so quickly and with such force I *needed* to talk about it. Not with Sam—I still had to formulate my thoughts before sharing this with him—but with Jasmine.

> Jasmine, I'm really sorry for swearing at you. And for not being honest with you about how I felt about Brian. You were right to warn me against having a fling with Sam. Because I did catch feelings. I've never felt this way before, Jasmine. But it's OK. Because he feels the same way about me.
>
> I'm going to be making some changes . . . Don't say anything to Mom and Dad yet. I can't lie anymore, and I'll tell them everything when I get home next week. Sam's a wonderful guy, and I know it will be hard, but after a while, they'll be happy for me. I know you will be, too . . . If you ever forgive me . . . Love you. Niki xox.

CHAPTER 29

*Y*ou're acting rather dodgy."

I tore my eyes away from my phone, glancing over at Sam. We were back at Mandrem Beach with Diya, Mihir, and their friends, although everyone else had gone for a dip in the water.

"Dodgy?"

"Odd." He squinted at me. "What are you doing over there, anyway?"

"Texting my dad," I lied, tucking my phone away.

"I love that you're close with your parents." Sam grazed his sandy foot against my bare calf, and I fleetingly felt bad for not telling the truth. "I bet you'll get on with your family in Amritsar just as well."

I squinted into the sun, smiling to myself. I was waiting until our big date tonight to tell him that I wanted to stay in Goa with him instead of visiting Amritsar, because it fed into another big secret I was keeping. One that, with each passing moment, I was more and more tempted to reveal.

You see, I could see the whole thing playing out without either of us having lived through it yet. Sam would come visit me in Seattle, and then he'd return to London, and we'd both resume our normal lives. He'd find new musicians for his band, and I'd get a new job, and although we'd visit each other every few months, at most, that would be just too hard, and one of us would have to move.

I would have to move.

Sam needed to be in London to pursue his music career, where he already had contacts and a big fan base, while I worked in tech. I could work *anywhere*. And after Jasmine still didn't text me back, I'd stayed up late working off the nervous, excited energy by doing the required research to put the plan into motion.

With a background in tech, I could likely get a visa to work in the UK. What's more, British workers got a ton of holiday time—more than double the piddly few weeks I got in my old job—which I could use to fly back to Seattle to visit my parents.

Ugh. My *parents*.

My stomach curdled at the thought of facing them. Of not only sharing the news that I'd met someone but that I was going to move across an ocean to be with him. They'd be disappointed in me—there was no doubt about that. They'd remind me that I'd only known Sam for a few weeks and that I'd never even been to London. But they'd understand once they saw Sam and me together how happy I was with him.

They'd forgive me. It's not like *they* hadn't left behind their parents to move to a different country, and at least they'd have Jasmine close by.

Yes. *Yes*. It would all work out. It *had* to. I sat up in the beach chair, and when I caught sight of Sam staring at me, every doubt and bad feeling melted away.

It had to work out.

"Let's talk tonight," I answered. I blew him a kiss, rolling over to my side to get a better look. He was reading a John le Carré novel. Yes, Sam was a voracious reader, just like I was. He was freaking perfect.

"What time is your flight tomorrow?" Sam asked without looking up from the page. "Have you booked it yet?"

"Sam," I whined teasingly. "I'll tell you later. OK?"

His sunglasses were hanging low over his cheekbones, and I couldn't read his face as he propped his head up on his elbow to face me.

"Niki, are you still leaving tomorrow?"

"Am I?" I answered vaguely.

"*Are* you?"

I swung my legs around and sat up from the chair, leaning forward. I was grinning ear to ear. "Well, I was going to tell you tonight." I knocked his knee with my own. "But I was *thinking* I'd stay here with you a bit longer."

I bit my lip impatiently, ready to spill the beans on the rest of my plans, too.

"How much longer?" he asked.

"Until I fly home—so about another week?"

"You won't travel to Punjab at all, then?"

My jaw stiffened. It was cooler today outside, but despite the breeze, my face felt hot and sunbaked. "I don't have to stay. I just assumed you'd want me to—"

"Of course I want you to stay, love," Sam interrupted, taking my hands in his own. He squeezed, pressing our palms together, and the tension—well, most of it—slipped away. "I want you as long as I can have you. I just thought you were keen to visit family."

I stared at the sand, my gut twisting. Sam was right. Over the past week, we'd talked a lot about family and how it felt like the right time for me to see Punjab, learn more about where I came from. It's what my parents were expecting me to do, too. My face flushed, annoyed by their voices in my head. But I always did what they wanted; wasn't it finally time to do something for myself?

"I'd like to stay with you." I paused, suddenly nervous to meet his eye. But then I sighed in relief when I looked up and caught sight of him, my Sam. My everything.

"If you'll have me," I added.

Sam paused. It was only for a second, but it made my stomach bottom out and my ears start to burn. But then his face unfroze.

"Yeah." Sam grinned. "Reckon I'll have you."

"You *reckon*, do you?" I asked playfully. My heart was still beating inexplicably fast, hummingbird on steroids fast. It took a good twenty minutes for it to settle down.

CHAPTER 30

*T*hat afternoon, we said our goodbyes to the rest of the group, who were flying out early the following morning. I had an extralong farewell with Masooma, who reminded me of our plans to get together when she was in Seattle in a few weeks' time, and of course, Diya and Mihir.

If I hadn't been let go from my job and had the rug pulled out from under me, not only wouldn't I have met Sam, but I would have missed out on the wedding of one of my very best friends in the world, and the experience of a lifetime. Spending time with the Joshi family, Pinky, and Manish in Mumbai. Celebrating Diya and Mihir's relationship. Going on their group honeymoon in a literal paradise. I wouldn't have been able to experience any of it.

It felt rather bittersweet, and Sam and I were quiet during the drive back to the apartment, our hands interlocked in a comfortable silence over the stick shift. As soon we got back to the apartment, I jumped into the shower. We were running late for our reservation at Frank's Café.

I was pleased that Sam still wanted to go for dinner that evening, even though it wasn't actually my last night. I suppose he had promised to take me out, just the two of us, and we *did* have a lot to talk about. As I scrubbed the sand from my body, I practiced what I was going to say to him and how I would say it.

I'll move to London for you.

I'll do what it takes for us to be together.

It sounded corny and clichéd, but—hell, I was ready to admit it—I was in love with Sam. I really was, and I knew this so clearly because I had never felt this way before, even with my ex. And everything about being in love suddenly *felt* kind of corny—the way he made me swoon or held my hand or the way his smile lit up the room as he did something as mundane as cutting fruit.

Then why did I feel so nervous? Quickly, so as not to waste too much water, I shampooed my hair and then added a bit of leave-in conditioner. Our conversation this afternoon had gone well but had left me unsettled, with a chalky taste in my mouth.

After I showered, I wrapped my towel around my head, changed into a pastel blue sundress, and then went to find Sam. He was upstairs in his room, his back flat on the bed, strumming on his acoustic guitar as he stared at the ceiling. He hadn't noticed me in the doorway just yet, and I smiled, watching him, imagining how the evening might unfold.

Over wine and what he promised me would be the best fish curry I'd ever taste, we'd talk about the future, our plans to be together. He would tell me he loved me, and speaking over him,

I'd say it right back, rushing out the words because everything just felt so goddamn right. I blinked, stepping toward him.

Who got to be this lucky? Who literally got to fall in love, like *this*, in a dream?

"I'm all done with the shower." I unraveled the towel from my hair, wringing out the damp ends as Sam sat up on the bed. "What time should we leave?"

"Soon." Gently, Sam set his guitar on the stand beside the bed. There was an odd quality to his voice, like a dull blade pressing up against something. It made my stomach flip.

"Too much sun today?" I asked, keeping my voice light. Sam didn't answer, and he seemed to be looking at everything in the room but me—the ceiling, the wood flooring. His feet. I swallowed hard, my muscles tensing. "Now you're the one being dodgy—"

"You left your phone downstairs," Sam interrupted. "On the dinner table. I didn't mean to look at it, honest."

My hands started trembling. Previews to all my texts and e-mails appeared on my home screen. What had he seen? Something from Jasmine? From . . .

"Was it Raj?" I hesitated, as I'd saved him to my contacts as his full name. "Rajandeep Singh Sahota?"

"No." Sam narrowed his eyes. "Who's Rajandeep?"

"No one," I said quickly, feeling stupid for saying anything. We hadn't been in touch since I was back in Mumbai, and there was no reason he'd suddenly reach out, knowing I was still on vacation. "We went on one date before I left town. Sorry."

"It's fine, Niki. I—no. It wasn't him." Finally, Sam met my gaze. "Did you cancel one of the job interviews you told me about? You have an e-mail from one of those companies you told me about. From what I read . . ."

He trailed off, waiting for me to interrupt him. I didn't want to do this here with my wet, tangled hair dripping water all over my neck, but it seemed like this moment wouldn't wait until our romantic dinner. I sat down on the edge of the bed, facing Sam, and took a deep breath.

"I canceled both interviews, actually."

"You did?" Sam beamed. "That's great, Niki. I think that's a wonderful idea."

I exclaimed in relief. "You do?"

"Absolutely. You have solid work experience, a good reference, sought-after skills." Sam tucked one of his legs underneath him. "I agree—you should only apply for companies you're *really* keen to work at. Somewhere you can feel passionate in your day-to-day."

I dug my fingers into the flesh of my thighs, squeezing. He'd missed the point, and my pulse started pounding again, this time in my stomach, as I tried to figure out how to clarify what I meant.

"You should hold out for the right opportunity. It won't take long. I'm sure of it." Sam paused, coming up for air. "What kind of company—"

"Sam." I cleared my throat, his voice ringing in my ear. "That's not why I canceled them."

"No?"

"I thought." I paused. "Well, I thought maybe I could look for a job in . . . London."

A moment passed, and then another, and then Sam's face didn't light up the way I'd dreamed it would. He didn't take me into his arms and whisk me away, metaphorically or physically. He didn't do anything with his arms, actually. He sat there like a limp noodle, not really looking at me, not saying a goddamn word.

"OK, then," I said dryly. My face was burning, confusion and hurt exhausting every limb of my body. "I guess I'll go finish getting ready—"

"*Niki,*" Sam pleaded, but he didn't say my name the way he usually said it, his tone loving and sweet, like a *gulab jamuun.* He said it like I was being a nuisance.

"Yes?" I fired back, looking for a reason not to walk away. I was hurt by his reaction, but maybe my idea had just taken him by surprise. When he still didn't say anything more a beat later, I tried to stand up.

"Don't leave." He tugged on my arm, pulling me back down, closer to him on the bed. "Sorry. I'm just in shock is all. This doesn't make any sense . . ."

Fear prickled my skin, crawling over me. Of course it made sense. It was the only thing that made *sense.*

"You can't move to London for me—"

"Why not?" My voice cracked. Was I crazy? Sam was the one who pursued me, convinced *me* that this couldn't just be a fling. "I thought you cared about me . . ."

"Of course I do. Niki, I want to *be* with you." He paused. "But this is so drastic, so soon—"

"Is it?" There was a lump in my throat, but I swallowed it down. "I know we haven't known each other that long, but this feels . . ."

"Different," he answered, and I nodded as hope coursed back

through my veins. "It is different. This is . . ." Sam groaned, lying back on the bed. "Niki, you know how I feel about you. How I've felt since I first laid eyes on you on Diwali."

My nose was dripping like a faucet, and I wiped my face on my towel and then tossed it on the floor. "Then what's the problem?"

"Mom gave up on her dreams for my dad, and they resent each other for it—you've seen them together. You know what their marriage has become."

"But it was her choice, Sam. And this is mine—"

"To leave your whole life behind, your *family*, just for me? I can't be your dream. I'm not enough."

"You mean *I'm* not enough."

"That's not at all what I'm saying," said Sam, but I didn't believe him. I felt like I'd been punched in the gut, and the tears had started pooling in the corners of my eyes and threatened to spill out.

"Then what are you saying?" I whispered.

Slowly, Sam sat back up on the bed. His hair was still salty from the beach, and he sighed hard as he ran his hands through it.

"There's nothing for me in London, either." He paused, my head spinning with confusion, even anger. "I'm not even sure I should go back."

"Sam . . ." I sputtered. I couldn't believe it. He was giving up on his dream? He couldn't. I couldn't let him.

"You said Dad will respect me if I respect myself, Niki, but guess what? I don't. He was right, this whole time. I should never have been so frivolous with my life choices." He smiled at me, but his eyes were far away. "I should have been more like you."

I laughed despite myself, and a single tear slipped free. Sam reached over and gently wiped it away with his finger.

"And you see how much my mother misses me. I've been toying with the idea of coming back to Mumbai, finding some sort of respectable job finally, and then on Diwali, I met you and . . ." Sam trailed off. "Anyways, we'll figure it out. We—"

"Aasha Auntie wouldn't want you to move home just to make her happy. She loves you," I said, finding my voice. "She worships the ground you walk on—"

"She doesn't expect a goddamn thing from me, Niki." Sam breathed out heavily. "She's so cool now, huh? She wasn't like that with Prem or Leena. She expected a lot from them, and she got what she wanted, and now I'm the throwaway child. Her little Sam who can do no wrong."

"That's not true . . ."

"It is. And my siblings resent me the *exact* same way you . . ." He trailed off.

The same way I resented Jasmine.

"It's time for me to grow up," Sam said. His voice was forced and hollow, and I wondered where the man I loved had disappeared to. At some point, he'd withered away into a shadow of himself.

And where had I gone? Practical Niki. People-pleasing Niki. The good Indian daughter Niki.

"So, what happens now?" My voice was small and weak, and I hated myself for it. I hated Sam, too. I stood up, my arms clutched over my chest, willing him to say something—anything—that put all the pieces back together. That made sense.

But then Sam looked up at me, his gaze narrow and weak,

and as the goose bumps prickled up and down my arms, I knew. I knew that we were over.

"I don't know," Sam said finally.

I don't know?

He did know; he just wasn't ready yet to admit it. It was just dawning on *me*, but Sam already knew that this was over. And suddenly, for the first time in more than a week, I felt like I was standing on solid ground. I sucked in air, slowly, and as I breathed it all out through my nostrils, suddenly it all made sense.

I picked up my wet towel from the floor, wiping away the last of my tears. "I think we're done here, Sam."

Sam had the audacity to laugh at me. He stood up, reaching for me, but I pulled away from his hug.

"Niki," Sam said, searching my face. "Don't. We'll figure this out. Together, with time—"

"No, we won't," I said evenly. I backpedaled one more step toward the door. "We can end this now. Or we can end it a year from now, after we've put each other through hell. Frankly, I'd rather not waste my time."

"Love, you're speaking nonsense. I—"

"I said I'm done."

Sam pleaded with his eyes, his hands, but I was immune to it now. I barely registered his words as I raced down the stairs and started throwing things into my suitcase as he banged on the bedroom door.

I thought I'd learned my lesson, but yet again, I'd gotten carried away.

I'd forgotten what was real.

CHAPTER 31

Five years earlier

*T*hat was a success!" said Gaurav's father as he put his feet up on the kitchen table.

My boyfriend Gaurav didn't say anything as his sister Sara elbowed me in the ribs.

"A success for *who*?" Sara mouthed.

I suppressed a laugh as she handed me freshly washed crockery to dry. Out of all the words that could be employed to describe tonight, "success" was the last one on my list. In fact, the entire evening had been a bit of a disaster.

Sara was getting married *tomorrow*, and no one really knew what was happening. The ceremony and reception were to be budget-friendly affairs at the local banquet hall, one of those places where you checked off what you wanted on a clipboard months ahead of time—food, decorations, and even the officiant—and just sort of showed up hoping the wedding would be what you asked for. But with only thirteen hours to go, no one had visited the hall to make sure everything was in order. No one even knew what time the family and wedding party were supposed to show up.

I wasn't in Gaurav's family yet, or the wedding party, but it seemed like I was the only one who was stressing out about it. With Sara's blessing, I'd politely asked her future in-laws to stick around after dinner so everyone could formulate a plan for the big day. They agreed, but after only ten minutes of going over the details, they claimed they were tired and took off with the groom.

"Should we take a break from the dishes and talk about tomorrow?" I asked Sara loudly enough so everyone could hear. "I can take notes."

"There are too many things to discuss," Gaurav's mom said, peering out from the pantry. "I don't even see the point now."

I bit my lip. I didn't want to push the matter—it wasn't really my place, and Gaurav had told me off before for sticking my nose in it—but tomorrow was destined to be a gong show if I didn't get involved. This family was lovely most of the time, but they couldn't even organize a dinner party to save their lives. At Gaurav's graduation party, nobody had remembered to buy any liquor, and I'd had to go out for it twenty minutes before it started.

"I don't mind," I said, trying again. I grabbed a legal pad from the top of the refrigerator and sat down at the kitchen table. "We might as well . . ."

The next fifteen minutes were painful. It was like pulling teeth trying to get everyone to commit to a schedule, to share the tidbits of information they alone knew, which when combined, would mean the wedding wouldn't be *totally* chaotic. Gaurav had remembered to organize the taxis, while his dad had indeed paid the venue and his mom had the seating chart "somewhere around here," which I volunteered to get printed at Staples first thing in the morning. And luckily, Sara had finally found a photographer, and one of her friends who worked at Sephora had offered to do her hair and makeup.

"Niki," Gaurav's mom said after the plans were finalized, and we all stood up from the kitchen table. "You will be in the wedding photos, too. *Hah?*"

My heart lurched. "Really, Auntie?"

"Of course!"

She returned to her tasks in the pantry, and immediately, Gaurav and his father disappeared from the kitchen. A few details for tomorrow still weren't finalized, but I felt better. Lighter. Gaurav's family was a bit messy at times, but one day, they were going to be my family. Sometimes I felt like they already were.

"Your *mehndi*," I said, staring at Sara's hands as she went back to the dishes. "Let's switch. I'll wash and you dry."

"Better yet, *Gaurav* should wash the dishes."

"You're right." I rolled my eyes, brushing past Sara. "I'll go get him."

I found Gaurav in the basement, where he always hid after dinner. Usually, down here he played StarCraft or shot at something on his new PlayStation, but tonight he had the TV on. He was watching a rerun of *Arrested Development*.

"Wanna come help?" I sat down on the armrest next to him

and planted a kiss on his cheek. He didn't answer, his eyes glued to the screen.

"Come on. Please? It's her wedding tomorrow . . ."

I sighed, studying Gaurav's face as he ignored me. Even though we were from the same Punjabi Sikh community, lately I'd been noticing how different our families were. Yes, Gaurav and I both grew up in houses with traditional gender roles, but while he and his father didn't even put their own plates in the dishwasher, Dad at least showed his respect and appreciation for Mom's domestic labor. Lately, now that his hours were better and he didn't need to work so hard, he'd even started to contribute.

Would Gaurav be like his dad after we got married? Would he expect *me* and our future daughters—but not sons—to do everything around the house even though I worked, too? Did he really think I would be OK if he farted around in the basement while I held the family together?

It was cold down here, and I rolled down my sweater sleeves to keep warm and decided whether or not to press him. It was the night before Sara's wedding, and I didn't want to start an argument. On the other hand, I knew I had to stop letting these things slide.

"Can we talk?" I asked him.

Gaurav flicked his eyes toward me. "About?"

"Sara's henna will get ruined if she does the dishes," I said. "Can you finish them?"

"Can *you*?"

My hands trembled at his tone.

I wasn't an idiot. I knew Gaurav wasn't a good boyfriend. The week before, Diya told me point-blank that he treated his "geezer StarCraft buddies" better than he did me. Ever since we graduated college, all he did was go to work, play video games, and act like hanging out with me, his *girlfriend*, was some kind of chore.

This was *his* family. This was *his* sister's wedding. Gaurav should be the one upstairs helping out, and he damn well knew it.

"What is up with you tonight?" I asked, my voice shaky. I hated having to ask. I hated when he made me feel like *I* was in the wrong.

"Nothing—"

"What. Is. *Wrong*."

He reached for the remote and turned off the television. The silence was deafening.

"Yeah?" I tried again.

"Mom didn't ask me about the pictures," he grumbled.

"She didn't ask you because you're the *brother*. It's a given you'll be in the family photos."

"No. Mom didn't ask me if I wanted *you* in the photos."

I pulled my legs onto the couch, processing what he meant.

"It's weird, right?"

"I don't know." I swallowed hard, the tears threatening to spill. "Is it?"

"We're not married, Niki."

"Yeah . . ." I trailed off.

But one day we're going to be.

"The last few months have just been a lot," he said, after a few moments slipped by. "Like, *a lot* a lot."

I nodded. Sara's engagement had been a whirlwind.

"So maybe you shouldn't come tomorrow."

My body shivered as something deep and dark unleashed inside of me. I couldn't breathe. I couldn't even speak.

"You understand, right?"

"No, I *don't* understand. What . . ." I was panicking. I was falling through the air. "Why? What are you talking about?"

"You've been so intense lately, Niki," he said quietly. "It's too much—"

"Too much for *you* that I helped your family organize that goddamn wedding?"

I didn't raise my voice often. Gaurav said it didn't suit me. But maybe, really, it didn't suit him. And as Gaurav looked at me with a facial expression I was becoming all too familiar with— *disdain*—it occurred to me that I didn't like who I was when we were in the same room. A woman who made herself quieter and smaller, even submissive. A woman who was made to feel bad for needing him to be a better boyfriend, for expecting . . . *respect*.

"If I don't come tomorrow," I said, my voice solid, "everyone is going to think we've broken up. Is that what you want?"

Gaurav looked at me, and a part of me wished I hadn't pressed him about the dishes. That I could curl into a ball, nestle myself close, and we could forget this whole conversation.

"Is that what you want?" I repeated.

I loved Gaurav, and I had been willing to stick it out. God knows why, I had been prepared to make the sacrifice.

And right then, Gaurav finally made it clear to me that he was not.

CHAPTER 32

*W*e can talk about it if you want."

Diya crawled into bed beside me. I was in their honeymoon suite bed back at Bardez, and Mihir, the thoughtful husband that he was, had gone for a walk to give us some alone time.

"I thought you wanted to stay neutral," I said. At some point, I'd stopped crying, and now I just felt stupid and numb. Mostly, just plain stupid.

"I suppose I do, yeah."

Diya didn't prompt me further, and even though I was tempted to talk about what had just happened, I didn't want to put Diya in an awkward position; she was friends with both Sam and me. She was loyal to both of us.

My mind was spinning a mile a minute; I didn't understand how I'd ended up here. I'd given myself a brief moment to pause to go off and live my life a little, and what's the first thing I did?

One look from a sexy musician had turned me into my old self, the sort of woman I swore I'd never be again.

The funny thing was, it took me years after the breakup to fully realize I deserved better. That I devalued myself by staying with Gaurav for so long. But I didn't have a frame of reference. Beyond a handful of junior high crushes on prepubescent boys, Gaurav was the first guy to really notice me. To think I was different and interesting and charming and all the ways we all want to feel when we're still figuring ourselves out and just want to feel special.

Gaurav had ticked every single box, so I hadn't even thought twice about bringing him home to the family—a nice Sikh boy I'd met at college with a good head on his shoulders who came from a nice family, who at first made me feel like I could be happy and still live the life my parents wanted for me.

Whenever he came up in conversation, I always told others that I didn't know why Gaurav ended it. But I did. Gaurav didn't love me. Regardless of the fact that he was not a good person, truly, he didn't love me. And I'd wanted our relationship to work out so badly I'd never even noticed.

"May I say something?" Diya whispered. Softly, she wiped the tears from my cheeks; I hadn't even noticed I'd started crying again.

"Sure."

"Sam really cares about you." She paused, my heart sinking into my chest as the tears came faster. "I know him. I can tell he might even love . . ."

Love me?

Two hours ago, I would have believed it. Now, it was hard to believe in anything.

"Remember how you were telling me not to freeze my eggs simply because I am afraid of the astrologer's prediction?"

I nodded.

"Well, do not give up so quickly because *you* are afraid. Sam's life is messy right now. He is confused—"

"Understood," I interrupted, smiling and trying to change the mood. I wiped my nose with my sleeve. "I think we need to go back to Switzerland."

Diya stroked my hair, and after Mihir came back from his walk, the three of us watched reruns of *The Big Bang Theory*, and I tried not to cling onto her words.

Maybe Sam loved me, too. Maybe Sam *was* confused. Deep down, I wanted to let her say it out loud. And I wanted to believe it.

But even more, I didn't want to get my heart broken again.

CHAPTER 33

*N*iki?"

I groaned at the sound of Mom's voice, rolling away from the door. Had I been sleeping? My mind felt foggy.

"Niki, *aaja!*" Mom bellowed again. Her voice was closer now, as if she'd left the kitchen and was now standing at the bottom of the stairs. My eyes closed, I could practically see her standing there with her hands on her hips, tapping a slipper. "Get up, you lazy girl! You can't sleep all day."

"Coming," I croaked.

I glanced at my alarm clock. It was past 6 p.m., three hours since I'd come upstairs to take a nap and ten hours since my flight had touched down in Seattle. I chugged the glass of water sitting on my nightstand and then threw my legs over the side of the bed, half surprised when my bare foot felt carpet and not the cold linoleum or hardwood flooring I'd gotten used to in India.

Everything and nothing were familiar to me in Punjab. I'd never explored the city of Amritsar or prayed at the humblingly beautiful Golden Temple, but somehow, it felt like I'd been there before. Although I'd never met in person the dozens of aunts, uncles, cousins, and other relatives, whether we were talking over *cha* or on a road trip through the farming communities where our ancestors had lived, it felt like I had known them my whole life.

I still didn't speak the language, and I'd never truly be "Indian," but over the course of the week, I started realizing that I was OK with that. I was happy with who I'd grown up to be, even if it meant I sometimes felt disconnected from my roots or confused about what label I should use. And I shouldn't have been reluctant to go to India because I was afraid of what I would see.

Because I loved every minute of my visit to Punjab.

Well, every minute I wasn't crying over Sam.

The last week had been a roller coaster, intense highs and lows, periods of overwhelming happiness while I was hanging out with my family, and moments of utter despair whenever I was left alone with my thoughts.

Sam had tried to call me once. I'd been meeting a few of my younger second cousins, and because they only had an hour before they had to go back to school, I declined the call, expecting that he'd follow up with a voice mail or at least a text.

But he didn't. Clearly, he had nothing to say to me. And I had nothing left to say to him.

I shampooed my hair, body clenched and trying to breathe

through it, doing my best not to cry. In the hot stream, I closed my eyes and took a deep breath, willing him to leave me alone. To leave me in peace. It would take me a while. But I knew I would get there. I'd pushed my way through heartbreak before.

After showering, I threw on a pair of old leggings and a UW sweatshirt, and then pulled my wet hair into a topknot. I'd been away for nearly a month, and it felt good to be home, to come barreling down the stairs and find my parents cooking together in the kitchen.

"Hey, Dad."

He looked up from the cutting board, a huge grin spreading across his face. While Mom had worked from home that day so she could pick me up from the airport, I hadn't seen Dad yet, who was still in his work clothes and looked like he'd just gotten home.

"Niki," he said as I rounded the kitchen island to give him a hug. "You look terrible."

"Hey," I whined. "Rude."

"You are looking dehydrated from your long flight is what I mean, *beti*. Have some water."

"I just did."

"Have some more."

I withdrew from the hug, and when Dad poured me another glass of water from the tap, I obediently drank the whole thing.

"Hungry? Do you want snack before dinner?" Mom asked. She was kneading *aata* with her right hand and texting with two clean fingers on her left.

"Not really. My body clock is all over the place."

"Your father is making jackfruit curry tonight. Let's see how it turns out."

"Yum." I eyed Dad. "Building your repertoire, I see."

"My curry is fit for the kings." Dad winked.

"Yes, but is it fit for your three *queens*?" Mom fired back. Smiling to herself, she tucked her phone in the front pocket of her apron and turned fully to the *aata*. "Jasmine is coming for dinner. She just pulled into the driveway."

I could feel a dull headache setting in, my heart rate slowly but steadily rising. Although we fought all the time, Jasmine and I had never sustained an argument for so long, and I wasn't sure if she had come over tonight to make amends or continue our battle face-to-face.

When she walked through the door, it hit me how much I'd missed her, how desperate I was to talk to her. She was wearing ripped jeans and a crisp collared shirt beneath an oversized sweater, her medium-length hair tucked neatly beneath a beanie. I held my breath as she greeted Mom and Dad, who were closer to the entranceway, and then watched her make her way toward me.

She stopped short a foot away, her head cocked to the side as if she was considering both of our next moves. I smiled, shrugging, hoping it was enough, and my heart burst a beat later when Jasmine grinned and threw her arms around me.

"Oh, thank god you're not still mad at me," I said quietly into her hair. "I'm so sorry."

"It's fine." She pulled away. "I'm sorry about giving you the silent treatment. We both needed to cool off—"

"What are you two whispering about?" Mom interrupted.

"Nothing." Jasmine winked at me. "So, what did I miss? You didn't start without me, did you, Niki?"

By the way she looked at me, I knew she was referring to Sam. My stomach bottomed out. I'd told Jasmine I was taking the leap with Sam and would break the news to Mom and Dad as soon as I got home, but because she'd never replied to my messages, I'd never bothered her with the update that I'd been kidding myself, and Sam and I were over.

"Start what without you? Dad asked.

"Nothing," I said.

"Nothing?"

I wanted to mouth, "Shut up! I'll tell you later," but I could feel Dad's eyes on me. Instead, I played dumb.

Nonchalantly, I reached for a banana in the fruit bowl. "I have no idea what you're talking about. Anyway—"

"Niki," Jasmine squealed. "I'm talking about *Sam*!"

I couldn't bear the sound of his name, and I started peeling the banana just to give myself something to do, somewhere to look. I bit my lip to keep it from trembling, and I dug my teeth harder and harder into the flesh.

"What about Sam?" Mom asked.

"*Nothing*." I swallowed hard, trying to keep my voice even. "Drop it—"

"Come on, just do it now." Jasmine shook my shoulder. "I'm so excited. They'll be excited—"

"Jas," I warned, glaring at her. "*Stop*."

"Niki, don't be a baby. "You're a grown-ass woman. Just—"

"Can you shut *up*!"

"Can *you*—"

"Sam and I are over, OK?"

The stool tipped over behind me as I stood up, and as Jasmine and my parents gawked at me, all I could hear was the steel seat wobbling on its axis against the linoleum.

"I lied to you," I said, after I worked up the courage to look over at my parents. "Sam is a close friend of Diya's, like I said, but Sam is a boy. He's a musician. We dated while I was on vacation."

I paused. I'd been rushing my words, and because I was only going to say this once, I wanted them to hear me.

"But it's over, OK? I'm home, and it's over, and you don't need to worry about me ever again."

*D*inner was . . . tense. Mom and Dad seemed incapable of understanding my subtle hints that I was not ready to talk about what happened and were on my case to "explain myself" until Jasmine not so politely told them to zip it on my behalf. Thank god for my older sister. She lightened the mood by regaling us with stories of her oddball colleagues, and eventually, Mom and Dad unclenched and started pitching in to the conversation, too. They had spontaneously decided to join a bowling league with a few of Mom's colleagues and invited us to go practice with them sometime, as neither of them had ever gone bowling.

Finally, by the time we were halfway through a dinner of jackfruit curry, *daal*, and *roti*, I felt as if I could open my mouth without bursting into tears or wanting to ram my fist into a concrete wall. Although I'd kept everyone generally updated on my whereabouts, I hadn't shown them many pictures from Punjab. Hunched over the table, I showed them all the photos I'd taken sightseeing or just hanging out with the relatives, videos from the cooking lesson Dad's *buaji* had given me on how to make traditional *saag* and *chole*.

I smiled, remembering them all, so thankful we had that precious time together. Many of my relatives were getting older, and who knew when I'd be able to go again, if ever. Everything happened for a reason. I was meant to be let go from my job. I was meant to go to India and be with Diya and Mihir on their wedding day. And I was meant to meet Sam so I would remember what was important.

Family.

It was late by the time we'd all scarfed down a full package of *kulfi* from the freezer for dessert and tidied the kitchen, and Mom and Dad disappeared upstairs for their nighttime ritual of stretching and watching BBC World News in bed until they fell asleep. But Jasmine lingered, and I appreciated it. I knew she wanted to be around if I was ready and willing to talk.

"So," she said, as we cozied beneath a blanket on the couch. We were lying end to end, my toes digging into the minimal flesh on Jasmine's bony butt. "Do you want to watch something?"

"Sure." I yawned. "Mindy?"

Jasmine laughed. We'd seen every episode of *The Mindy Project* at least five times. *"Again?"*

"Come on. Let me pick." I pouted, joking. "I'm *so* sad."

"I can tell."

I tilted my head up from the headrest to get a good look at her, and I could tell she was trying to figure out how far I wanted to be pushed.

"Fine," I sighed. "Just *ask.*"

"Can I see a picture?"

I laughed despite myself. Of course that would be Jasmine's first question. I scrolled through my camera roll, deciding which one to show her. We'd taken a ton of photos in Goa, just the two of us and with the group, but for whatever reason, the Sam in those photos wasn't the way I pictured him in my head. I went further back in time to my snapshots in Mumbai and stopped on a selfie Sam and I had taken together the night we met.

I'd forgotten my phone in Diya's car, and Sam had been the one to take the picture, catching me off guard as we sat side by side on the edge of the pool. I was midsentence, my lips in a half smile as I gave him the side-eye, while Sam was grinning ear to ear, his exuberant, happy, full-of-life self.

I could feel my hand shaking as I handed Jasmine my phone.

"Oh damn, he's . . ." She trailed off as she caught my eye. "He's hideous. You dodged a bullet."

At some point, my nose had started running, and I used the sleeve of my sweatshirt to wipe it. "Shut up."

"Seriously. Your babies would have looked like little goblins," Jasmine declared. She tossed the phone on the blanket between us, and it slid off until dropping quietly to the carpet. "He's absolutely disgusting—"

"No, he's not," I groaned, pressing my hands into my face. "He's a babe."

"A babe who hurt you, so as far as I'm concerned, he has warts on his face, his hair line is prematurely receding, and he has three and a half balls."

I choked on a laugh as the tears started to come. As vivid as Jasmine's loyalty was, hearing her say out loud that Sam had hurt me made it all the more real.

He had hurt me. The truth of it was very simple.

"When was that photo taken?"

"The night we met," I whispered. I was crying, again, and staring up at the ceiling. "On Diwali."

"Do you want to talk about it?"

It turned out I did want to talk about it, and Jasmine listened to every word, every single detail, over the next half hour, both of us huddled beneath a single blanket, even though there were extras right next to us on the floor.

"And you were right," I said, after I told her the part where I'd stormed out. "I caught feelings. I got my heart broken."

Jasmine hadn't said much during my story, and was particularly silent during the part where I'd admitted that for a twenty-four-hour period, I'd actually convinced myself that I was willing to move to London. I lolled my head to the side to get a better look at her. She was sitting upright now, her legs crossed, staring at me. Her face was blank.

"What are you thinking?"

"What am *I* thinking?" she echoed.

"You're thinking . . . I told you so." I laughed. "I should have listened to you. I should never have tried to have a 'fling.'"

"No." Jasmine's voice was flat and even. "Honestly, I was thinking that this is *good*. This is really good, Niki."

I sat up, confused by her meaning.

"You know what it feels like to really be in love," she continued. "And to *feel* loved. For the future, you finally know what you deserve."

I nodded sadly, remembering the way Gaurav used to treat me. How insecure'd I felt about myself those few years. Yes, Sam had hurt me, but he had made me feel good, too. Around him, I felt like I was worth it. And even though we weren't going to be together, that feeling lingered. I *was* worth it.

"You were right, by the way," Jasmine said a little while later.

"I'm right about a lot of things," I joked.

She smiled. "You were right not to tell me you weren't Brian's biggest fan. Because I realized something recently . . ."

I dug my toes into her side, prompting her.

"I never told you that I didn't like Gaurav."

"You didn't like him?" I laughed. "Why didn't you at least tell me after he dumped me?"

"I dunno." She shrugged. "You were already so sad. Mom and Dad were broken up about it, too. And I didn't want you to think about how much time you wasted over that piece of trash."

"For the record," I said, "I don't think Brian is a piece of trash. I just don't know if you're a good fit."

Jasmine nodded, smiling stiffly as she leaned her head back on the armrest of the couch.

"But I'm not in your relationship. I don't see everything, and sometimes I think I look for reasons to judge him." I paused. "I'm happy if you're happy, OK?"

Jasmine stared up at the ceiling, and the room got quiet, except for the sounds of BBC News coming from upstairs.

"Are you happy?" I asked her after a few minutes had passed.

Wryly, she said, "I haven't decided yet."

CHAPTER 34

*J*asmine must have said something to my parents, because over the next few weeks, they never asked me about Sam or how I was doing or if I wanted to talk to them about what happened. Because I didn't. I knew that lying to them about who I was staying with in Goa and "dating" some guy I'd met on vacation was a crushing blow for them, something they didn't expect from their good daughter. And saying everything out loud all over again would only make me feel worse.

We avoided all talk of Diya, the wedding, and the week I spent in Goa, and when we talked about my time in India, we instead focused on the few dozen more phrases of Punjabi I'd picked up with the family. Mom's *pinni*, which was a hit with every host. The warm, familiar tingle I felt spending time with my relatives.

I got over my jet lag pretty quickly, and because my parents

worked all day and I was unemployed, I pulled my weight around
the house more so than usual—cleaning and cooking dinner for
them every night, sometimes Indian, sometimes a cool new rec-
ipe I found on Chrissy Teigen's Instagram. I could only spend so
many hours per day watching television, going to the gym,
searching for jobs, or doing whatever else I could find around the
house to keep myself focused, my mind anywhere but on Sam.

On how much I missed him.

By the second week of December, even though I was as miserable and unemployed as ever, the whole world seemed to be on
serotonin-inducing drugs as the city got ready for the holidays. I
couldn't go grocery shopping without hearing Ariana Grande's
"Santa Tell Me" or try out a spin class without the instructor
mixing Justin Bieber's rendition of "Drummer Boy" with an
EDM beat to keep us sweating. I tried my best to get into the
spirit, but sometimes I just needed to tune out the world, stare at
the ceiling, and listen to something angsty from my adolescence,
like My Chemical Romance or Simple Plan.

Mom and Dad were out every other night at some work holiday party or community function, and although Jasmine had
been coming home often to check on me, she, too, became in-
creasingly busy, balancing her workload with her and Brian's social calendar. Even without a job, I found myself leaving the
house more and more, and wearing clothes that weren't sweat-
pants, however much I didn't feel like it. Having given them the
bare bones of what happened with Sam via our group chat, my
girlfriends dragged me out of the house for movie nights or wine
nights, occasions where I'd let them indulge me for no more than

fifteen minutes before making a show of turning over a new leaf and enjoying the rest of the evening.

My old boss Oliver also invited me for drinks with the old work crew, and although I declined his invite to crash the office Christmas party—boy, would that have been weird—I did meet up with my old team in the city at the same pub we'd all been going to for years. It was good to see them and tell the same jokes and talk about the same work politics as ever, but it made me realize that getting let go really was a blessing in disguise. I was content with them, but I wasn't happy, and unless something had forced me out of my inertia, I may never have left. I may have never figured out that although I cared about them and learned a lot while working there, it was well past the time for me to move on.

When I was still in Punjab, I'd reached out to both companies who'd wanted to interview me to see if I could backtrack on my cancellation. The first told me it was too late; they'd found another candidate. The other one brought me in a few days after I got back to Seattle, but I could tell within the first ten minutes that I wasn't going to get the job. Despite three espressos and a pep talk in the restroom just before the interview, my performance was entirely lackluster, and I came across as a sad, boring former data analytics manager who couldn't care one way or another if they offered me the job.

But wasn't that true? I wasn't supposed to be thinking about Sam, but every time I scrolled past yet another job I was technically qualified for but not exactly enthused about, I remembered how proud of me he was when he thought I was only going to start applying for companies I really cared about, where I would feel passionate. I remembered how much faith he had in me. And it made me want to one day believe in myself, too.

Halfway through the month, I was a bundle of nerves when I woke up to a DM from Masooma reminding me that she was in town for work and wanted to grab dinner. Although Diya and I had texted frequently since I got back to Seattle, we had both steered clear of He Who Shall Not Be Named, referring to Sam only in passing, or incidentally to Diya asking me if I was holding up OK. He hadn't tried to reach out to me since I got back to Seattle, and because he hadn't posted a thing on social media, I had no idea where he was or how he was doing, if he'd ended up telling his family and his friends that he wasn't going back to London, or if he changed his mind in the end and was there right now. If he just hadn't wanted me to go with him.

I was tempted to bail, fake the flu or some appointment, but Jasmine encouraged me to go. And she was right. After all, I'd gotten on well with Masooma and wanted to stay friends with her, and she was classy enough not to pry. So I suggested a trendy tapas bar near her hotel and put on waterproof mascara, just in case Sam made it into the conversation. Just in case, yet again, I turned into a total idiot.

Masooma was running late from her meeting, and so I waited for her in the bar area, snagging the last free stool. The place was always busy, very popular with the late twenties and thirties crowd, and it was unusually packed tonight. I ordered a beer and passed the time by people-watching—longtime couples on dates, would-be couples trying to pick each other up, small groups of friends having a laugh.

One month earlier, I would have sat here and imagined what they were saying to one another, created backdrops and stories and even silly little songs, but what was the point of all of that? I didn't need an outlet for my fantasy. I'd lived through a real one—well, *almost*.

"The prodigal daughter has returned."

It was a man's voice, no more than a foot behind me. I blinked long and hard, and as my whole body trembled, I allowed myself to think for one fleeting moment that it might be Sam.

I swiveled around on the stool, using the bar edge to propel myself, and as the body behind the voice slowly came into view, I realized that of course it wasn't Sam.

But it was a friendly face.

"Rajandeep. Singh. Sahota," I said, my lips slowly curling upward. "Aren't you a sight for sore eyes."

"You can call me Raj," he teased, echoing the words he'd said when we first met for lunch.

I smiled, giving him a quick hug as he pecked me on the cheek. "You're saved in my phone that way, and it's how I remember you."

"So you do remember me," Raj said, clutching his chest. "Because I've been waiting by my phone for months."

"Months?" I laughed.

"Weeks, then." Raj rested his forearm on the back of my stool. He had his sleeves rolled up, and when his skin made contact with my back, a shiver shot down my spine. I bit my bottom lip as he smiled at me in that knowing way. I'd forgotten how handsome I'd once found him.

Raj stood next to me as I gave him a very brief (and edited) overview of my trip to India, and he told me about his latest rotation, how, as the new resident, he was on back-to-back call shifts throughout Christmas and New Year's.

Purely because of space limitations, our knees were touching, and the bar was so loud that every time one of us spoke, the other had to crane their neck out to hear the other person. I could smell the cologne on his neck and the whiskey on his breath, and our faces were so very close together that when I noticed Masooma hovering nearby, I felt like I'd been caught red-handed.

"Masooma, hi!" I hugged her, noticing how exhausted she looked. "Busy day? Here, take my seat."

"Thanks." She dropped into the stool like she was throwing herself down a set of stairs. "The fucking jet lag, Niki. What was I thinking, arriving one day early only?" She shook out her hair and then looked from me to Raj. Her eyes narrowed.

"Where are my manners," I said, suddenly nervous. "Masooma, this is Raj. Raj, Masooma. She's visiting from Mumbai—"

"*Oh.* Nice to meet you, Masooma." He shook her hand firmly. "Are you the friend that just got married?"

Masooma threw me a sideways glance, shaking her head. "That's Diya, another friend of ours." She gently squeezed my forearm. "Lots of friends, this one. *Very* popular."

"Right." I laughed.

"So how do you two know each other?" Masooma asked.

Before I could think of a reply, Raj answered. "This one here stood me up."

I scoffed, crossing my arms. "I did *not*—"

"Don't listen to her, Masooma," Raj said, ignoring me. "We had the most wonderful date"—he set his hand on my waist—"and she promised to call me when she was home from India but never did."

They both turned to me, Raj's eyes teasing and half-drunk, Masooma's unreadable. I bit my lip, both flattered by Raj's attention and worried about what Masooma would think of me if I flirted back. If I acted as if Sam, her and Diya's friend, was the last thing on my mind.

I reached forward to grab my beer. I didn't want Raj's hand on me with Masooma watching, and thankfully, he let me go. I took a big sip.

"Well, Raj," I said carefully. "You never called me, either."

Raj grinned, and I could tell he'd had a few drinks. "The cheek on her, Masooma. I'm telling you."

"I think our table is ready," I said suddenly. "Masooma, shall we?"

She nodded, and we gathered our things and said our good-byes to Raj, who took the free stool as we walked away.

"Make sure she calls me," he called out to Masooma. "I'll be waiting by the phone!"

The host led us to a table at the back of the restaurant, and we spent the next hour eating tapas and catching up.

It was nice to get to know Masooma and dive into subjects that we didn't necessarily want to talk about in a big group setting and around a bunch of other people, like our families and the struggles each of them had faced settling into new cities and countries. But we talked about lighter things, too, like Shah

Rukh Khan, and our weird, nerdy love for pandas software documentation.

But eventually, as we worked our way through small plates of calamari, *patatas bravas*, and garlic prawns, it was inevitable that we talk about our trip to Goa. It was inevitable that we talk about Sam.

"I was sorry to hear that it didn't work out," Masooma said after she mentioned having brunch with him back in Mumbai.

"Thanks." I shrugged, my stomach twisting into knots. "It's OK. I do live in another country."

She smiled, her friendly mouth stretching wide. It wasn't a look of pity, which I appreciated; it was one of understanding.

"There are enough eligible men in your own town, I suppose." With her eyes, Masooma gestured to the bar area, where she'd seen me with Raj. My cheeks heated up. "He was cute. What's his name again?"

I sipped my water. "Raj."

"Raj," she repeated. I couldn't get a read on what she was thinking. "Do you think you'll see him again?"

"Maybe." I laughed. "I don't know. Maybe if he calls me . . ."

Masooma grinned. "Good idea. Guys like that need to make the first move."

I didn't know what she meant by that, but before I could ask, she continued.

"Diya will be happy you are doing so well. She sent me as her emissary to check on you."

"Really?" I teased. "And what will you report back?"

She raised one eyebrow. "That you're doing much better than Sam."

My lip started to tremble. There were two croquettes left on the table, and so I skewered one of them with my fork and popped it into my mouth. I was doing better than him? If Masooma had seen me on literally any other day in the past few weeks, I was sure she'd have formed a different conclusion.

Chewing, I tried to decide whether to press further on the subject. It was strange to have confirmation that Sam was struggling, too. Comforting. But maybe that had nothing to do with me.

"Is he still in Mumbai?" I asked, after I'd swallowed the croquette.

She nodded. "He finally told us. The age of Perihelion is over."

My body tensed. "Has he told his—you know what? Never mind. Sorry. It's not my business."

"It's OK, Niki. Chill." Masooma smiled at me. "And, yes. He did tell Pradeep Uncle."

"Did he react as badly as Sam expected?"

"That, I'm not sure. But Sam and Aasha Auntie have left Goa and have shifted back to Mumbai." She smiled limply. "With the three of them in one apartment, I suspect that time will either solve their problems, or very soon I'll be reading about a murder in the *Indian Express*."

I giggled, shaking my head. I was happy to hear that Sam was trying to move forward with his life, even though it would never include me.

"I am not aware of what happened between you and Sam," Masooma said. She paused, considering me. "But he is feeling really bad. If he hurt you. He didn't mean to—"

"You don't need to apologize for him," I said, waving him off. "And he didn't hurt me. It was just a fling."

"Right," she answered. "*Good.* I just wanted you to know, he really is a good guy."

I smiled brightly as my stomach twisted into a palpable, painful knot. What was I supposed to do with that information? Where was I supposed to store it, inside, where I could keep it safe from my heart? I knew Sam was a good guy, and he hadn't meant to shred me to pieces. That, in some alternate reality, he could have been *my* good guy.

That's what made this so fucking hard.

CHAPTER 35

*H*ow was the big interview?" Brian asked me.

"Yeah, fine." I shrugged. I'd interviewed that afternoon for a data analyst role at one of the big, impersonal banks in town. It would be a step down in title but paid better than my former job, and I wasn't sure I would take it even if they offered it, but I needed to at least give it a shot.

"I'll find out next week."

"Who knows," said Brian. "You might get a job offer as your early Christmas present."

I made a show of beaming at him, and Brian, in turn, gave me an awkward thumbs-up. Jasmine, Brian, and I were squished around their dinner table, which was only meant to seat two people. We were packed in so tightly our plates touched, and I couldn't help but kick both of them when I crossed my legs. I'd suggested we eat on their sectional, as the living room of their condo was much more spacious, but Jasmine had set the table just for me and wanted us to all eat here.

"This is really good," I said, watching the analog wall clock. No one had said anything in thirty, now thirty-one seconds. I looked back at Jasmine and Brian when they didn't respond. They were poking at their salmon. "Teriyaki?"

"Yep," Jasmine said flatly. "Brian cooked."

"Nice." I smiled at him again as hard as I could. "Thanks, Brian."

"Anytime," he answered, spinach and salmon still in his mouth. "This sauce is unreal. You can whack it on chicken, too. Takes like two minutes."

Jasmine stiffly set down her fork and glanced over at Brian. It was so quiet all of a sudden I could hear my heart beating. Hell, I thought I could hear *Jasmine's* heart beating. Although she hadn't given me a lot of details, I knew she and Brian were having problems. That she was thinking things over, and he was making more of an effort in their relationship. I wondered if cooking dinner for his girlfriend's little sister was part of that effort.

"Well, it's *delicious*," I said, smiling at both of them. I had promised Jasmine I would try, too, and was determined to hold up my end of the bargain.

My phone buzzed beside me on the table, and my muscles tensed when I saw the caller display.

"Who is it?" she asked.

I held up the phone.

"Rajandeep Singh Sahota," she read slowly, and a beat later, her eyes brightened. "Oh, *him*. Answer it!"

"We're eating dinner—"

Jasmine grabbed the phone from my hand and set it to speakerphone.

"Hello?" Raj's voice blared through my phone, and I kicked Jasmine hard under the table as Brian voluntarily took his plate into the bedroom.

"Hey," I said finally. My voice was weird, so I cleared my throat. "Hey, *Raj.*"

Jasmine rolled her eyes at my tone, and I had to press my hand over my mouth to keep from giggling.

"Did I catch you at a bad time?"

"Not at all," I managed to say. I paused, composing myself. "Having dinner with my sister. What are you up to?"

"Oh, you know," he answered. "I'm just in my car, listening to a power ballad, wondering why you never called me. *Again.*"

"Poor you." I raised one eyebrow at Jasmine, who was devouring her salmon and nodding approvingly. "Sounds like you're having a terrible night."

"It could get better."

"Could it?"

Raj laughed. "I went into the hospital just now thinking I was on call, and turns out, I'm not. I have the night off."

"Lucky you."

"I'll be lucky if you meet me for a drink."

I bit down on my bottom lip. I was smiling. I was flirting. For the first time in weeks, I wasn't feeling out-of-my-mind depressed. It had been three days since I'd run into Raj at the tapas bar, and although I hadn't felt ready to make a move back toward the dating world, now that I was talking to him, I was kind of . . . excited.

I glanced up at Jasmine, for permission. She was nodding at me like a crazy person, and making rather lewd gestures with her hands. I grinned.

"Where and when?" I said slowly, into the phone.

"Michael's on Fifth," Raj answered. "Give me an hour?"

"Michael's on Fifth," I repeated. I'd been to that bar before, but only once; it was a little too swanky for my taste. "Well, if you're lucky, I'll see you there in an hour."

I ended the call without saying another word and immediately started shoveling the rest of my dinner into my mouth. It would take me about twenty minutes to drive there, and I knew Jasmine would insist on an exhaustive grooming routine before she let me out of her sight. I was barely wearing any makeup, and I'd borrowed Mom's middle-aged-woman-looking cardigan for the interview.

"*So,*" I heard Jasmine say, and I looked up from my dinner. "Since *when* did you learn how to flirt?"

"I learned from the best," I winked, my mouth full of food.

"You'll need to brush your teeth," Jasmine said dryly. "We have an extra toothbrush somewhere. Brian's teriyaki always makes my breath stink."

I finished chewing, studying Jasmine's face. "I don't have to go. I'm really enjoying our dinner . . ."

"*Right,*" she smirked, lowering her voice. "It sucks. You'll be doing me a favor if you leave."

I couldn't tell if she wanted me to go or if subconsciously she needed me to stay. "Jasmine——"

"Please. *Go*." She smiled. "Go figure things out with *Rajandeep*." She glanced through the doorway to the bedroom. The door was ajar, and on the other side, we could just hear the distinctive, whiny noises of some video game. "You and I both need to figure a few things out."

*O*ne hour and thirteen minutes later, I walked into Michael's on Fifth and spotted Raj in one of the booths. I had swapped out Mom's cardigan for one of Jasmine's funky tops and was wearing lipstick about two shades darker than I usually wore, my big sister's signature Mac shade, Viva Glam. I smiled brightly and pulled back my shoulders when he caught sight of me, trying to look the part of Confident Girl Goes on a Second Date, when really my insides were squirming.

"I was just about to give up on you," Raj said as I sat down opposite him.

"Traffic." I pulled off my coat. "Everyone must have a Christmas party to get to."

Raj flagged down our server, and I ordered a cocktail off the menu. I was feeling better than I had since I left Goa, and as the tingle of prosecco and Aperol warmed my cheeks and released the tension in my chest, I found myself having a good time. No. A *wonderful* time.

Sam who? I felt like shouting it out loud, although that would have been weird because I was in public and on a date with someone else. With someone who realistically could be a part of my life. Raj was outgoing and sweet, and there was a touch of something wild about him that gave the impression we'd never run out of things to talk about.

Sam lived in India. He was in the past. And this flirty, handsome, parental-approved guy here in Seattle could be in my future. Right?

After our second round of drinks, I was bursting and excused myself to the restroom, and took the opportunity to apply a bit more lipstick and return Jasmine's text checking in on me. I replied with a handful of select emojis and then left the restroom.

But when I fully pushed open the door, something made me linger in the entranceway. Raj was still at the booth, facing away from me, and our server was back even though she'd only just checked on us five minutes earlier.

It was clear they were flirting, the way she was smiling and twirling her hair. I couldn't see Raj's face, but when he turned his head, I caught sight of his profile and that toothy, slightly drunk-looking grin of his.

I didn't want to jump to conclusions, and I was about to brush it off and make my way back to the table, but then the waiter placed something on the table.

My eyes narrowed. It wasn't the bill. It was too small. It was a business card. She was giving him her phone number. Raj studied it for a moment, and when he slipped it into his jacket pocket, everything fell into place and hit me over the head like a frying pan.

All night, I'd thought it was dorky, even cute, the way he always seemed to be looking off into space, distracted by his own thoughts, when now it was fairly evident his eyes wandered every time our server was nearby.

I inhaled sharply, as bits and pieces of information, red flags, and outright warnings all came rushing back.

Our first date, he'd been a relentless flirt, gotten me drunk at the sushi bar, and invited me back to his place. Twice. I thought he'd been joking, but maybe he wasn't; he'd been trying to take a sad, vulnerable, and very drunk girl home. And now that I *thought* about it, Raj had stopped texting me back in India only after I started to show more interest and messaged him back more quickly. Even the tapas bar where I'd run into him days earlier was a notorious place to pick up people. And what was it Masooma had said about him?

Guys like that need to make the first move.

Guys like *that*. I laughed, shaking my head. Even Masooma had seen right through him, and she'd known him for about five minutes.

Our server had her legs pressed against the table, and when Raj started stroking her inner thigh, I backtracked into the restroom, my jaw hanging open, and went to stand over the sink.

I evaluated myself in the mirror, top to toe, wondering how on earth I could have been so naive. I'd assumed that Gaurav would automatically be a good boyfriend because he was a harmless, nerdy Indian boy. That Sam was an insincere player—when he was anything but that—just because he was a musician. And later, that it was rational to move mountains to be with him without exploring any of our other options.

And just now, I'd assumed that Raj might be interested in settling down just because our *families* had introduced us. Without knowing anything beyond Raj's ability to check a few of the right boxes, I'd been on the verge of getting carried away on a fantasy all over again.

"I like this place," I said to Raj, after giving him another three minutes to feel up our server. She'd returned to her post behind the bar, and I quickly glanced in her direction. "Do you come here often?"

"Not often, no." Raj smiled vaguely. He took another sip of his martini, studying me. "Are you all right?"

"I'm perfect."

He bit his lower lip. "You are."

I beamed at him, but inside I was gagging.

"How about a third round?" Raj asked. He'd finished his martini, and I was on the dredges of my second drink, a beer. I picked up my glass and downed the last of it.

"Can't. I'm driving."

"What happened to fun Niki from our first date?"

"The kind that gets drunk on a Wednesday afternoon?"

"That's the one."

"She's had a long day, Raj."

"You don't want to make it a *bit* longer?" He was trying to be seductive, his tongue rolling around in his mouth just a bit too much for comfort. Ten minutes earlier, I would have thought it was a joke, but now I knew he wasn't kidding.

I flirted for fun, for laughs. He flirted to get laid.

When the server brought over our check, I played dumb and reached for the billfold before Raj was able to, reminding him it was my turn, as he'd paid for our lunch date.

"I'll get it next time," Raj said only after our server had taken payment and was out of earshot. "I'm thinking. A heavy red. Dinner." He paused for effect. "My place for dessert?"

"Absolutely," I lied. I now knew what I deserved and what kind of guy deserved *me*, and Raj was not it. "Sounds like a blast."

CHAPTER 36

I listened to Spotify on the drive home, shuffling through my liked songs, relieved that I'd figured out my pattern of behavior just in time to save myself from Raj. When I was nearly home, "Guess the Star" by Perihelion came on, and even though I was tempted to skip the track, I didn't.

Shoegaze music was dream pop, otherworldly, and this song, which Sam wrote, was one of the best I'd ever heard of the genre. My hands trembled on the wheel during Sam's bass solo whenever I could clearly hear his voice singing in harmony to the lead's during the chorus, but I pushed through it. I loved his music. And I wanted to get to a point where I could listen to it, or even think of him without feeling sad.

I wasn't there yet. Not even close. But one day, I knew I would be.

I could hear the television on in my parents' bedroom when

I arrived home to a dark house. I was a grown woman, and I didn't have a curfew, but my parents always waited up for me. They said they couldn't sleep unless they knew I was home safe.

I trudged up the stairs and found them both in bed in their pajamas, Dad half asleep with his head lolled to the side while Mom flicked through channels at random. I watched them for a moment before making my presence known, inexplicably happy to see them like this together. To know that, as annoying as it was, they always, *always* waited up for me.

"I'm home."

Dad snorted himself awake, and they both turned to look at the same time. I came into the room and flopped down on the end of their bed.

"Fun night?"

"Sort of."

"Did Brian really *cook*?"

I nodded, propping myself up on my elbow to face them. "Salmon."

"*Curry?*" Dad mocked.

I shook my head, smiling. It wasn't so long ago that Mom and Dad couldn't even hear Brian's name without storming out of the room. They'd come so far as immigrants and as parents and as part of a generation who were forced to accept their children's choices if they wanted to keep them in their lives.

Why had I always been so desperate to please them? Jasmine was part of the reason. But maybe I was just scared. Maybe I was too afraid to do anything that they didn't support—music, boys, travel, *anything*—because what would have happened if it didn't turn out the way I planned. If I'd laid all my cards on the table—made up my *own* mind—and I was wrong.

"I left Jasmine's around eight," I said quietly. It was nearly eleven now. "I went out after."

"With friends?"

"With Raj."

It was funny watching my parents' reactions. Dad suddenly was very occupied with wiping down his lenses with the edge of his pajama shirt, while Mom turned off the television and tried not to hyperventilate. I didn't want to get their hopes up, and so as quickly I could, I told them the truth about what had happened on my date.

"*Badmash*," Mom exclaimed afterward, shaking her head. "How could he do such a thing?"

"I will alert his parents." Dad reached for the phone. "Rajandeep cannot get away—"

"Dad." I laughed, interrupting him. "You are *not* calling his parents."

"Why not?"

"For one, it's none of their business. Two, you don't even know them. It was his uncle who set us up, wasn't it?"

Dad was so upset he'd nearly gone cross-eyed, and he and Mom took turns insulting Raj in both Punjabi and English, using expressions and curse words I wasn't aware they even knew.

"What if he does this to another girl in our community?" Mom said, still appalled. "We must *warn* them—"

"Mom," I groaned. "They'll figure it out just like I did, OK? Don't worry. Lots of guys are dicks—" I grimaced, and avoided eye contact with my dad. I hadn't said that word in front of him before. "Players, sorry. Lots of men *and* women can be players. And we can't warn every girl in the Seattle area that Raj may or may not hit on their server when they leave the table."

Mom and Dad were both looking at me long and hard and disturbingly all-knowing.

"I'm sorry," Mom said quietly. "I suppose we are not very good matchmakers."

"We haven't had any practice," Dad joked.

"It's OK." I paused but then decided not to lie and just get this over with. "And *I'm* sorry I lied to you. I should have told you who Sam really was from the beginning."

"It disheartens me that you felt the need to lie to us," Dad said, after I'd told them the truth about what happened in India, or as close to the truth as I could get. (My parents definitely didn't want to know how attracted I was to Sam and how my senses went on overload every time he touched me.)

"I didn't want you to be disappointed in me," I answered plainly. "Jasmine gave you such a hard time—"

"You shouldn't compare yourself to your sister," Mom said. "And I shouldn't have encouraged it. You are both your own women, and you must lead your own lives."

"It would have been foolish, though. I was ready to move to *London* for him." I laughed at myself, at how ridiculous it sounded when I said it out loud. "I was ready to throw my life away for him."

"Did you love him?" Dad asked, and I nodded.

"I think so."

"Well, then." Dad grimaced. "If this Sam character had been a smart boy and not an idiot for letting you leave"—I laughed—"then how is it you would have been throwing your life away?"

I shrugged. "You and Mom have had such a solid marriage. I always wanted to live up to you two. To find someone that made sense for the family, who was Sikh, who—"

"Niki," Mom interrupted. "Do you really think that your father and I got married because we have the same faith?"

I paused, looking between the two of them. "Well, wasn't it?"

Mom smiled, leaning forward to squeeze my hand. "The fact that we are both Sikh, had the same culture—of course it made a few things easier—but it was never the reason we got married."

"I married your mother because, as Jasmine likes to say, she is a straight-up hottie!"

"Dad!" I blushed.

"And, of course, because I loved her very much," he finished. "I would have 'thrown' my life away for her."

Mom smiled at him, and my heart filled with so much love my chest was at risk of ripping right open. I always knew I was lucky to have parents who genuinely loved each other, but I'd always assumed that the love came later. That it wasn't the foundation of their partnership but a fortunate side effect.

I supposed, when it came to love, it didn't really matter who we were and where we came from. The only thing that mattered was that each person made space for and respected the other.

"Can I ask you guys a question?"

Mom's face went red. "Is it the same question Jasmine asked me last week, because I don't want to discuss—"

"No," I said, shaking my head. "Wait, what did she ask you?"

"Nothing!"

"Mom—"

"She asked if your father and I 'waited' until marriage, and I told her it was none of her business, so don't you ask me, either!"

I laughed at how embarrassed she was, Dad, too, and I shuddered as I realized that her cagey nonanswer was an answer in and of itself.

"No," I said, after gaining control of my giggles. "I was not going to ask that." I paused. "I was going to ask why you never taught us Punjabi."

Dad furrowed his bushy brows at me. It was such a simple question, and I wondered then and there why I'd never asked.

"You always spoke English to us," I said. "Why? We would have learned it anyway at school."

"I'm sorry. We should have," Dad said finally, glancing at Mom. "We should have taken you to India when you were children, too."

"Dad, it's OK." I smiled. "We didn't have enough money—"

"We did. But we spent it on other things. Like this house. At the time, the public schools in this neighborhood were the best in Seattle."

I bit my lip. They'd never told me that's why they chose this area instead of the ones closer to the *gurdwara*, where their Punjabi friends tended to live.

"You see," Mom continued, "very early on, your father and I were so concerned about creating a life *here*, trying to be American, that we didn't . . ." She paused. "We didn't take care to connect you both to your roots. This is our mistake—"

"And by the time we started to notice . . ." Dad started, and even though he didn't finish his thought, I knew what he was getting at.

It was only when Jasmine and I were approaching adolescence that my parents started getting stricter, came down on us for not behaving or speaking like good Indian girls. They made life particularly hard for Jasmine, who had been marching to the beat of her own drum since she was a toddler, and pushed her so hard that it had been inevitable that she would rebel.

"It wasn't a mistake," I said finally, smiling at them. "It is what it is. It's in the past."

"We could have done a better job—"

"You couldn't have," I said, interrupting Mom. "There is no better or worse," I said, curling my feet under me. "Or right or wrong."

Without getting sad, I fondly remembered how Sam had playfully pinched my nose and called me "an American" for thinking my life was better than my family's in India. The way I felt about myself and who I was when I was around him, a guy who respected me and valued me and made me feel like I deserved love.

"I love how you raised me," I said to Mom and Dad before getting up to go to bed. "Because I love exactly who I turned out to be."

CHAPTER 37

*H*ere were the things I was doing to occupy myself during unemployment:

1. Going for my dream job.

I'd been relieved that the bank I'd interviewed at turned me down, and it made me realize that Sam had been right. Even though it might not work out, I at least needed to try going after what I wanted. But what *did* I want? What sort of company could I see myself working for? After hours and hours of researching my various options and potential career paths, I still didn't have an answer, but at least I was a little bit further along into answering these questions.

2.   Getting off the couch and onto my piano bench.

The last few years, I'd been very content to spend my evenings in front of the TV, my tired body sinking into the plush cushions as I got lost in some rom-com or Netflix original. But I'd been making a concerted effort to cut back on my bingeing and start playing at my keyboard again, and the more I practiced and the more the songs and skills came back to me, the more I wanted to play. Now, I didn't even have to force myself. I was wailing away up there for hours every day, everything from Debussy to Bach to Vanessa Carlton. I was playing so much that my parents had not so politely requested that I occasionally plug in my earphones to "give their ears a break."

3.   Diving headfirst into the Christmas spirit.

The festive weeks between Diwali and Christmas were always my favorite time of year. It was time to sit indoors with a good book; Mariah Carey's Christmas album; and a cup of cocoa, *cha*, or mulled wine. To get dragged along to some family friend's Christmas party with a Punjabi twist, where the beardiest uncle would dress up as Brown Santa for the kids and hand out *ladoo*.

It was the time to be *cheerful*.

There was going to be no more whining, longing, or pining for Sam, or wishing things were better or different. Not when I had a million things to be thankful for and to look forward to, and a group of wonderful people already in my life. I had parents who loved me to pieces and, it turned out, had never judged me as hard as I'd always judged myself.

I had Jasmine. We always loved each other as sisters, but now we were starting to love each other as friends, too. The resentment I'd been hiding my whole life had dissolved—completely—and it had left a space for so much more to bloom.

I also had a great group of friends. There was Diya and now Masooma, who lived half a world away but still occupied my thoughts, my DMs, and my heart almost every single day. I had my crew in Seattle, who were like a second family, and two of them, potential *roomies*. Their other housemate was moving out in the new year, and they'd asked if I'd like to take her spot. I was thinking about it seriously, and my parents were very supportive of the idea. (A little *too* supportive, even.) We all knew it was time for me to put myself out there, and not just when it came to dating, which I'd be ready for sooner or later. But in *life*. I couldn't use Mom and Dad as an excuse anymore to stay home and not try new things and experiences. And I no longer wanted to.

A few days before Christmas, I dropped Dad off at work and then took his car downtown to go shopping. My family had been doing Secret Santa since I was in college, and for the first time in years, I had Jasmine, the only person in my family who was easy to shop for. I could glance at a table of books at Barnes & Noble and know exactly which one she'd pick up first, and the same went with makeup and clothing or even kitchen gadgets. I'd already bought us matching reindeer onesies, but I wanted to gift her something she could actually use more than once a year.

I parked the car and wandered through the streets, smiling

so wide my cheeks hurt. Although the weather was cool, the sun was miraculously out, and storefronts were decorated with red bows, wreaths, and twinkling lights, Christmas music blaring whenever I passed by a door. I thought back to Diwali as I skipped over a crack in the cement, and the way that holidays could bring people together and make us see the good and the light in that which was already right in front of us.

The way, right now, it had even seemed to temporarily dull the pain of heartbreak.

I ended up finding Jasmine the perfect pair of brown leather boots at a department store not too far from my old office, and on an impulse, I decided to do a walk-by. Now more than ever, I was happy I'd been laid off. It had forced me to take a plunge into something new. Still, I was curious about how it would feel being there again, a place where, until two months earlier, I'd spent most of my waking life.

When I rounded the corner, I spotted my old window two floors up. Instinctively, I flicked my eyes ahead at Juliet's coffee cart. I grinned. Romeo was in line.

Nervously, I walked up behind him. He was much taller than he'd seemed from my window and more handsome, too. I was tempted to tap him on the shoulder and introduce myself, but that would have been weird, right?

Hello. My name is Niki, and I used to watch you flirt while you ordered your coffee.

Yeah. Pretty weird.

"Hey, Jules," he said, when he got to the front of the line. "How you doing?"

"Hey, Tom."

So that was his real name!

"I'm doing fine, yeah." Juliet paused, smiling oddly. "The usual?"

"The usual."

They went quiet as she took his reusable mug and started preparing his coffee. I took a step to the side to try to see their faces and get a read of things. Unlike before, Juliet's gaze was fixated on the coffee rather than Romeo—I mean Tom. And *he* was . . . on his phone?

What the hell had happened? Had the flirting and sexual tension fizzled out, or had I imagined everything?

I stepped back in line, a little bummed out, but then I saw Juliet reach for her own phone. She giggled, and then flicked her eyes up at Tom.

"Sure," she said slyly. She put her phone away and then handed him his coffee. "I'll go out with you again. I can't say no to Thai food."

I pressed my lips together to try to remain casual. *Yes!* It had finally happened for them!

"I'm glad to hear it." Tom had his hands pressed against the edge of her cart, his body leaning forward. I held my breath, taking a slight step forward so I could see them better.

"Because I had a good time last night."

"Last night *was* good," Juliet whispered. "But this morning, it was even better—"

Damn, Juliet!

I laughed, a little too loud, and when they both swiveled to look at me, I pressed my palm over my face and pretended it was a cough. Doing my best to seem oblivious, I bent down to tie my laces, and a moment later, they resumed chatting in low voices.

There was hope for all of us! Not only for would-be couples in romance novels and movies and my fantasies, but right here IRL. I stood up, wanting to cheer them on and congratulate them on finally—*finally*—getting together.

But again, that would have been a little bit weird.

CHAPTER 38

I went to sleep on Christmas Eve with a full belly and an even fuller heart. Our family celebrated Christmas the same way we did Diwali or Thanksgiving or any other special occasion that called for good food, music, family, and a few glasses of Dad's Johnnie Walker Red Label.

Jasmine would have Christmas dinner at Brian's parents', and so he had come over, and the five of us played board games like Twister and Scattergories and even one round of Cards Against Humanity, after which Mom, who I could tell found some of the cards *hilarious*, feigned modesty and made us put the game away. Even though evenings with Brian were always hit or miss, everyone actually seemed to have had a good time. Jasmine and Brian's relationship was still majorly on the rocks, but even she was in a good mood tonight, and every so often, I caught her staring at me with a grin on her face.

Jasmine slept over, and the next morning, she woke everyone up at the crack of dawn, blaring "All I Want for Christmas Is You" from the stereo. Mom, Dad, and I came downstairs to eggs and bacon frying and the smell of coffee roasting, and after eating breakfast, we opened our presents by the tree. Mom gifted me a stack of books I'd been eyeing and some makeup, and Jasmine loved her presents from me. We put on our matching reindeer onesies immediately.

"So, what now?" I asked as we folded up all the wrapping paper and saved it for the following year. "Should we bake sugar cookies? Watch a movie?"

"Why don't we go for a drive?" Jasmine suggested.

"Sure," Dad said.

"Good idea." Mom slapped her thighs as she stood up from the ground. "*Chalo.* Let's go—"

"A drive?" I whined. We occasionally went for walks as a family, but it was pissing rain outside and dreary as hell. "Why?"

"Why not?" Dad asked. He didn't meet my eye but started whistling, grabbing his keys from the side table. "We should get out. We should stretch our legs—"

"Stretch our legs by sitting in a *car*?"

Nobody answered me, and so reluctantly, I dragged myself up from the floor.

"I'm going to change, I think," Jasmine said, pulling down the hood of the onesie, the antlers falling down by her neck. "Niki, join me?"

"I'm good." I smiled. "It's cozy."

"But we're going out—"

"And we're staying in the car, aren't we?"

Jasmine didn't press me any further and ended up staying in her onesie, too. We filed into the backseat of my dad's car the way we used to as kids. It was strange to be going out for a drive, which we'd never done just for the hell of it. I was surprised Dad didn't complain that it would be a waste of gas.

Everyone in the car was oddly quiet, and after ten minutes of almost near silence, Jasmine leaned forward and turned on the radio. "A Holly Jolly Christmas" was playing, and dorkily, we all started singing along.

We stayed out for more than an hour, sticking to the coastline and the more scenic parts of Seattle. It was late morning by the time we got home, and I was ready for my second coffee of the day. I bounded up the driveway to make everyone a fresh pot.

"Who has the key—" I stopped short as I reached the front door, my hand on the knob. I turned around. Mom and Dad were taking their sweet time getting out of the car, but Jasmine was right behind me.

"It's unlocked," I said suspiciously.

"Oh?" She didn't look up from her phone, but there was a smirk on her face. "I must have forgotten to lock it."

I swiveled my body back around and slowly pushed open the door, half expecting a serial killer to jump out at me. The lights were out like we'd left them, but there was an odd flickering coming from below. I glanced down. In the center of our foyer, there was a single *diya*.

"What the hell . . ."

My stomach somersaulted when I caught sight of another glimmer, the light of a second candle down the hall. I followed it, walking slowly, until another *diya* came into view. And there was another one after that.

My limbs shook as I followed the trail of *diya*, my breath catching in my throat when I saw they led up the stairs.

Could it *be*? No. *No . . .*

My heart was beating so fast I could barely contain myself, and I tripped on the last step and stumbled onto the landing. Up here, there were even more *diya*. And they were all leading to my bedroom.

The door was open, and when I rounded the corner, I didn't recognize my room. The lights were on low and there were *diya* on every surface—my bedside table, dresser, and keyboard. Even the floor, too. I took a step forward. There was a narrow path carved through them, leading to the window. The drapes were shut, but by the flicker of the candlelight, I could just make out his silhouette.

"Merry Christmas," he said, stepping out of the shadows. My gut twisted as he fully came into view. It was Sam from the Band, standing in my bedroom, in Seattle, wearing the same *sherwani* he'd been wearing on Diwali. Setting the scene of the night we met. His eyes locked on me, pulling me closer to him as my hands trembled, and I realized why he was here.

"Merry Christmas . . ." I stammered. "When did you—" I stopped, took a deep breath. "*Why* did you . . ."

I couldn't finish that sentence, either, my body tense as Sam threw me a sheepish grin.

"I flew in early this morning. Jasmine left the door open for me."

I hid a smile. Of course Jasmine was behind this.

"And as for your other question." Sam paused. "Simply put, I was a wanker, letting you go like that. And I'm sorry."

I crossed my arms across my chest, almost as if they would protect me from him. "Is that it?"

"No. I also wanted to tell you that you were wrong."

"You mean *you* were wrong—"

"No, actually," Sam interrupted, "I was right."

I cocked my head to the side, studying him. That confident smirk on his face I'd first seen when he'd been playing on Diwali was back.

"I couldn't let you move to London for me on a whim. It was rash. And it wouldn't have been good for either of us."

I nodded. I knew that now. I'd just felt so desperate to make it work at the time; it seemed like the only option.

"But, Niki. Just because we don't know *how* this will work, or even how long, doesn't mean we can't give it a go. It doesn't mean we can't have a little faith—"

"But Sam. Come on." I sighed. "You live in Mumbai, and I live here—"

"Yes. So?"

"And we're both unemployed."

"How very millennial of us."

I smiled, biting my lip.

"I shouldn't have let you go." Sam nodded stiffly. "But you shouldn't have left. We have to try. We have to at least give this our best shot."

I let my arms fall to my sides, my body trembling. "You couldn't have just called me to say that?"

"You're a romantic," Sam whispered. "I knew a grand gesture wouldn't go unnoticed."

I laughed, tears forming at the corners of my eyes. He was wearing me down, and we both knew it.

"And I did call you—"

"Once," I reminded him. I wiped my cheeks with the back of my hand. "And you never tried again."

"Everything at home is so complicated right now. My life is complicated, and I thought I needed time to sort myself out first, to be on my own. I didn't think I deserved you yet." Sam paused. "You were right about my dad. He's not going to respect my choices until I do."

"And do you?"

"I'm working on it."

I wanted to know what he meant by that, what his being back in Mumbai or him standing here in Seattle now meant for his future, for his relationship with his family. I wanted to ask him so many things, but first, I asked him, "What changed, then? Why did you really come, Sam?"

A shadow crossed his face. "Masooma called. She said—"

"Oh." I cut him off, my jaw tight. "You're here because you're jealous."

"No. I'm here because I didn't want to miss my chance." He took another step forward. Now there were only a few inches between us. He reached his palm forward and gently clasped my wrist. "Niki . . ."

My breath caught in my chest as I let him tug me toward him. "Yeah?"

"I'm here because I'm in love with you."

I gasped, my knees buckling as he wrapped his arms around me.

"You know that, don't you?"

I did know that he loved me. I loved him, too.

Who knew what steps either of us would take next, and if they would send us packing in different directions or lead us down the aisle. But Sam was right; our love—this almost chemical, spiritual, and totally chaotic connection between us—was enough for right now. It was enough for us to give it our very best shot.

"Say something," Sam whispered. He pressed his body against me, and I could feel his breath on me as I tentatively let my forehead fall into the crook of his neck, fingered the embroidery on the neck of his *sherwani*. I'd forgotten what he smelled like and how much I missed him.

"Oh, Sam," I whispered.

"Yes, love?"

Fortunately, I hadn't forgotten how much I loved to tease him.

"It's too late."

I felt Sam's body stiffen beneath my touch, and my face deadpan, I took a half step backward.

"It's that Raj bloke, isn't it?"

I let out a huge sigh, forcing my body to tremble as I unwrapped myself from his arms.

"We're betrothed."

Sam's eyes narrowed.

"We've had the *rokka* and everything."

Sam caught on, the edges of his mouth curling up into a sly smile.

"You should leave before he gets here," I said, swallowing a laugh as I tried to keep my expression neutral. "Otherwise, there will be hell to pay."

"Will there, now?" Sam set his hands around the small of my waist, squeezing. "Shall I challenge him to a duel?"

"Do you have a sword?"

"I have a bass guitar—"

I giggled, the charade over, wrapping my arms around Sam. I pulled him into me again, hard, rocking back and forth against his body.

"You gave me a fright there for second," he whispered into my hair. A beat later he kissed me sweetly on the forehead.

"You thought I'd run off with the doctor?"

"No," Sam said dryly. "I thought I'd have to *fight* the doctor."

I laughed and reached up to kiss him. I was halfway to his lips when the antlers on the hood of my onesie bonked him in the face.

"Can you take these off?" Breathing heavily, he pulled down my hood, antlers and all. "It's cute, but it's in the way."

"Only in a Bollywood movie would the heroine be dressed up in a reindeer suit."

Sam pulled me tight, his mouth close to mine. "No Bollywood movie I've ever seen."

This time, there were no antlers in the way when our lips

touched. I melted into him, into the kiss, our hearts beating fast as I wound my hands through his hair and hung on for dear life. A kiss that was full of love and hope and mystery and . . .

We pulled away in a daze, the overhead lights blinding us. I spun around, wiping my lips with the back of my hand. Mom, Dad, and Jasmine were in the doorway.

"Hey . . ." I took a giant step away from Sam. "Um, so this is Sam."

He took a step forward, touching his hands together and bowing. "*Sat Sri Akaal*, Uncle-ji." He turned to Mom and flashed her a smile. "Auntie-ji."

I was impressed that Sam had used my community's greeting with my parents, and Mom seemed to be, too. In fact, her eyes were rather shiny, and she seemed to be completely taken with him.

"Nice to meet you, *Sam*." Mom glanced around the room, eyeing the *diya*. "Jasmine mentioned this would be happening. It is a very nice gesture."

"Indeed." Dad cleared his throat. "Welcome. How long will you be leading on my beloved daughter this time?"

"*Dad!*" Jasmine and I exclaimed simultaneously, just as Mom jabbed him in the ribs.

"No, it's OK." Sam held eye contact with my father, who had puffed up his shoulders and was doing his best to come across as a scary uncle. "I made a mistake. And I intend to work hard to earn back your daughter's trust and respect." Sam paused, bowing again. "And yours, too, Uncle-ji."

Dad glared at Sam for three more seconds, and I was about to think that maybe Sam would actually have to fight someone to-day when Dad eased up. He grunted his approval, and I let out a sigh of relief.

"Well, that was quite the speech," Mom said demurely. She rolled up her sleeves, ready to get back to the day. "But Sam. *Beta*. I hope you know. You will be sleeping the guest room."

Eleven months later

A cool breeze blew off the ocean as we arrived at the beach, the sparkling Goan sun sinking into the horizon. We laid out blankets on the sand, unearthed the beer and Limca from the cooler, handed out plates of *samosa* and mango salad. The new single from Blackpink started playing on the Bluetooth speaker, and I smiled, catching Sam's eyes from a few feet away. Tonight's playlist didn't feature your typical Diwali music. It had everything from TLC and D'Angelo to India's Top 40. Jennifer Lopez circa 2001 to John Denver's "Take Me Home, Country Roads."

It was a playlist Sam and I had created together. Like our yearlong relationship, it was a compromise.

"Does anyone have matches?" Pradeep Uncle asked suddenly.

"Right here." Sam patted his shirt pocket before retrieving the small box. "Would you like some help?"

"Sure." Uncle smiled, sitting back on his heels. "Thanks, son."

The evening grew darker, and I tried not to watch Sam and his father working together, lighting the *diya* Aasha Auntie and I had laid out in the shape of a mandala. Sam and his father had come a long way that year, mended the fabric of their relationship together. From what Sam had told me, they still had a long way to go, but small, civil exchanges were a very good start.

Eating and drinking, we huddled together as the air cooled, and even though I was shivering, I felt warm inside. Not only was I spending Diwali with Sam, but we were back in Goa with both of our families. Aasha Auntie and Pradeep Uncle had a full house, all three of their kids home for the holidays, spouses and grandchildren in tow. Even Mom, Dad, and Jasmine had accepted Aasha Auntie's invitation to come visit and had found our family an apartment in the same complex.

I know. I know. Holidaying with both sets of families?

"Holy *wow*—like, no pressure!" was how Diya phrased it after I'd told her about the trip. But Sam and I had been very clear with our parents before we booked the trip: we were in a serious relationship, but we were no way near ready for marriage. I mean, how could we be? This past year, we'd barely even seen each other.

After spending two weeks together in Seattle last Christmas,

Sam and I didn't see each other again for six whole months, and the distance nearly finished us. We were both working hard in our own cities and at creating our own lives. There was simply no time to fly halfway around the world to visit each other.

Sam found an assistant job at a record label in Mumbai and, on top of that, had gone back to school; having graduated from business school more than seven years earlier, he'd decided to take a few supplementary classes online through his alma mater, UCLA. Meanwhile, I started taking on freelance projects while I waited for the perfect job, and within a few months, I had enough clients to go solo. These days, I work for myself, and provide data analytics services and consulting to companies all over the country. I had a handful of big soulless clients that paid enough for me to move out of my parents' house, buy a car, and rent a desk at a trendy coworking space. But I also had more than a dozen other clients that I worked with because I wanted to, like a music streaming start-up and my favorite romance fan fiction app. I could even afford to work with a few nonprofits and charity organizations for reduced rates or pro bono.

With Sam in Mumbai and me in Seattle, it would have been all too easy to say goodbye, and there were moments I felt it seemed inevitable. With our unpredictable work schedules, sometimes we'd go days without video chatting, and the twelve-and-a-half-hour time difference made the distance even harder. There were so many reasons for Sam and I to go our separate ways, but I supposed there was another one that motivated us to stick it out: we loved each other.

This past July, Sam's boss finally gave him a week off work, and I met up with him in LA so we could both have a holiday. We stayed at his sister's house in Pasadena and spent each day basking in each other's company, being total tourists at the Santa Monica Pier, Rodeo Drive, or Hollywood Boulevard. One afternoon, we even took Sam's nieces and nephew to Disneyland.

Sam showed me around UCLA, the bars where he used to play gigs, and one night he joined me for dinner with my favorite client, Emilio. Emilio was the chief operations officer and cofounder of the music streaming start-up, and he and Sam got along like a house on fire. Emilio even let slip that the start-up was getting a cash infusion from investors, and they'd soon be expanding the team, creating a platform with more global content.

And that, very soon, they'd be hiring.

Sam and I tried not to get our hopes up. It was a long wait and a long shot, too, but the investment cash arrived. Emilio came through on his promise to get Sam an interview. And just two weeks ago, finally, after months of anticipation and four separate Zoom interviews, Sam was offered a job. The company was impressed by Sam's background in business and real-world music experience in London and Mumbai. They wanted someone like him in their content strategy department and for Sam to move to LA by February.

"Should we tell them now?" I whispered to Sam, scooting up next to him on the blanket.

"I'm so nervous."

"Don't be." I cozied into him, hooking my arm through his. "Our parents will be happy for us."

"I'm not nervous about telling our parents we're moving to

LA," Sam said. "I'm nervous about telling *your* parents we'll be *living* together in LA."

I shushed him, giggling. We were planning to make the "we're not getting married" announcement later tonight, and nobody knew except Jasmine. I had tried to keep the secret from her, too, but slipped up within a few hours.

I would miss Jasmine and my parents terribly, but the more I thought about the move, the more excited I became. I had always loved visiting LA, and working freelance, I could be mobile; I could fly back to Seattle and work remotely from my old bedroom as often as I wanted.

I also had the sneaking suspicion they'd visit Sam and me often, too. Mom and Dad had always talked about retiring someplace with more sun and less rain, like California. Maybe I would be the excuse. And now that Brian was out of the picture and Jasmine was looking for her next big adventure, maybe my best friend and big sister would come, too.

Sam was similarly thrilled about going back to a city he knew and loved, and where his parents already visited often to see Leena and her family. He was starting to let go of the pursuit of being a rock star, because I think he finally realized he'd already lived that dream. No, he wasn't Mick Jagger, Jimi Hendrix, or Bowie, but Sam had accomplished what he'd set out to achieve. For years he'd lived a full, exciting, passionate life as the bass guitarist of Perihelion, and now it was time to turn the page and start the next chapter. To build a new sort of career in the music industry, one he never even knew was possible.

It seemed almost too good to be true, like one of my little

fantasies, the way things were starting to work out. The way that what was best for both of us as individuals was the best-case scenario for us as a couple, too. But wasn't that how it was supposed to be? Being in love wasn't just about how you felt about the other person. It was how you felt about *yourself* when you were with that person. It was knowing, without a doubt, that *you* were living each day as the best version of yourself.

The first burst of light shot off in the distance, and a hush came over the beach as everyone settled in together for the fireworks. I rested my head against Sam's shoulder, and while everyone was distracted, I reached up and kissed him.

Diwali was the Festival of Lights. The celebration of the goodness in this world over darkness. A holiday that could be whatever anyone wanted it to be. And for Sam and me, having first fallen for each other on Diwali, I knew it would always be the day we celebrated our love for each other, too.

Acknowledgments

I am so thankful for my family and friends for their ongoing love and support. Thank you to Martha Webb and everyone at CookeMcDermid. I am so lucky to have you in my corner.

Thank you to Berkley, particularly Kerry Donovan, Brittanie Black, Fareeda Bullert, Mary Baker, Vikki Chu, and Will Tyler, as well as Penguin Random House Canada for championing me here at home. A huge thanks also to Federica Leonardis and Stephanie Caruso, as well as to the librarians, booksellers, bloggers, event organizers, and more who have supported me and my books.

Finally, I want to thank my husband, Simon Collinson. You are the reason this romance writer is a romantic.

A Holly Jolly Diwali

SONYA LALLI

Questions for Discussion

1. Why do you think Niki agrees to being set up with Raj?

2. What do you think pushes Niki to throw caution to the wind and book the last-minute trip to Diya's wedding in Mumbai?

3. When they meet on Diwali, Sam teases Niki that it was fate that brought them together; Niki was meant to lose her job so she could come to India. What do you think of this? Have you ever experienced a setback in life, only for it to lead you somewhere better?

4. Why doesn't Niki stand up to the "sour-faced auntie" in the restroom who comments on Niki's caste and skin color? And why do you think the interaction affected her so much?

5. Niki and Sam were drawn to each other the first moment they laid eyes on each other. Do you believe in love—or lust—at first sight?

6. Aasha Auntie is a modern auntie who revels in defying stereotypes about "auntie culture," which often portrays South Asian middle-aged and older women in a negative light. Did anything surprise you about her character?

7. As a child, Niki is teased by her peers for mispronouncing *jeera,* leading her to wonder why her parents never bothered to teach her to speak their language. Why do you think Niki's mom and dad made the choices they made?

8. What do you think about Niki's impulsive decision to look for a job in London, and why do you think Sam reacted so poorly to the news?

9. Sam has a complicated relationship with his father, who never supported Sam's musical ambitions. In what ways did this affect Sam's decision-making when it came to both his career and romantic life?

10. Niki often doesn't tell her parents the whole truth in order to protect the image they have of her as the "good

daughter." Could you relate to anything about Niki's relationship with her mom and dad? Did you enjoy how it evolves over the course of the novel?

11. Sam followed his dreams, while Niki played it safe and chose a stable career. What did you think about where each of them ended up? Is there a right and a wrong choice?

12. Niki often wrestles with her self-identity and the expectations that come with the labels "American" or "Indian." How do you think her trip to India helped or hindered her personal growth over the course of the book?

13. In India, Niki discovers there are so many ways to celebrate and experience Diwali—both religious and secular. Can you relate with any unique holiday traditions in your own life?

Don't miss Sonya Lalli's next novel,
featuring Jasmine, coming 2023 from Berkley!

Photo by Ming Joanis at A Nerd's World

Sonya Lalli is a romance and women's fiction author of Punjabi and Bengali heritage. Her debut novel, *The Matchmaker's List*, was a Target Diverse Book Club Pick, and Sonya's books have been featured in *Entertainment Weekly*, NPR, *The Washington Post*, *Glamour*, and more. She lives in Vancouver with her husband.

Ready to find
your next great read?

Let us help.

Visit prh.com/nextread

Penguin
Random
House